THE HEART OF PANGAEA

Lindsey Kinsella

Also by Lindsey Kinsella:

The Lazarus Taxa (2022)

Copyright © 2023 Lindsey Kinsella

All rights reserved

Hardcover First Edition 2023

ISBN: 9798394160264

Edited by Donna Marie West

Cover Art by Giorgio Rizzo

Our beautiful planet is indeed worthy of our study; it was once our cradle—it will soon be our grave.

-Gideon Mantell

Prologue

The earth glowed orange as rock liquefied under intense heat. Comets rained from the gloomy heavens, scattering globules of semi-molten rock with every impact. The air was thick, heavy, and toxic, and lightning streaked relentlessly across the sky. The oceans barely clung to their liquid form, spewing steam from the waves as they simmered close to boiling. Beneath the surface, the seafloor was lined with scalding volcanic vents and magma flows.

This was the Hadean Eon.

Despite a name deriving from Hades, the Greek god of the underworld, this place was not Hell, but rather, Earth in her youth.

You might think such a place would surely be devoid of life, yet, if you were to delve to the bottom of the seething seas, towards those volcanic vents, upon that red-hot rock, you may just find something living.

Tiny, microscopic life, but life, nonetheless. If you were especially fortunate, you might even find one particularly important microbe—your very own ancestor. In fact, the ancestor of every single living thing today. Science refers to this as the "Last Universal Common Ancestor," or simply "LUCA."

From this single entity, far too small to see with the naked eye and barely surviving in an inhospitable setting in time and space, evolved our vast and complex tree of life. LUCA's descendants included the fish, the insects, the dinosaurs, the mammoth, the neighbour's noisy dog who will not stop barking at 2:00 a.m.—and you. Every living thing on this little blue sphere we call home can trace its family heritage to one single individual living four and a half billion years ago in a broiling hellscape.

And so, it seems, regardless of how humble one's origins might be, great things—perhaps the greatest of things—can come from anywhere. A single bright spark in a world of darkness can light the way for us all.

Robyn and the Dimetrodon

Do you know what a *Dimetrodon* is? Of course, you don't... or maybe you do. I can't tell how you answered because that's not how a book works. For now, let's assume you don't.

The *Dimetrodon* was a truly ancient creature, one which predated even the earliest dinosaurs by tens of millions of years. It looked, to the untrained eye, like some kind of German-shepherd-sized lizard. Upon the back of this beast, you would find a crescent-shaped sail made of a thin membrane of skin stretched over a row of tall spines. It was one of the first hyper-carnivores on land, stalking the ancient landscapes of Pangaea for prey. Pretty cool, right? In fact, it was probably the coolest animal to ever walk the Earth.

I know what you're thinking: this sounds pretty biased. Did a *Dimetrodon* write this? Well, yes. One did.

My name is Ed. Ed the *Dimetrodon*. I'm sure you're wondering how an almost three-hundred-million-year-old synapsid came to be writing a novel. To get to that, I need to first introduce you to a young lady named Robyn Croll.

What can I say about her? Well, Robyn is easily the smartest kid in her class. She's also a talented artist and do you know, she has won the sports day hundred-metre sprint four years in a row? But if I'm being honest, what really makes her special is her imagination. Yes, yes, I know—that's incredibly cliché, but it's true. Indeed, I wouldn't even exist were it not for the power of her inventive mind.

Despite all she excels in, however, she hasn't ever fit in. Other kids just don't seem to understand her. In truth, she hasn't ever understood them either. Perhaps being an only child left her without those particular social skills. And so, when the real world didn't accept her, Robyn created a world of her own.

And that's where I come in. So, specifically, I'm Ed the imaginary *Dimetrodon*. My prehistoric form may seem odd to some—most children with imaginary friends will dream up another child, a clown, or a puppy. Something... sweet, I guess. But sweet is boring, if you ask me. I, on the other hand, am an ancient, awesome, dragon-mammal.

The reason for my rather unorthodox appearance lies within Robyn's greatest passion—natural history. Ask her anything, literally anything, about prehistoric life, and she'll know the answer. From the woolly mammoth to *Triceratops* and from the Cambrian explosion to the most recent Ice Age. So, naturally, when the time came to imagine herself up a companion—she chose well.

Our story begins on what was a preposterously hot summer day. Robyn sat by her dressing table with some paper and coloured pencils, sketching. The sun blazed through the wooden blinds and caused her well-brushed, but otherwise unfussed, auburn hair to glow and her emerald eyes to glint. Her skin was pale, lightly freckled, and a little sunburned thanks to the current intense summer weather. She had inherited her fragile complexion from her father and, thanks to that, was punished every time the sun so much as peeked through the clouds. Her mother would joke that Robyn might burn if the brightness setting on the television was too high.

Every window in our small, semi-detached house was wide open in a futile attempt to allow in some cooling airflow. It was certainly too hot to be outside today—not that Robyn had any friends to play with anyway. So, instead, she did what she usually did to pass the time—she drew.

It was a simple pastime, but she was rather good—I reckoned she had a bright future as a famous artist. And she did more than draw. Every sketch, every painting, every doodle on a napkin—it all contributed to her own wonderful fantasy world. She called it "Pangaea," after the prehistoric supercontinent, and it was filled with all of her prehistoric creations from every geologic era, all mixed up together. Each image was pinned to her wall in a vivid collage of ancient life. With such worldbuilding skills, perhaps she also had potential as an author—though maybe she would be wiser to get a proper job.

I would often admire the wall of Pangaea for hours on end. I had my favourites, of course. Her *Meganeura*, an ancient dragonfly the size of a large bird, was brightly coloured in striking shades of green and purple. In contrast, her *Microraptor*, a small flying dinosaur with wings on its arms and legs, was dark and brooding with its black feathers and subtle blue highlights—probably her most mature piece.

Each picture was wonderful, but together? A masterpiece. Perhaps I'm prejudiced—after all, I did feature right in the middle. The proud *Dimetrodon*. I loved how she nailed my copper skin tone, my crisscrossing black stripes, and even my tiny little whiskers on the end of my nose.

This afternoon's addition was a beautiful, purple marine reptile. With its comically long neck, I recognised this particular example as one of Robyn's favourites—*Plesiosaurus*. Think of an ocean-dwelling *Diplodocus*, but with an even longer neck and flippers instead of feet. You've seen the Loch Ness Monster photos, right? Then you get the general idea.

While shading the underside, Robyn stopped and squinted at this particular image.

"It's missing something," she pondered, taking off her rectangular-framed glasses and giving them a wipe with her t-shirt.

"Hmm… looks pretty good to me," I replied.

"No, there's something… it needs something."

I looked back at my own body for inspiration. The orange and black colouration on my scaled skin, which was covered in a light, almost imperceptible coating of fuzzy hair, seemed to me like the best possible option.

"Maybe it should be orange?" I suggested.

"You think everyone should be orange." She giggled.

"How about some stripes then?"

"Hmm… actually…"

Robyn reached into her vast art case and retrieved a coloured pencil—a darker shade of purple this time—and began to sketch in some subtle striping along the reptile's back in a similar fashion to my own.

"You're a genius, Ed," she exclaimed as she triumphantly dropped her pencil onto the desk.

As she held her photo proudly aloft, Robyn's bedroom door swung open, and in stepped her mother. Carol was a kind woman and, even though she wasn't aware of my presence, I loved her almost like she were my own mother. She was short with rounded features and the same magnificent, emerald eyes sported by her daughter. Her pale blue shirt was made from shimmering satin which glinted in the sunlight streaming through the window. On her head was the black and green floral headscarf I had become accustomed to seeing her in.

It was strange how quickly that had become normal. Carol's illness had only come to light a few months ago and her hair had fallen out shortly after. Yet the headscarf now felt entirely ordinary. That being said, neither I nor Robyn truly understood what cancer was. Carol assured Robyn that she just had to take some medicine for a while and then she would be fine. I was sure she would look forward to regrowing her hair since she used to take such pride in it.

"Dinner is almost ready, darling," she announced softly.

"Okay, Mum," Robyn chirped. "I'm just finishing up here."

"Oh, what's this then?" Carol enquired as she peered down at Robyn's drawing. "A *Diplodocus*, right?"

"Not quite," Robyn replied with a chuckle. "It's a *Plesiosaurus* for my wall. I'm going to call her Mary, like the palaeontologist Mary Anning."

"I see. Well, it's a very cool dinosaur."

It was clear Carol didn't have a clue what a *Plesiosaurus* was, but she seemed genuinely pleased to see her daughter so passionate about something. Of course, *Plesiosaurus* wasn't a dinosaur. Rather, it was a plesiosaur, but Robyn chose not to correct her mother on this occasion.

"And this wall," Carol remarked, looking from one end of it to the other. "You'll be running out of space soon."

"Maybe I'll have to add some to the ceiling."

Carol smiled broadly.

"You certainly could. I like this one here, the orange dinosaur."

I rolled my eyes in despair as she pointed at the picture of me. Normies. They think everything extinct is a dinosaur.

"He's not a dinosaur," Robyn replied with another giggle. "That's Ed—the *Dimetrodon*."

"Oh, yes, he's the one you... see."

Robyn nodded enthusiastically. However, it was obvious my presence worried Carol. She was probably concerned that an imaginary friend was likely to hinder the process of making any "real" friends.

"He's a... sin... Sinatra?"

"Synapsid. They were more closely related to mammals than to reptiles, you know."

"Interesting. Well, he's very handsome," Carol concluded.

"Okay, Carol," I said smugly. "Well played. I'll let the dinosaur comment slide."

Not that Carol could hear me, of course. Perhaps one day she would, I thought.

The Lonely Beach

The unusually hot weather intensified further that day and Robyn's father insisted she head outside and "enjoy the sunshine." She had slathered a thick layer of sunscreen on every bit of exposed skin but, from experience, I knew fine well she would burn anyway. It was like a superpower, or whatever the opposite of a superpower is. Regardless of how much sunscreen she wore, or how often she skulked in the shade, she would burn to a crisp at the slightest hint of sunshine. Nevertheless, we headed out to make the most of it. I, of course, didn't have to worry about the heat. That big old sail on my back? It's not just for display. Rather, it's an ingenious thermoregulation device. Very useful in the height of summer.

Together, we wandered through the picturesque seaside town of Lyme Regis on the famous English Jurassic Coast. The town had been Robyn's home her whole life and she knew every inch of it. Today, we made our way past the new Mary Anning statue and along the coast towards her favourite spot. We called it the Lonely

Beach—it probably had a proper name, but it had always been the Lonely Beach to us.

It was covered in sharp stones, slippery moss, and deep, seaweed-filled rock pools. What did this mean? Well, it meant it was a fairly wretched beach. But that had one main advantage—there was seldom anyone else there.

We clambered down the steep, sandy access path and onto the rocky beach. Before us, stretched the sparkling English Channel while the iconic Blue Lias cliffs wrapped around the coastline. It was quite a view—one which neither of us ever got bored of.

"Look," Robyn exclaimed while pointing at the cliff face.

She skipped towards the cliff and pulled a fist-sized rock which looked ready to fall. It was a pale grey, but with white veins running through it. These were fairly common around here, and Robyn knew what to do with it. She crouched and smashed it on the ground several times, causing it to split in half. The two halves fell away to reveal a spiral-shaped fossil inside.

"It's an ammonite," she chirped excitedly.

"Neat," I replied with an approving nod while admiring how well preserved it was. "What's an ammonite?"

"An ancient cephalopod," she clarified. "It was like a little squid in a shell—it's just the spiral shell that's preserved. I talk about these all the time. How do you not know about ammonites?"

"I zone out a lot," I admitted with a shrug.

After spending some time examining the fossil, Robyn stuffed it into the pocket of her baggy, green shorts and wandered closer to the sea. By the shorefront, she stopped and scanned the ground intently. After a few moments, she found what she sought—a small, flat stone perfect for skipping. She grasped it tightly, stretched her arm back, and launched it into the channel… where the stone proceeded to simply plop beneath the waves. Robyn had many skills, but rock skipping wasn't one of them. Her dad had promised to teach her, but he never seemed to find the time.

"Nice throw, Croll," came an unexpected voice from behind.

It was a voice Robyn and I knew all too well, and it wasn't a welcome one.

We turned around to see a blond girl in white denim shorts and a pink, glittery vest top. It was Hannah. Hannah Owen was an especially unpleasant young lady who attended the same school as Robyn. I reckoned every time her name was spoken, somewhere in the world a small child dropped an ice cream cone.

For some reason, Hannah revelled in any opportunity to tease those around her—and Robyn seemed to be her favourite target. Today, to make matters worse, she was also backed up by two friends. I didn't recognise them, but an audience always made Hannah more vicious.

"H-hi, Hannah," Robyn stammered. "The good beach is back that way."

"Maybe I like this beach."

"Oh, I just thought you might be lost."

Robyn turned away and picked up another rock before tossing it into the sea. She was attempting to appear calm, but I could see a slight tremble in her right leg.

"Me and my friends want it to ourselves," Hannah snarled, approaching Robyn ominously.

"What? But... I was here first." Robyn replied, almost in a whisper.

"Well, I don't want to look at your cheap, ugly clothes," Hannah sneered while plucking at Robyn's yellow sports t-shirt. "They don't even fit you properly."

Her accomplices began to circle behind Robyn as Hannah became visibly angrier. She gave Robyn a forceful shove, from which she stumbled backwards several steps. One of the other girls then pushed her back towards Hannah, who shoved her once more. For several long minutes, all three girls took turns pushing Robyn around—cackling the whole time.

"Stop," Robyn begged. "Please."

Robyn's glasses were shaken loose from her face and clattered onto the stones—only for Hannah to kick them into the distance.

When Robyn finally broke free of the cycle, she strode away. She didn't want to run—she wanted to retain at least some dignity, but she took long, fast strides. After a quick scan of the area, she crouched to reclaim her glasses. She took a quick look to assess their condition and found one lens to be missing and the other cracked. Fighting back tears, she stuffed her broken glasses into her pocket.

"I saw your mum the other day," Hannah sneered. "Nice haircut."

That was a low blow. Normally, Robyn would simply have walked away, but something caused her to stop.

"Completely bald, by the way," Hannah explained to her friends, who began to giggle. "Probably the stress of having such an ugly daughter that did it."

"She's sick, actually," Robyn grumbled.

"Oh, no!" Hannah replied with a dramatic imitation of despair.

Her two friends, seemingly devoid of any personalities of their own, dutifully giggled some more. But I, for one, didn't think Hannah was funny. Neither did Robyn, but I knew she wasn't one for conflict. She lowered her head and skulked away. I wouldn't be chased off so easily, though. I lined Hannah up, dipped my head, and charged.

Of course, I knew fine well it would have no impact. The biggest downside of being a figment of a child's imagination is that you can't interact with the real world. I would do what I always did—float right through her and she would be none the wiser. It would make me feel better, though. It usually did, and the visual entertainment would make Robyn feel better too. Except, this time, something strange happened.

As I charged, the stones felt unusually solid beneath my feet. With each step, loose stones flicked up behind me and, as I reached my target, my head made a solid, jarring contact with the girl's chest. I looked up to see Hannah Owen hurtling backwards through the air before splashing into a small, but deep, rock pool.

She sat, her mouth wide open in surprise, with her legs pointing into the air and her backside wedged into the bowl-shaped pool. Her friends looked on with confusion, noting the several metres between Hannah and Robyn. After a moment of disbelief, Hannah scrambled to get back to her feet but only found herself slipping on the moss and falling back into the water repeatedly. She screamed and swore as her face grew redder and redder.

I looked at Robyn, concerned that I had taken things too far. However, while clearly a little surprised, my old friend was trying desperately to contain a snigger.

After finally hauling herself out of the water, Hannah flicked several strands of seaweed off her previously white shorts, now stained a brownish-green, in disgust.

"*Eugh*," she screeched. "You did this, you little witch!"

"I've been way over here," Robyn replied, desperately disguising a smirk.

"I'll make you sorry!" Hannah screamed before storming off into the distance.

I looked on rather proudly as that horrible specimen of a child retreated in defeat, but there was something more profound to consider.

"How did you do that?" Robyn asked once the girls were out of sight.

"I have no idea," I replied honestly. "It felt good, though!"

"Maybe she fell, and it just happened to be when you charged."

"I don't know. I felt it. It felt the impact, it was... solid."

"It can't have been, you must have imagined it."

"You're the one who does the imagining around here," I insisted. "I know what I felt."

"But Ed—and I mean this with love—you're not real."

"Tell that to Hannah."

"Do you think she'll tell her parents? I don't want to get in trouble."

"We'll burn that can of worms when we open it."

"Okay... wait, what?"

"What?"

"That's... that's not the saying."

"Sure, it is. Her outfit looked expensive, didn't it?"

Robyn and I paused for a moment and glanced at each other before bursting into hysterical laughter. There was no way that green stain would wash out.

Granny's Macaroni

Robyn and I returned home that night in a rather cheerful mood. Neither of us understood what had happened, but there was a quiet pleasure in having watched Hannah dunk into the slimy rock pool. Whether there was some inexplicable power rendering my imaginary body physical, or merely an odd coincidence, justice had been served.

The Crolls were a young family, having had Robyn in their early twenties, which made for tight finances, but they provided all they could for their daughter. Their home was a simple, two-bedroom terraced house with tan-coloured roughcast on the front which had begun to crumble in places. The front garden needed weeding, but it was one of the more presentable houses on the street. It wasn't a mansion, by any stretch, but it was home.

"Hi, Dad!" Robyn chirped as she strode into the kitchen.

"Hey, pumpkin pie," Michael Croll replied cheerfully, glancing up from his cooking. "Where are your glasses?"

"Oh, I dropped them at the beach," she lied, extracting the broken pair from her pocket. "I'll go get my spare pair."

"Please be more careful, honey. Those repairs aren't cheap," he said, while tapping his own glasses which had also been recently mended.

"Sorry, Dad."

"That's all right, pumpkin." He gave Robyn a kind smile. "You've burned your chest."

Robyn raised a hand to her collarbone and winced as she felt the sting of sunburn. She had forgotten to apply sun cream above her neckline.

"Robyn in name, robin in appearance," I teased.

She rolled her eyes in response before turning her attention back to her father.

"Look what I found today." Robyn thrust her fossil on an outstretched hand under Michael's nose. "It's an ammonite. I wonder how old it is."

"Well, does it have three bums?" he asked.

"What?" Robyn replied with a giggle. "No."

"I guess we can rule out the Triassic then."

Robyn rolled her eyes once more and groaned while a self-satisfied smirk spread across her father's face. Michael was an overgrown child at heart. Wearing a blue Cookie Monster jumper—despite the heat—and performing a disjointed dance to "Karma Chameleon" on the radio, he emptied half a block's worth of grated cheddar cheese into his bubbling pot of macaroni. His bouncy, black hair flopped around in time with his uncoordinated dance moves, which added to the amusing spectacle. He was definitely the "fun" parent—at least when he had the time.

Robyn's parents had met while they both studied in Scotland. I used to wonder why they chose to move to Carol's hometown after Robyn was born rather than staying up north, but then we spent a fortnight in Glasgow for a wedding and it all became clear. It rains there. A lot.

Robyn opened the fridge door and extracted a large jar of gherkins. She twisted off the lid, dipped her fingers into the yellowish vinegar, and pulled one out before tossing the whole pickle into her mouth.

"We're running low on pickles," she mumbled, her mouth still full of partially chewed gherkin.

"I'll get some more tomorrow," Michael said with a chuckle. "At the rate you eat them, I'll have to get two jars."

"Sounds good to me," she replied with a cheeky grin.

"Are you ready for some of Granny's mac?"

"Always!"

He called this particular meal "Granny's mac" as it was a recipe he had inherited from his mother in Glasgow. However, I had seen the recipe and it was certainly not the same meal Michael produced. His heavy use of garlic showed complete disregard for the recipe and the quantity of cheese bordered on disdain for it. But man, did it smell good.

"Is this the recipe with a metric tonne or imperial ton of cheese?" Robyn joked.

"Pumpkin, I've told you a million times not to exaggerate," Michael replied with a smirk. "But metric, always metric. We're not savages. Would you like some lemonade?"

"Oh, yes, please."

Robyn's father proceeded to pour some lemonade into a glass while also continuing to stir his pot. In his attempt to multi-task, he soon overfilled the glass and lemonade overflowed, spilling onto the counter.

"I think that's plenty," Robyn teased.

Michael mumbled a curse word to himself before dabbing the wet counter with a dish towel.

"Well, you know me, I always give a hundred and ten percent."

Recently, Michael had been somewhat preoccupied. Not only did he work full-time as a schoolteacher, he also spent an increasing amount of time tending to Carol, who seemed evermore dependent on her dutiful husband. She had her good days, but she also had long spells when she was unable to even get out of bed. Then, of course, there was all the work to be done around the house—cleaning, dishes, laundry.

He never once complained, but I often wished he had more time for us. Robyn missed spending quality time with her father and, in truth, so did I. Michael may not have been able to see me, but he was the only adult who didn't become awkward around the topic of Robyn's "imaginary friend." Indeed, he embraced it. He was the only person other than Robyn to ever properly accept my existence.

"Granny's mac smells delicious tonight," remarked Robyn.

For all his other qualities, Michael was also a fine chef—a fact that made me wish I was actually capable of consuming food. A rich, smoky scent filled my nostrils and made me drool.

"I hope it tastes as good as it smells," he replied. "I added some smoked ham this time. Here, taste it."

Michael proceeded to scoop a small sample of macaroni out of the pot and thrust it towards Robyn's face. He dropped a piece of pasta onto the floor as he did, which produced a small splatter of cheese sauce. Robyn enthusiastically chomped on the sneak preview of the meal to come. It was obviously hot, so she chewed with her mouth wide open, inhaling large gulps of air to cool it inside her mouth. Finally, she scrunched her eyes closed in pleasure.

"Hmm, it's okay," she replied with a cold, analytical expression and a shrug.

"You don't exactly seem overwhelmed."

"I mean, I'm not underwhelmed. You could say I'm sufficiently whelmed."

Michael narrowed his eyes and stared at her with a smirk.

"Your poker face is terrible—it's delicious, isn't it?"

Robyn's stony expression failed and transformed into a broad grin.

"It's your best one yet."

"Well, your dad is the best cook in the world," he said with a wink. "Now, you can't be winding me up like that in a few weeks when I transform from Dad into Mr. Croll."

"Oh, God, don't remind me. It was bad enough having Mum in Year Five."

Robyn was in the rather unfortunate position of having both parents work as local teachers. Carol taught at the primary school, while Michael educated the teenage delinquents in chemistry at the secondary school.

"Well, you'd best pay attention. Chemistry is important if you're going to be a big shot palaeontologist, like you said. Will you be joining me for chess club?"

"Mum!" Robyn called through the house, hurriedly changing the subject. "Mum, you have to come taste Dad's macaroni."

I stared longingly. Easily the worst thing about being imaginary was the inability to eat. Oh, how I craved food. What I would have given to chew on a burger or slurp an ice cream. I stared at the stray piece of macaroni on the floor with a heart, or I suppose a stomach, full of longing.

"You know, Robyn," I began. "With what happened today… maybe I could just try some of that macaroni. Maybe I'm more real than I realise."

She rolled her eyes.

"Nothing happened," she whispered. "She fell."

"It wouldn't hurt to try, though, right?"

She sighed.

"Dad, could you maybe leave a plate out for Ed?"

"Of course," he replied with a smile. "Can't have the poor little guy going hungry. He might go extinct."

That level of lazy humour was sadly all too common, but I forgave it. Besides, occasionally he was mildly funny. What I did appreciate was the complete lack of hesitation at the prospect of feeding Robyn's invisible friend. Any other adult, even Carol, would have at least paused awkwardly before reluctantly humouring her. But not Michael. He embraced her as she was.

Michael's face then dropped as he turned to face the kitchen door. I followed his gaze and saw Carol standing, propped against the door frame. She was pale, paler than I had ever seen her.

"Carol?" Michael said. "Carol, are you okay? You don't look too well."

"Oh, you're all compliments today," she replied with an eyebrow raised sarcastically.

Despite her teasing response, Michael was right. She didn't look well at all. Before anyone could say anything else, she collapsed and crumpled onto the floor.

"Mum!" Robyn screamed.

Michael rushed to Carol and rolled her over onto her side. She began to convulse awkwardly with her eyes pinned open. I'd seen her seizures before and her blank, unfocused gaze haunted me every time.

"Robyn, get me my phone," Michael directed in a surprisingly calm fashion.

But Robyn didn't even hear him, not really. She gazed in horror as her mother began to drool onto the floor and grind her teeth loudly.

"Robyn," he repeated, more sternly this time.

She scrunched her eyes and snapped back to reality. Spinning around, she fumbled for the mobile phone. I kept my eyes focused on Carol. While to the others she seemed to stare blankly into space, it seemed as though she was looking me right in the eye. A coincidence, I was sure, but it was odd, nonetheless.

"Hang in there, Carol," I whispered.

I knew she couldn't hear, but it made me feel better to say something.

A New Prognosis

I felt slightly guilty for thinking so, but having the chance to ride in the back of an ambulance was a lot of fun. Sure, I was concerned about Carol, but this wasn't her first seizure. Indeed, I could recall at least four—all as a result of her illness. On previous occasions, though, Carol's mother had been on hand to look after Robyn, so this was the first time we had ridden to the hospital with her. I found myself rather pleased that Robyn's grandmother had gone to Lanzarote for the week.

However, the hospital was most certainly *not* as exciting as the ambulance. Carol finally came around, exhausted as always, which was followed by endless waiting. We waited for nurses to check her blood pressure and shine torches in her eyes. We waited on doctors to discuss her symptoms. We waited even longer for specialists who each asked the same questions over and over again.

The latest in a long line of doctors to question Carol and Michael was a familiar one. Doctor MacGregor was her name, and she was an... *oncologist*? I think that's what they called her. I had no idea what an oncologist did, but she was friendly. As per usual, she greeted Robyn with a gentle smile.

"Hello, Robyn," she chimed. "How are you today?"

Robyn shrugged.

"Don't be rude," I insisted. "At least pretend not to be bored."

"Uh, I'm okay, I guess," Robyn said with a forced smile.

"Nice weather today."

"Thanks."

"Thanks for the weather?" I teased.

"Well, not *thanks*, it's not like I made the weather. I mean... yes. Yes, it is."

"Smooth," I added.

"Here, why don't you take this and get yourself something from the vending machine?" Doctor MacGregor said while handing Robyn two golden, one-pound coins.

It was obvious Doctor MacGregor simply wanted some privacy with Robyn's parents—but Robyn wasn't so nosey as to turn down free chocolate. As such, we both headed down the corridor for snacks. Of course, the snacks were only for Robyn, but I was still keen to attempt the whole "food" thing. I might have been delusional, but it was worth a shot.

"What are you getting?" I asked as Robyn scanned the machine.

"A Bounty, I reckon. I'll never understand why people don't like them."

"Maybe I could try?" I requested. "I didn't get any macaroni, after all."

Robyn's Bounty tumbled into the well at the bottom of the machine before she crouched to retrieve it.

"I don't know about that. Sharing pasta is one thing, but *chocolate*?" she teased. "That's a big ask."

"Come *on*," I pleaded.

Smiling, she peeled the wrapper away and extracted one of two small milk chocolate bars which, as I gathered, were filled with creamed coconut.

"Here," she chirped, holding the bar towards my face. "It won't work, Ed. I know you think what happened at the beach was—"

"Just let me try," I insisted.

This was my moment. I could *do* this. I had interacted with the real world before—with Hannah. I knew in my heart it wasn't a coincidence. It *had* happened. It *was* real and, for a brief moment, so was I. Now, the ultimate experience for any real-life, physical being... chocolate.

I opened my mouth wide, much wider than needed, and chomped enthusiastically. As my teeth closed over the silky milk chocolate, my tongue was flooded with the sweet taste of... *nothing*. My jaws passed straight through the Bounty as if it were a hologram.

"Oh, come on," I moaned.

"I told you so," replied Robyn.

"That you did," I conceded, trying to hide my disappointment.

"Mum will be okay, won't she?" Robyn asked after a brief silence.

"Of course," I replied as we began to walk back towards the hospital room. "She always is. Remember the one after Christmas? That was worse than this one."

"True, she hit her head pretty hard that time."

"Yeah, she had a black eye and everything. This time wasn't so bad; she'll be home tomorrow."

We arrived back at Carol's hospital room to find the privacy curtain drawn. From behind the curtain, we could hear Doctor MacGregor speaking with Robyn's parents. Robyn stopped to listen to what sounded like a fairly downbeat discussion.

"So, what does this mean?" asked Michael.

"I think we have to be realistic," replied the doctor solemnly. "The cancer has progressed much faster than we expected—it's clear the treatment isn't working."

"So, she'll need a different treatment?"

There was a brief pause as Doctor MacGregor seemed to mull over her response.

"I'm afraid we've exhausted all treatment options."

"*No,*" snapped Michael. "She's only thirty-four. She's strong, she can fight it. There has to be—"

"So, I'm dying?" interrupted Carol with surprising calmness. "How long?"

"I couldn't possibly say for sure. It could be weeks."

"Weeks?" gasped Michael.

"Maybe days."

This was followed by a long silence. I couldn't believe what I was hearing. I had become so accustomed to the illness—it had simply become part of our lives. I had heard so many times that everything would be fine, but now the doctor thought Carol was...dying?

I looked up at Robyn, whose eyes seemed to glaze over. She was understandably in shock. Slowly, the news began to sink in. Her eyes welled with tears as she acknowledged that her mother might only have mere days to live. Her bottom lip quivered before she turned and stormed out of the room.

"*Wait,*" I called as I followed her out.

She ignored me and broke into a run, heading for the exit.

"Robyn, please!"

Robyn sprinted through the waiting room, almost knocking over a young boy in the process, and burst through the rotating door into the cool evening air. She crumpled to her knees and cried as I had never seen her cry before. She wailed, unconcerned by the many onlookers. I did the only thing I could. I pressed in tightly to the only physical part of the world I could feel—my dear Robyn. She wrapped her arms around my neck and hugged me tightly, tears dripping onto the top of my head as she did.

I desperately wanted to help—more than anything I had ever wanted. Robyn was hurting. She was feeling unimaginable pain. Every sinew of my being longed to take it away.

If only there was a way.

***

"Robyn," I hissed through the darkness. "*Robyn.*"

Robyn rubbed her eyes slowly before pulling the duvet over her face.

"Wake up, Robyn."

"What do you want?" she mumbled.

"I know how to help your mum."

She paused for a moment before throwing the covers off of herself and staring into my eyes. She reached her hand over to click on her lamp, revealing her brows furrowed in confusion.

"What are you talking about?"

"I've been awake all night thinking… Remember what happened with Hannah?"

"Sure, you yeeted her into a rock pool."

"Exactly! Wait, yeeted? That doesn't sound right. Is that really the past tense of yeet? Yote, maybe? Yet? No—"

"Ed, focus."

"Right, Hannah, yes, I yote her into the pool. But that should have been impossible, right?"

"It *is* impossible, Ed. She fell. It just looked as though you pushed her."

"But what if she didn't?"

"Then you'd have eaten the Bounty."

"Look, let's just practice. Maybe I can do something else."

"And how would that help Mum?"

"Just… just humour me for a minute."

Robyn sat herself up and sighed deeply.

"Fine, Ed. What do you suggest we do?"

"I… I don't know," I said as I scanned the room. "What about this?"

I pointed my nose at a plastic cup which sat on Robyn's desk. It was a disposable, green cup with white polka dots which she used to wash her paintbrushes.

"If I can knock this over…" I suggested.

"Go for it," Robyn replied with a shrug.

I could tell she didn't have high expectations, but I had to make this work. I raised my right paw and swiped. My claws rushed through the air as I focused on that little green cup. It was going to work. I *knew* it.

My heart dropped as my paw glided straight through as if it wasn't there, or, rather, as if *I* wasn't there. I swiped again, and again, and then once more—each time with the same outcome.

Robyn scowled at me. "Can I go back to sleep now?"

"Do you not get it?" I snapped. "This could be our ticket. If you can make me real, then you can make *anything* real."

"Anything? Like what?"

"Anything like *anything*, Robyn. Anything you could imagine. And what would you want more than anything else in the world right now?"

"For Mum to get better," she replied, her eyes dipping towards the floor in sadness.

"You just have to want it."

"Of course, I want it, Ed," Robyn hissed. "But this isn't a fairy tale. Things don't happen just because I want it."

"But you did want Hannah to meet some sweet, soggy justice, did you not?"

"I guess."

"And that did happen?"

"That doesn't mean—"

"Just focus and we can do this. I can do this, I *know* it!"

"You can't *do* anything, Ed."

"I can if you…"

I took one more futile swipe at the plastic cup which once more remained stubbornly atop the table. Robyn reached over, pulled the chord on the lamp, and plunged the room into darkness.

"How can you give up so easily? I'm trying to help!"

I marched over to the bed and pulled the lamp chord, turning the light back on.

"Why are you being like this?" I scolded.

Rather than respond, Robyn simply stared at me blankly. It was as though she didn't even care—like her mind was elsewhere. I knew I could do this if she only had some faith.

"All I need is a little bit of conviction from you," I ranted. "You have to believe too, not just me. *Really* believe, and then maybe—"

"Ed?" Robyn whispered, her eyes wide.

"*What*?" I snapped, irritated that she had interrupted me.

"You switched on the lamp."

Carcinisation

Have you ever seen an octopus eye up close? Granted, it's hardly an everyday sort of thing to see but, if you had, you might have noticed one peculiar thing. The eye of an octopus is remarkably similar to your own. Why is this so peculiar? Perhaps because the last common ancestor between yourself and an octopus was a flatworm three quarters of a billion years ago. So how did both of you end up with remarkably similar eyeballs?

This is due to a strange phenomenon called convergent evolution. In effect, with similar needs and pressures placed on different animals over time, they will sometimes evolve similar adaptations. For example, bats and dolphins both faced hunting in low visibility and so, both separately developed echolocation, a characteristic that allows them to use echoes from sound waves to hunt—even in total darkness.

However, there is one type of convergent evolution which is especially bizarre—because it happens again and again. It's called carcinisation and is the tendency for crustaceans to evolve into crabs. You see, all the animals you would consider to be crabs are likely not all related. In fact, crabs have evolved separately at least five times.

So, maybe we are all destined to become crabs one day. Or perhaps, regardless of the final form it takes, destiny is simply something which comes knocking for all of us—humans and crustaceans alike.

The Primordial Forest

She was right. The lamp. Robyn sat bolt upright and ran her hands through her auburn hair.

"Try it again," she whispered.

I reached over and grabbed the chord between my paws once more—feeling the string as I gripped it. I pulled it down until it clicked twice. The bulb died before bursting back into life.

"It works," I mumbled in shock.

"How?"

"I have no idea."

"Wait, how will this help Mum?"

"Well, you made me, and you made me real. Now you just imagine your mum getting better, I guess."

"Just imagine?"

"Sure, it's not rocket surgery."

"I don't—wait, what?"

"What?"

"Rocket surgery?" she asked.

"What's wrong with that?"

"That's not the saying."

"Sure, it is."

"Whatever—the point is I don't think it's so simple to just imagine a cure."

"Trust me. Imagine what a cure might look like. How about some kind of miracle—I don't know… a miracle soup?"

"Soup?"

"Well, I've never taken medicine before, have I? Your mum always gives you soup when you're unwell."

"With a cold, Ed. I think cancer needs more than a bowl of soup, however miraculous it might be."

"Well… a pill, then?"

"It might seem a bit odd if I hand her a mystery pill."

"Okay, so, what I'm hearing is that soup is back on the table."

"Okay, fine. One bowl of magical, medicinal soup coming up. Soup… soup…"

Robyn rose from the bed and strode over to her desk. She stared down and focused hard on the wooden surface.

"A cure," she whispered. "A cure, a cure a cure."

We both stood, eyes fixated on the desktop—waiting for the bowl to appear.

"I don't think this is how it works." Robyn sighed.

"How do you mean?"

"Well, I imagined you knocking the cup over, I imagined you eating the chocolate, but I didn't imagine the lamp, or you knocking Hannah over. Those things… they just kind of happened."

"How did you make those things happen then? How do we recreate it?"

"I don't know. It was subconscious, I guess."

Before Robyn could finish, there was a loud cracking sound from the far wall. We spun around to see that the painted plaster had begun to split. A thin, twisting branch reached upwards from the floor, cracking the wall further as it burrowed through. A second branch then sprouted to the left and soon, both stretched almost to the ceiling. They curved inwards at the top until they met, forming a wooden archway. The remaining wall between them began to deform and shrivel as ivy vines bridged the gap until the wall couldn't be seen for a thick covering of vegetation. A faint light seemed to shine through from the vine leaves.

"What is that?" I gasped.

"It… it looks like a door," Robyn whispered.

"How does a door help your mum?" I asked, somewhat perplexed.

"I have no idea," Robyn replied honestly.

"Did you think of the soup?"

"Yes, I thought of the soup, Ed. But instead, I got… this. I told you it wasn't that simple."

"You think the cure is on the other side? Maybe it's like a medicine cupboard."

"Maybe."

For several long minutes, we sat and stared at the strange door which had grown through Robyn's bedroom wall. It was crooked and twisted and seemed ancient despite having only grown a few moments ago. It was oddly intimidating. Switching on a lamp was one thing, but this was something more. Much more. Robyn had only become aware of this abstract ability and yet it now manifested itself brazenly.

"So, you should probably go first," she suggested nervously.

"Chicken," I teased with a smirk.

However, I was, admittedly, somewhat nervous too, so I couldn't blame her. It might have been the product of her imagination but, as she had alluded to before, it seemed to be a subconscious construction. Robyn had no more control over what lay beyond that door than I had.

I stepped forwards with my head held high. The door didn't have a handle of any kind. Rather, it was simply formed of intertwined branches. I pressed my head against it and shoved. It didn't open easily. As it began to shift, a warm breeze streamed into the bedroom and a stunning, yellow light shone through the thin crack which grew wider as I pushed. I leaned hard and heaved. Even with the door now fully opened, the glare was too bright to see what lay beyond.

"Oh my God," I gasped as I stepped through.

"What's through there?" Robyn called from the other side.

"You'll have to come through and see for yourself. You'd never believe me otherwise."

"Is it… is it safe?"

"Just get over here, Robyn."

Robyn took a deep breath and crept through the door after me. She gasped and grabbed onto my sail, propping herself up—presumably, a precaution in case she were to faint. We stood at the top of a tall, grassy hill and, for as far as I could see, a great rainforest stretched out below us. Miles of endless, luscious, green canopy under the bright sunlight and almost entirely cloudless sky. Birds fluttered, insects buzzed, and mysterious beasts called and roared in the distance.

"You… you made all this?" I muttered, dazed by what I saw.

"I don't know. I guess so…"

"This a bit more than a bowl of soup."

"It's probably a dream, right?"

"Maybe," I conceded. "That would make the most sense. We do have a habit of sharing dreams."

"How would we know?"

"Hmm…"

I swung my tail around and swept Robyn's legs from beneath her. Her feet flew forwards and she thumped onto her back.

"What was that for?" she exclaimed, shooting me a furious gaze from the ground.

"Did it hurt?"

"Yes, it hurt!"

"Huh… probably not a dream then, I guess."

Robyn clambered back to her feet, clearly annoyed, but it was the only test I could think of. Take it from someone imaginary—you don't feel real pain in a dream. If it hurt bad, then it was real.

"A little heads up would have been nice."

"I needed it to be authentic," I replied.

"So, what now?"

"I don't know. I suppose the cure is out there somewhere. Shall we go for a stroll through your imaginary jungle?"

"Is that a good idea? We don't know what's down there."

"There's one way to find out."

"I guess it can't hurt."

"I think we've established it can," I remarked with a smirk.

We descended the hill, wary as to what we might find in the forest. As we reached the bottom and the trees loomed large over us, the bright sun disappeared. The forest floor was stifling and humid—the air felt heavy and sticky. The undergrowth hummed with flying insects and a rich cocktail of earthy smells.

As I looked around, I began to pick out some interesting details. For one, many of the trees weren't like the trees back home at all. In place of bark, they had what I could only describe as dragon scales. Smooth and ridged, they were like the skin of some monstrous reptile.

"Check out these trees," I said.

Robyn gasped.

"Those are *Lepidodendron*."

"They're what, now?"

"Scale trees. From the Carboniferous Period."

"Carbon… you mean prehistoric?"

"Very prehistoric. These guys went extinct like three-hundred-million years ago—a lot of their remains became coal, you know."

Above my head, flitting between two trees, I saw a small, black, feathered creature with wings on both its arms and legs. It glided from branch to branch, like a strange cross between a bird and a flying squirrel. I recognised it instantly—a small, arboreal dinosaur named *Microraptor*. Then, darting around above the undergrowth, was a pigeon-sized dragonfly which glittered green and purple.

I knew these animals—they were from Robyn's wall. Robyn hadn't just created a world in her subconscious—she had created a world filled with the ancient creatures she obsessed over. This was a prehistoric paradise.

"Robyn, this is amazing," I said, gazing around us.

"I know, right?"

"You know what this is, don't you? This is Pangaea. It's not just on paper anymore. You've… you've brought it to life."

Looking shocked, Robyn gaped for a moment. "I don't understand it, but… I guess so. I have no idea where to go, though. This jungle looks like it carries on forever in every direction."

"Maybe we should… wait…"

Something had caught my attention. It was a sound; an unsettling, deep, slightly metallic gurgle. I turned to be faced with an alarming sight. What stood in the shadows of the scale tree canopy was a huge, heavily armoured crocodile. It had an almost wolf-like stance, standing tall on muscular legs which were tipped by what could only be described as hooves.

"Robyn," I whispered. "You wouldn't imagine up anything that might do us harm, would you?"

"What do you mean?" she asked as she turned to be greeted by the fearsome reptile. "Oh… oh my."

"What is that, Robyn?"

"It's… it's a *Boverisuchus*."

I feared as much. It gurgled louder yet and took a step towards us. Its leathery skull passed through a glistening sunbeam which highlighted its focused, narrowed eyes. There was no doubt in my mind, whether a creation of Robyn's imagination or not, this animal meant us harm.

"Stay back," I warned. "I'll have you know I'm a black belt in, um, chai tea."

"We should run," suggested Robyn.

The only saving grace when faced with a modern crocodilian is it probably wouldn't chase you far. Sure, crocodiles and alligators can move quickly, but usually only over small distances. This was not true of *Boverisuchus*. Running from it was surely futile. However, I saw no alternative.

We turned and fled. Robyn's feet pounded against the dirt while my paws padded alongside. Unfortunately, neither her bipedal gait nor my short, outwardly protruding legs made for an especially fast mode of locomotion. The galloping hoofbeats of the *Boverisuchus* bore down on us embarrassingly quickly and the great beast clamped its vice-like jaws around Robyn's ankle. She fell face-first into the dirt before being dragged back. I needed a Plan B—it looked like I would have to fight.

I sprang over the top of Robyn and thudded onto the crocodilian's osteoderm-covered back, causing it to crumple into the ground. The momentum carried me forwards and I tumbled onto my side. Looking up, I realised I had been overzealous. I now lay on the ground in a highly vulnerable state with a large predatory reptile charging at me. It closed in with its jaws open wide.

"Oskar," called a soft voice through the forest. "Oskar, what's going on?"

The *Boverisuchus* halted and looked towards the source of the call.

"Spies," he growled back in a strong German accent.

I had considered it to be some rabid, wild beast, so the revelation it could speak caught me by surprise.

"Spies, you say?"

Through the trees appeared the oddest of creatures. It was immensely tall, easily four times Robyn's height. Its plump, round, heavily feathered body was supported by two comparatively short legs while its head, which sat atop a long and slender neck, was small, narrow, and tipped with a blunt beak. Most curiously, and most intimidatingly, were the long arms which hung limply in front of its belly, adorned with enormous, sharp, sword-like claws.

I was struck by how beautiful the creature's plumage was. It was a shimmering, iridescent shade of blue, while emerald-green wing feathers fanned outwards from its forelimbs. The enormous herbivore gazed down upon me as I scrambled to my feet and backed away from Oskar.

"What is a *Dimetrodon* doing in the jungle, might I ask?" interrogated the beast. "One might think a creature so far from its natural habitat is... suspicious."

The creature was eloquent. He had an aura of authority around him in a way I hadn't expected. I wasn't sure why, but the inhabitants of Pangaea being anything other than mindless beasts surprised me. I suppose, rather selfishly, I had assumed myself to be the only one whom Robyn's imagination would bestow with a personality. That being said, despite the intimidating circumstance, it was oddly pleasing to have someone other than Robyn see and speak to me. Not only that, but he hadn't mistaken me for a dinosaur either.

"Uh, nothing suspicious here," I replied with a shake in my voice. "We're just passing through."

"We?"

"Over there," grunted Oskar. "Some kind of fish with legs."

The feathered giant turned its head towards Robyn.

"A legged fish? Oh, my goodness," he gasped. "Oskar, you imbecile. That's no fish, what kind of fish have you seen? This is a *Homo sapiens*—a human. A young girl, no less. Which must mean… you find the Architect strolling through her own jungle and you attack her!?"

"Architect?" Oskar gasped. *"Mein Gott."*

"A human girl! Who else do you suppose it could be?"

"I didn't think—"

"That's nothing new," the creature lamented. "Please, miss, do accept my apologies. My friend here is new and somewhat over-enthusiastic."

The feathered reptile let down a vast, clawed hand for Robyn to grab onto before pulling her to her feet. She grimaced as she put weight onto the bitten ankle but seemed mostly unhurt.

"You… you're a dinosaur," she stammered. "A *Therizinosaurus*."

"Indeed. Doctor Boggs, at your service, madam."

"Nice to meet you, Doctor," Robyn replied with a nervous smile.

"A doctor?" I asked.

Robyn looked at me and then Doctor Boggs with wide eyes and smiled.

"It's you," she remarked.

"I beg your pardon?" the doctor replied.

"I tried to imagine a cure, but instead I found you—a doctor. You can cure my mum."

Doctor Boggs raised an eyebrow.

"Your mother, you say? Is this why the Architect is in the jungle? You seek a cure?"

"For my mum's cancer."

"I'm afraid I'm not that kind of doctor, but I do believe there is one who can assist you. Please, let me take you to my master—the ruler of these lands. The king will wish to meet you."

The Golden Citadel

A king? I hadn't seen that coming. Given we had already established the residents could speak, perhaps it shouldn't have been such a surprise. Far from being a wilderness, it sounded as though Pangaea might be somewhat civilised.

This was confirmed as, after a short hike, we wandered beyond the tree line of the rainforest. The low sun blinded me for a moment but, as my eyes adjusted, I saw a great city before me. The ground sloped downwards away from us, allowing a spectacular view of the sprawl of gothic architecture. From here I could see what looked like cathedrals, monuments, and bell towers, all with beautifully intricate masonry. Towards the centre, the buildings grew taller and were adorned with stained glass which glinted in the sun.

At the centre of it all was a vast, golden citadel. It was an impossibly tall, spire-shaped building with a myriad of windows and balconies. The main structure was flanked by two towers of almost equal height. The citadel dominated the city skyline, towering over the streets below. This golden marvel was surrounded by a shimmering lake and connected to the rest of the city by a series of arched stone bridges.

The city itself brimmed with life. *Pterosaurs* flocked around the rooftops while creatures of all shapes and sizes marched around the streets. High above the bustle was a network of cable cars, soaring silently across the sky.

"What is this place?" I asked, blown away by the magnitude of the urban sprawl.

"This is the city of Tanis," Boggs explained. "It's the oldest and largest city in Pangaea—and the capital."

Almost prancing with excitement, we proceeded to the gated city walls. Rather than pressing straight on through, as I very much wished to do, Boggs led us up a staircase on the inner side of the huge, stone wall. Once at the top, we were greeted by a sleek, pill-shaped, metal cable car painted in glossy red and accentuated by gleaming chrome fixtures.

"This will take us directly to the citadel," he announced. "We would be best to avoid the crowds of the city given your... status."

I wasn't sure what he meant by that, but a cable car ride didn't seem so bad. As we soared above the city, I gazed in wonder at the streets below. They were filled with swarms of creatures—from tiny birds to vast, long-necked dinosaurs. In places, it was so crowded it simply looked as though the ground were a living, swelling sea of life. I found my gaze drawn to a large, open square near the heart of the city which featured an enormous, golden statue of what appeared to be a giant lizard of some kind.

Both above and below us, hundreds of cable cars whizzed back and forth in a remarkably intricate web. They converged on a large, stone turret tower near the lake's shore. Oddly, it looked to be blackened on one side with bamboo scaffolding wrapped around.

"What happened there?" I asked.

"Ah, yes, we had a small fire last month," replied Boggs. "Don't fret, all the necessary repairs have been completed."

Our cable car stopped atop the turret. Once disembarked, we climbed down the spiralling stairs of the tower and strolled onto a broad, flat bridge which connected the mainland to the citadel's island.

The bridge itself was constructed of huge blocks of sandstone which, on closer inspection, each preserved a trilobite fossil within. Robyn knelt and inspected a crumbling piece of the bridge. She picked up a small, flat disc of stone which contained a perfectly preserved trilobite. After admiring it for a second or two, she stuffed it into her pocket as a keepsake.

"Behold, Architect," announced Doctor Boggs as we climbed the stairs towards the vast doors. "The Golden Citadel. This is the seat of power, the home of our king."

"It's beautiful," Robyn replied, slack-jawed in amazement.

"It kind of feels like… home," I added.

"We're all children of the Architect here," Boggs said with a smile.

With his great clawed knuckles, he pushed on the heavy doors, forcing them both open. We would have easily fit through one door, so opening both seemed unnecessary, but it certainly made for a good entrance. Inside was a huge, circular hall with a pair of gleaming, marble staircases which curved around against the outer edges and came together high on the far wall. Where the stairways met was a wide balcony which notably had no bannisters or barriers.

Standing on each side of this balcony were two creatures I had hoped not to see. They were huge, barrel-bodied, theropod dinosaurs with vast jaws and tiny, two-fingered forearms. Stupid little arms—little more than clawed nipples as far as I was concerned.

"Ugh, T. rex?" I scoffed at Robyn. "I thought your imagination had more originality."

"I mean, apparently I did also imagine up a dinosaur city and a giant, golden castle," she replied while gazing, wide-eyed, at her surroundings. "That has to count for something, right?"

"I suppose it does," I conceded.

Upon closer inspection of the two fearsome dinosaurs, I noticed how remarkably dissimilar they were. The rex on the left was covered in rough, reptilian scales which were a diffuse shade of green with dark, dappled patches all over.

It was lean and muscular with a steely focus in its eyes. I could see its gleaming white, sharp, serrated teeth protruding from its maw.

The second *Tyrannosaurus* was rather more unappealing. Its skin hung loosely from its plump, fatty body which was coated in a thick, scruffy coat of matted, black feathers. The unkempt plumage on its neck was puffier and reminiscent of a lion's mane, but a rather sickly, unclean lion. The feathering stopped at the top of the neck, with its head instead covered in lumpy, uneven, black skin with blood-red stripes around its snout. Flaps of rough skin hung from its neck while large, wart-like lumps covered the ridges above its eyes. It reminded me somewhat of a vulture. Unlike the other rex, this one had lips which disguised its fearsome teeth.

"Doctor Boggs," said the muscular rex in a deep, booming voice. "Who do you bring before the throne unannounced? The king is resting. Don't think yourself so esteemed as to intrude on the crown whenever you please."

"Spare me the lecture, Sir Barnum," Boggs replied. "As his most trusted advisor, the king will be interested in what I have for him."

"And what makes you think that?"

"Well, while I'm aware intellect is far from your defining quality, I'm sure you recognise that I bring before you a human girl."

"Unusual in these parts, but not exactly worthy of royal attention."

"Specifically, a *Homo sapiens* girl."

Both tyrannosaurs stood a little taller, suddenly taking the giant herbivore more seriously.

"The Architect?" the shabby tyrannosaur hissed.

"I believe so," Boggs replied.

"Young lady," said Barnum, shifting his gaze onto Robyn. "Is this true?"

"Uh, s-so I'm told," she stammered.

Barnum stared at her in silence for several moments, seemingly deciding whether to believe her. Upon apparently reaching a conclusion, he emitted a thunderous call which bellowed from his abdomen without the beast having to open his mouth. The walls shook and Robyn flinched with fright. After a few seconds, the upper doors burst open. A shimmering white light shone into the hall and a silhouette emerged into focus. It was a beast—huge and muscular.

"All hail King Richard," announced Barnum.

"What is the meaning of this?" demanded a raspy and aged voice.

As the doors behind him slammed shut, the king became fully visible. He was a creature of vast proportions, even rivalling the tyrannosaurs in size, a huge reptile who stood on four legs and sported a long, lizard-like head which was filled with sharp teeth. The weight of his head was supported by a massive hump of muscle over his shoulder blades while his robust tail dragged along the floor behind him. His skin was a mosaic of flat scales which had a deep red colouration. He resembled a sort of giant monitor lizard, but with the build of a rhinoceros.

"What is that thing?" I whispered to Robyn.

"*Megalosaurus*," she replied in a hushed tone, "but a really outdated one."

I quickly realised she was right. King Richard was a living embodiment of the earliest reconstruction of the first known dinosaur—like a piece of Victorian palaeontological history brought to life. Upon his back was a red velvet cloak, trimmed with black fur and golden stitching.

"At least you didn't make one of the rexes king," I whispered to Robyn. "That would have been unimaginative."

She offered a wry smile in response.

"Your Majesty," said Boggs confidently as he and Oskar bowed onto their knees.

The king waved at them dismissively. His movements were slow and lethargic. Above him, blue flames erupted from a metal ring suspended from the ceiling. Even from the distance at which we stood, I could feel the heat. It reminded me somewhat of a gas stove, but seemed to act as a heat lamp. Slowly, under the intense flame, the cold-blooded *Megalosaurus* seemed to regain his strength—standing upright and raising his head.

"Doctor? You had better have good reason for your intrusion."

"I do, Your Highness. Please accept my apologies for interrupting your well-earned rest."

I was sure that ruling as king had to be tiring, but I did think it odd the king had seemingly been asleep during what looked like the middle of the day. I wondered how time here related to the real world, since it had been nighttime back home, yet it was broad daylight in Pangaea.

"Sire," hissed the feathered tyrannosaur. "Doctor Boggs claims this girl is the Architect."

As the scruffier tyrannosaur spoke, a foul odour travelled in his breath. It smelled like old, putrid meat.

"Nonsense, Gigas," the king scoffed.

"It's true, my liege," Boggs insisted.

"Hmm…"

King Richard narrowed his eyes as he examined Robyn from his elevated vantage point. He then glanced at me and back at Robyn before opening his eyes wide in excitement.

"By the stars. Doctor, come."

The huge, feathered beast acquiesced and lumbered up the stairs. Once on the balcony, he and the king conversed in hushed tones, both glancing in our direction once or twice.

"My dear, come closer," the king finally commanded. "And you, *Dimetrodon*, loyal companion to the Architect, join her."

Robyn edged nervously towards the staircase to our right. Now, I wasn't usually one to be bossed around by a dinosaur, particularly not by one that wasn't even scientifically up to date, but he was a king, after all. He was certainly commanding and, as silly as their little arms were, I did find his guards rather intimidating. Sure, tyrannosaurs are dumb, but they're also enormous. We climbed the sweeping stairway until we, too, reached the king's balcony.

"Since I was but a hatchling, I have been told stories of the Architect," the king continued. "It has long been said she would return and bring a golden age to Pangaea. I never truly believed the day would come to pass, yet here you are." He stopped to cough loudly, a deep, chesty, painful cough. "Tell me," he rasped. "Why have you come now?"

"Uh, well," Robyn mumbled. "We hoped we might find some soup."

"Soup?"

"A cure," I clarified. "For her mum. She's sick."

"An ailing mother? A humble cause for such a historic moment."

"I, uh, is it?" Robyn stuttered.

She stared at the ground and fidgeted with her foot. She didn't deal well with social interactions at the best of times, but she was clearly feeling the pressure of a royal inquisition.

"Surely the Architect has a more important purpose. Your arrival has been foretold since the dawn of time, and all you seek is medicinal aid for another human?"

"There's no more important purpose," I interjected, a little annoyed by the king's suggestion that Carol's life was somehow insignificant. "We're here to save a life, the life of someone dear to us both. It's a noble cause."

The king furrowed his brows and glared. I don't think he was used to being challenged, but it seemed to pass quickly. A forced smile returned to his face.

"But of course, we dinosaurs know all too well the importance of motherhood. We imprint on our mothers at birth; those who don't are driven mad. Perhaps I can help."

"You can?" Robyn replied with a squeak.

"Perhaps. It is said there is an object of great power within the ancient Mausoleum of the Archean. They call it the Heart of Pangaea."

"The Heart of Pangaea?" I enquired. "And how will that help?"

"If the stories are to be believed, the heart is the source of all life and a cure for any ailment—some even say it is the secret to immortality. More yet, it is claimed only the Architect herself may enter the mausoleum. It would seem like this is fate after all."

Robyn turned to me with a huge smile across her face.

"You hear that, Ed? There's a cure."

"And where is this mausoleum?" I asked, a little sceptical but intrigued, nonetheless.

"In the mountains across the Tethys Sea in the land we call Laurasia," the king replied. "I can arrange passage for you. It would be my honour to assist in the Architect's quest."

"Oh, thank you," Robyn gushed. "That's very, very kind of you."

"Go north, until you reach the coast. On foot, it should take three hours… perhaps four with your little legs. You will find a port there. Ask for Mother Mary."

Robyn smiled and croaked out a few more thanks, desperately trying to display her gratitude despite her social discomfort.

"But please," the king added, "allow me the distinction of offering some royal hospitality. Come. Let us eat."

***

That evening, we found ourselves standing around an impossibly long table made of a single vast slab of polished, purple amethyst. The king sat at the head while his two tyrannosaur bodyguards towered at either side.

Robyn and I sat beside the leaner of the two—the one they called Sir Barnum. Across from us were Doctor Boggs and Oskar the crocodilian.

There were no chairs. It seemed, with such vastly differing physiologies, it would have been impractical to store the necessary varieties of chair. Instead, we simply stood on the stone floor. It felt oddly informal for a royal feast.

But what a feast it was. The table was piled high with all sorts of fruits and vegetables. There were bowls of boiled eggs the size of rugby balls, roasted birds larger than an ostrich, and plates stacked high with vast, grilled sawfish. Best of all, it was real. Or perhaps it wasn't, but it was real for me. For the first time in my life, I ate. I ripped into a drumstick which was larger than a baseball bat and stripped the barbecued meat from equally large ribs, the juices dripping down my chin and onto the floor. It was more food than anyone could possibly eat, but I gave it a good try.

"Do you have any pickles?" Robyn asked.

"Pickles?" asked Doctor Boggs.

"You know, gherkins."

"What are they, exactly?"

"They're cucumbers, I think, soaked in vinegar until they shrivel up really small."

Boggs seemed to recoil at Robyn's description.

"No," he stated. "No, we don't have those. You eat that?"

"They're my favourite."

"I'd love to try one," I added. "I need to see what all the fuss is about."

After shrugging off the absence of her favourite pickled snack, Robyn smiled broadly and dug into a huge trifle. Upon realising the dessert tray was out of my reach, she gestured towards the sweet treats.

"Do you want some cake, Ed?" she asked.

"Uh, does the pope poop in the woods?" I replied.

"Okay, here… wait, you did it again."

"Did what?"

"That's not the saying."

"Just pass the cake, man."

Robyn shrugged and slid over a bubbling, sticky, toffee pudding.

I felt sluggish and dense by the time I had eaten my fill and now fatigue consumed me. Unable to stand any longer, I sat on the cold stone floor.

"Have you eaten a little too much?" Robyn asked with a snigger.

"I think so," I groaned. "I feel a bit sick."

"Have you eaten to… crapulence?"

We both giggled. That had been a running joke at home, with Carol finding the word crapulence—which simply meant to feel ill after overeating—hysterical. She would use it whenever she could.

It seemed the king recognised my weariness.

"My friends, it's late and the jungle is not safe after dark. Please, stay for the night. Rest and begin your quest at dawn. The main guest room in the north tower is available."

"We can stay in the castle?" I replied before flashing Robyn an excited glance. "It has been a long day."

"I can imagine," King Richard replied with a smile. "Doctor Boggs, please show our guests to their quarters."

"Yes, sire," Boggs replied with a respectful nod.

"Sleep well," said King Richard.

"Goodnight," added Sir Barnum.

"Uh, yup," replied Robyn. "Sleep night to you too. I mean, good well, no—"

"Please, this way," said Boggs, beckoning.

I skipped up the curving staircase behind the feathered giant while Robyn crept along behind. The room itself was as luxurious as one would expect from a king's castle. I flopped myself onto a huge, golden, four-poster bed and almost disappeared into the fluffy, burgundy duvet. Robyn hopped onto the bed and lay curled up by my side.

"Tomorrow, Ed," she whispered, staring into my eyes with a hopeful smile. "Tomorrow, we save Mum."

An Elusive Reality

"No, no, no, no!"

I awoke to Robyn's panicked cries as she tore the duvet off me. I lifted my eyelids and gazed upon the collection of drawings which hung on Robyn's bedroom wall. It took me a moment to realise we were home. The four-poster bed, the castle, Pangaea—it was all gone. I instantly shared Robyn's sentiment and my heart sank.

For a moment, I had allowed myself to believe it was all true, that we could save Carol, but I had been naïve. Now, I had to once again accept that there was nothing we could do to help her. The feeling of hopelessness was like a crushing, suffocating weight, as though I had been plunged into the deepest, coldest depths of the ocean.

"We have to get back, Ed," Robyn yelled. "We have to!"

She began to pad her hands against the wall where the door had once been, willing the portal back into existence.

"Robyn," I replied solemnly. "Robyn, it was a dream. I'm sorry. I was wrong."

"No," she huffed, sliding down the wall to sit on the floor.

***

Later that day, Michael drove Robyn and me to the hospital to visit Carol. He tried repeatedly to spark up a conversation, but Robyn gave short and distant responses. Her mind was elsewhere. I couldn't tell if she was simply dismayed to find that Pangaea wasn't real, or if she was angry with me for giving her false hope. I hoped it wasn't the latter—I had just wanted to help so badly.

After taking the long walk through the hospital ward, we arrived at Carol's room. As Michael pulled the partitioning curtain back, she greeted us with a weak smile.

"Oh, my darlings. It's so good to see you both."

It's funny. Of course, I knew she couldn't possibly see me, but I was nonetheless mildly annoyed that she only acknowledged Robyn and Michael. I knew this was irrational, but I couldn't help it. Being invisible to the ones I love can be difficult.

Robyn responded by sprinting to her mother and embracing her incredibly tightly. Michael flinched, likely for fear of hurting his wife, but the pair were deep into the hug before he had a chance to react. Instead, he simply tended to the flowers on the bedside table which needed to be changed. He had brought an outrageously large bunch of flowers, a subtle blend of pale pinks, purples, and whites. I didn't know what kind of flowers they were, but they were beautiful. Michael was thoughtful like that.

I couldn't help but notice how fragile Carol looked. Without her headscarf, I could see her balding head where only a few wisps of thin, discoloured hair remained. Her complexion was so pale she almost looked grey and, despite having only seen her the night before, I could swear she had lost weight. Her cheekbones seemed to protrude more, and her eyes appeared to have sunk into her skull. She seemed small. I reared onto my hindlegs and, despite only raising my eye line marginally above Carol's, it felt as though I towered over her failing body.

"How are you feeling, Mum?" Robyn asked.

"Oh, I'm fine, pumpkin," Carol croaked. "I'm sure I'll get home in a few days."

"Oh, that's fantastic," chirped Robyn excitedly. "We should go on a trip somewhere before the end of the summer—how about the zoo?"

"I think your mum could do with some rest after she gets home," Michael responded with a cautious smile.

"I think the zoo is a wonderful idea," Carol said with a smile. "You know I love the penguins."

"You know penguins are dinosaurs, right?"

"Yes, I remember." Carol giggled. "All birds are dinosaurs, even the cute ones."

"Especially the cute ones," Robyn joked.

It was clear to me that both Robyn's and Carol's thought processes were similar—if they weren't to have much longer together, then they had better make the most of it.

"Well, we can see how your mum is feeling," Michael replied. "How about I go and grab us some sandwiches?"

"That sounds lovely, dear," Carol replied.

Michael set off towards the café without taking any orders. Of course, he had memorised everyone's favourites a long time ago.

"How are you really feeling, Mum?" Robyn asked politely.

"Honestly, I'm fine, honey. Just a funny turn. You know how it is."

There was a sadness in Carol's eyes as she lied to her daughter. I wasn't entirely sure why she lied, but I suspect she couldn't bear to break such devastating news to her only child. Perhaps she simply hadn't yet found the right words. However, she didn't have to. Robyn burst into tears and Carol's mouth fell open while her eyes widened in surprise as the pair embraced tightly once more.

"What's the matter, sweetie?" she pleaded.

"I heard the doctor yesterday," Robyn sobbed. "She said you're going to die."

"Oh, honey, I'm sorry. I'm so sorry, I should have told you."

"What will we do?"

Carol pulled back from their long hug and looked into Robyn's eyes, offering a sad smile.

"I don't know, but we don't give up, not in this family."

"Are you really going to die?"

There was a long pause as Carol gazed at her daughter.

"I am, Robyn, but until that day comes, I am going to be here by your side."

"I don't want you to leave us," Robyn cried as a fresh deluge of tears ran down her cheeks.

The ever-wise Carol seemed at a loss as to how to respond. I could see her conflict. She was desperate to reassure her child that everything would be fine, yet she was unwilling to supply her with any more false hope. In the absence of comforting words, she simply held Robyn tightly for several long minutes.

"You know, something odd happened the other night," Carol whispered as her chin pressed against the top of Robyn's head. "When I had my seizure. I've never remembered anything from any other episode, but this time I could swear I saw something."

"What did you see?" Robyn mumbled, still buried in Carol's shoulder.

"Your friend. The one you drew. Ed."

This caught us both by surprise. Robyn raised her head out of her mother's embrace and flashed me a glance, eyes wide with surprise, yet her brow furrowed in confusion. I returned the sentiment. I thought back to that night and how I had been briefly convinced she had looked right at me while she lay on the floor. Not near me or through me like usual, but at me.

"You saw Ed?"

"Yes. Silly, I know. I suppose your brain does strange things in those moments. Hallucinations. It was nice, though, it felt like a peek into your wonderful little mind."

"Mum, what was he doing?"

"He was staring at me, right in the eyes. He looked worried and whispered something to me. 'Hang in there,' or something, I think he said."

"I did say that," I interjected.

"You did?" asked Robyn, who had begun to breathe quickly.

"Who are you... oh, is it Ed?" Carol finished the latter comment in a whisper.

Robyn quickly stood and began to frantically rummage in her hoodie pocket. She then stopped abruptly and stood still for several moments with a vacant expression and her eyes wide.

"What is it?" I asked with some concern.

She retracted her hand from her pocket to reveal a small stone with a perfectly preserved trilobite held within.

"Oh, what's that?" asked Carol. "A stone? Oh my, it's a fossil. From the beach?"

"She can see the fossil, Robyn," I stated.

"You can see the fossil," Robyn repeated blankly.

"Of course, I can," Carol replied with her eyes narrowed in confusion.

"It's not from the beach."

"So where—"

"It wasn't a dream, Ed. It was real."

"Robyn, what are you—" Carol began.

"Sorry, Mum, I have something important to do."

Robyn and I spun and strode quickly towards the door. As we left, Michael was returning, sandwiches in hand.

"Hey pumpkin, I got you tuna… Uh, where are you going?"

Robyn snatched the tuna sandwich from his hand and strode past.

"Thanks, Dad, I have a thing."

"A thing?"

"A big thing," Robyn replied, turning to face her father and pacing backwards. "A really big thing. I think I do, or maybe I've gone mental—I don't know."

"You're not making any sense, Robyn."

"I know. It doesn't make sense to me either. Not yet." Robyn broke into a run before calling back. "But I'll figure it out. Don't wait for me, I'll get the bus home."

The Number 63 to Pangaea

Robyn and I boarded the number sixty-three bus at the stop just outside the hospital to head home. There, we hoped Robyn might be able to recreate the door to Pangaea. Neither of us knew how, but we had to try. I felt bad to have abandoned Robyn's parents at the hospital, but time was vital. There was no telling how long Carol had left—every minute could count.

As we arrived back in Lyme Regis and approached our stop, we anxiously made our way to the front of the bus. The journey home was long enough for a level of doubt to creep into our minds. After all, we'd had our hopes dashed only this morning. Even if it were real—and the fossil did seem like proof—how would we reopen the doorway?

Such worry proved unnecessary. The bus drew to a stop and, to our amazement, the door slid open to reveal the sweltering forest of Pangaea. I looked around at the other passengers on the bus and no one flinched. Few even looked up to acknowledge the departing passengers. Through the windows of the bus, I could still see the suburban housing of our street, yet directly through the doors was a luscious prehistoric jungle. We stood for a moment with our jaws hanging loose.

"Well?" asked the driver, confirming that he saw nothing out of the ordinary. "You getting off?"

"Oh, um, yes," stammered Robyn.

"Remember to thank the driver," I added.

"Oh." She turned back to the driver. "You're welcome."

He raised an eyebrow.

"I mean thanks. Thank you. For driving… thanks."

Eyebrows still raised, he offered a forced smile. "No worries, kid."

"Well, that was painful to watch," I teased.

We stepped out into the forest and were hit with a thick wash of hot, humid air. Sunbeams shimmered through the canopy and dappled onto the fern-covered ground. I glanced behind me to see a strange, rectangular window floating in the air through which the bus driver continued to eye us suspiciously. Then, as the door slid shut, the window into the real world sealed.

"That was easier than expected." Robyn shrugged.

"Yeah," I responded. "The number sixty-three to Pangaea. Who knew?"

"So, where now?"

Luckily, we were quickly able to determine our approximate location as the peak of the golden citadel was visible above the treeline.

"Well, we're still near the city. The king said north, right?"

"That's right, north," Robyn replied, glancing around nervously. "North, north, north."

"You don't know which way is north, do you?" I asked dryly.

"Do you?" she snapped.

"Of course not. I'm a creation of your overactive grey matter. I only know what you know."

"That can't be how it works. I imagined everyone here. Like the king—he told me about the mausoleum, didn't he? I didn't already know that."

"That's true."

"Well, the sun moves from east to west, so we can figure out which way is north from that."

We both looked up, but the thick canopy ensured we couldn't locate the sun.

"Hmm, I don't know." I pondered. "The mausoleum is imaginary too. Maybe you did know. Just... subconsciously."

"Well, then maybe subconsciously I do know which way is north. Let's go..." Robyn spun around a few times before pointing over my shoulder. "This way."

And so, with a direction picked at random, we started to walk—hopeful the realm of Robyn's imagination would help us out by orienting us the right way. I admittedly had little faith in this plan. Neither did Robyn, and it showed. There was a long, awkward silence as we both internally contemplated the consequences of wasting time wandering the wrong way through the jungle. After trudging on for some time in silence, I finally broke the tension.

"So, the Architect. You're sort of like a god to these people."

"I wouldn't say that. I don't know… more like a parent."

"A parent? They have a mausoleum only you can enter. You did create a world; that's sort of the first requirement of godhood."

"A god would know which way north is."

"That's a fair point. You're not exactly omniscient."

"Do you reckon it's true?" she queried. "This Heart of Pangaea, I mean. It doesn't seem too good to be true, does it?"

"Oh, it sounds entirely too good to be true. I'm sure it won't be as easy as it sounds."

"You think it could be real, though?"

"I have no idea what's real anymore. Is any of this real? This world, these trees, the king… am I real? But that fossil was definitely real, Carol saw it."

"What if it's all in my head? What if there's no cure?"

I looked up at her to see her face drooping with worry.

"Don't think about that, Robyn. Focus on the task at hand. We will save her. One way or another."

Robyn checked her watch regularly to judge how close we should have been. The four hours, after which the king suggested we would have reached the port, came and went. By the fifth hour, Robyn slumped onto the ground against a tree and groaned loudly.

"I don't think I chose north, Ed."

"It would seem not."

"This should have been easy."

"We just need a local, someone who knows the terrain."

"Like who?"

"I don't know. There's bound to be someone around. The place was crawling with dinosaurs and killer crocodiles yesterday. I haven't seen so much as a bug today."

"Strange."

I didn't want to say out loud, but it was almost as though the forest's residents knew something we didn't. Perhaps there was good reason not to be in the jungle today.

As if to confirm my assertion, a loud shout rang out through the forest. I couldn't tell what had been said, but it sounded like a woman's voice—fierce and urgent. It was a more dramatic way to find a local than I had hoped for, but we were desperate. Without saying a word, Robyn stood, and we ran towards the source of the commotion.

After sprinting through the forest for a few short minutes, I heard something from the trees above. A sort of gasping sound.

"Do you hear that?" I asked.

Robyn nodded. We looked into the tree to see a slender, tan-coloured mammal of some description clinging to the trunk. I couldn't make out what it was, but it had short fur and a sort of dark, striped pattern on its back. Whatever it was, it was breathing heavily as though it had run for miles.

"Hey, you okay?" I asked it.

"Oh, g'day, mate," the animal replied in a decidedly male voice. "Yeah, I'm all right, thanks."

He sounded young and spoke with a smooth, yet strong Australian accent.

"Are you sure?" I pressed.

"Are you in some kind of trouble?" Robyn asked.

"I mean, I guess so. It's just the Golden Guard looking for mammals again. No biggie, though I would appreciate it massively if you could pipe down a little. Best not to give me away."

Suddenly, three fear-inducing beasts came racing through the forest. All were carnivorous theropod dinosaurs—the type which stand on two legs—and towered over us at twice Robyn's height. Two were heavily feathered dromaeosaurs, or "raptors" of some kind. They were covered in glossy, hazel plumage with white feathering on their necks and tails, and fanning out from their forearms like wings. In some ways, they were beautiful, like magnificent, terrestrial eagles, yet the huge, sickle-shaped claws on their feet struck horror into my core.

The third, who led the group, was more intimidating yet. Its head, mounted atop a snaking, S-shaped neck, was large and adorned with two tall crests which ran along the snout in a "V" formation. Filling its slender jaws were long, ferocious, recurved teeth. Notable was a notch in the upper jaw near the tip of its snout, giving the tip an aggressive, downward curve.

I recognised the leader as a *Dilophosaurus*—the "two-crested reptile." It was one of the largest early, hyper-predatorial dinosaurs. Unlike what you might have seen on television, they weren't venomous, nor did they have an expanding neck frill, but they were fearsome hunters, nonetheless.

The *Dilophosaurus* was also covered in feathers, but these were unlike the raptor's rich, beautiful plumage— these were course, matted, hair-like proto-feathers. This coating was almost entirely white while the beast's eyes were fiery red.

As this pale dinosaur laid eyes on us, it growled loudly. Its eyes burned fiercely, and it foamed at the mouth as though rabid.

"You," she snarled in a husky, gravelly, yet female voice. "Have you seen a marsupial around here?"

"A marsupial?" I asked.

As a marsupial was a type of mammal which raised its young in a pouch, such as a kangaroo, I knew she most likely referred to whichever animal was currently hiding in the tree above us. But there was something deeply troubling about this dinosaur. I certainly didn't much feel like assisting them in their search.

"Are you deaf, lizard?"

"I'm not actually a lizard—"

"You wouldn't lie to me," she snarled menacingly, slowly approaching until she was almost pressed against my face. "Would you?"

"I'm always honest," I replied. "That's why I feel obliged to let you know your breath smells like a coprolite."

The albino growled loudly in anger, likely considering clamping her jaws around my head. For all my bravado, I hoped she didn't—she would have made short work of me, I'm sure. Thankfully, Robyn took the more intelligent approach.

"Actually," she announced. "I maybe did see a marsupial. Back that way."

She pointed into the distance the way we had come. The beast finally broke eye contact with me and glanced at Robyn, narrowing her red eyes in suspicion.

"You'd better be telling the truth, amphibian. Let's go, boys."

Before walking past, she made a point to shove me to the side with her clawed hand. I staggered a little but stayed on my feet. She kept her eyes locked onto mine until she had passed completely. Then, the guard broke into a sprint once again.

"Did she call me an amphibian?" Robyn asked with an eyebrow raised in puzzlement.

"I don't think many around here have seen a human before," I suggested.

"The crocodile thought I was a walking fish, yesterday," she recalled with a chuckle.

"What were they? The two lackeys looked like *Velociraptors*."

"No, they were way too big. *Velociraptors* were about the size of a turkey. Those were *Utahraptors*, I think."

"The dilo was seriously creepy."

"Yeah, let's hope we don't run into her again."

We waited until the so-called Golden Guard were out of sight before attempting to help the stranded creature out of the tree.

"You hanging in there?" I called out.

"Nah, yeah, I'm all right," he replied. "You wouldn't mind giving me a hand down, would you? It's a bit iffy up here."

I glanced nervously towards Robyn.

"Well?" Robyn replied.

"Don't look at me. Do these paws look like they were meant for climbing? You're the monkey here."

"Ape," she corrected.

"An ape who's stalling. You evolved to climb; get up there."

"It's quite high," she replied, gazing upwards. "What if I fall?"

"Then I'll console you."

"I don't think I should—"

"My friend Robyn is going to come up and help you," I called up the tree.

"That's all right," the mystery creature replied. "I'm sure it'll be easier if you just catch me."

"Okay… wait, what?"

I stared as the creature came tumbling towards the ground. He might not have been especially large, but he was falling at considerable speed.

"Oh, no, no, no, no," Robyn stammered while attempting to scramble out of the way, realising she was directly below him.

Her attempt was futile, and the full weight of the stranger came pounding down on top of her. She collapsed under him and thumped into the dirt.

"Aw, cheers, mate," he said. "I'm sure lucky you were here."

"Please get off me," she wheezed.

The small, dog-like animal hopped off and Robyn hauled herself to her feet. As she dusted her shorts off, I inspected the stranger. He was much slimmer than most dogs, built not entirely unlike a greyhound, but with a more robust snout and some attractive dark striping upon his hindquarters. I noticed his eyes were mismatching—one with a green iris, the other brown.

He was a thylacine. Or, as they are more commonly known, a Tasmanian tiger. Of course, that doesn't mean he was a tiger. That was a colloquial name thanks to the aforementioned striping. Nor was he a dog of any kind. Rather, as a marsupial, the thylacine was more closely related to a kangaroo than to any placental carnivore it may have resembled.

"This is Ed," Robyn said. "And I'm Robyn. Nice to meet you."

"Bonzer to meet you both. Name's Benjamin."

"What were they after?" I asked, referring to the squad of theropods.

"Oh, the General? She's hunting down mammals. They caught me off guard since I was releasing a dirt snake into the wild."

"Oh, I love snakes," Robyn replied.

"Luckily for me," Benjamin continued, "it all turned into some awesome tree-climbing practice. Pretty ripper experience, really."

"That's one way to look at it, I guess," I replied with an eyebrow raised. "Not much meat on you, if you don't mind me saying."

"Meat? They weren't hunting me to eat me, ya silly drongo. I'm an outlaw."

"An outlaw? What did you do?" asked Robyn.

"What did I do? Blimey, you've been living under a rock, haven't ya? Mammals are all outlawed in Gondwana. It's because of our high metabolisms, you see? We eat too much food, which causes a shortage. It makes sense, I guess. I'll be taking the trip to Laurasia soon; that's where I belong."

"They hunt you for eating a lot? That's awful."

"Ah, it's all right, it keeps me on my toes."

"Speaking of metabolisms..." Benjamin looked up at Robyn. "What are you? Some kind of featherless bird?"

"What? I'm a human."

"Oh, that sounds very modern. I guess that makes you a mammalian outlaw too. Don't worry, I reckon the lack of fur makes you pretty inconspicuous. What brings you out this way?"

"We were trying to get to the port. Do you know the way?"

"Bloody oath—are you two lost? Don't stress, mates, I'll take you there."

The Demon of Tasmania

Around two million years ago, on the continent we now call Australia, a peculiar kind of animal evolved. Thylacinus cynocephalus, or simply the thylacine, was most closely related to other marsupials, and yet the uninitiated would swear it was a dog of some kind. Indeed, so similar are the skeletons of the thylacine and a dog that zoology students are often given the skull of one or the other to identify as a final exam.

The thylacine, along with much of Australia's megafauna, disappeared from the mainland under mysterious circumstances thousands of years ago. Perhaps it was a change in climate, human overhunting, or even the arrival of the dingo dog which drove this catastrophic collapse. Regardless of the cause, the thylacine persisted in one last haven—the forest island of Tasmania, a paradise for the last of their kind.

However, it didn't remain a paradise forever. In the early seventeenth century, European settlers arrived, and the Tasmanian tiger's island refuge began to change. Forests were slowly replaced by open fields. The emu and bandicoots were replaced by strange, new, domesticated animals. Still, there was mostly peace between the island's apex predator and the newly settled colonists.

This was short-lived. Early in the nineteenth century, farmers began to suspect the thylacine of preying on livestock. It's not clear if this was true. Feral dogs were far more likely culprits, but the people of Tasmania considered the predatorial marsupial to be guilty. Over time, fear grew of the mysterious, wolf-like creature which prowled through the woods and emerged under the dark cover of night. They considered it a monster—a vampiric beast which mutilated animals and drained their blood. The thylacine was declared an enemy of the people to be hunted. And how they hunted it.

Bounties were placed on their heads, leading poor townsfolk to take up their rifles. The aim was clear—the annihilation of the species. Thousands upon thousands were shot and killed. The persecution was relentless, the butchery brutal, yet it was celebrated. The last known wild thylacine was shot in 1930, and the last specimen in captivity died in Tasmania's Hobart Zoo in 1938. With that, the Tasmanian tiger was erased forever.

Why, when dogs were just as dangerous to livestock, if not more so, was the ill-fated thylacine singled out? Why do the dogs persist while their marsupial counterparts were exterminated in the most merciless fashion?

It seems in times of hardship that people often look to those in power for help, but those in power are often directly responsible for and actively profiting from said hardship. This delicate situation calls for one thing—a scapegoat.

It's a tactic as old as civilisation itself. Too often have the most vulnerable paid the highest price for the crimes of the powerful.

I thought of this as Benjamin led us through the forest. It saddened me that, even here, in this paradise for lost species, he and his kind still experienced such persecution.

Hangenberg

Emerging from the forest, we came to a stretch of small dunes peppered with tall, harsh grass which stabbed into my belly as I walked through it. Once we cleared the peaks, I saw a spectacular, glistening, blue-green sea stretching out to the horizon, where it met a pristine, cloudless, sapphire sky. The sound of the gently lapping waves and the smell of salt were rather soothing.

By the shore was a small village. Stone houses lined the coast. Some were painted white or grey, but most were pretty, pastel hues. What struck me was the variation in size—some of the houses were around the size of a shoe box while others, despite clearly being styled as a house, were large enough to pass for a cathedral. I supposed it made sense; the inhabitants of Pangaea weren't exactly homogeneous, but it was striking nonetheless.

"So, where to?" asked Benjamin.

"Uh, I'm not sure," Robyn replied. "We're to speak to someone called 'Mother Mary.'"

"I've heard the name, but I can't say I know where she'll be. I guess we should ask around. Pub?"

"Pub?" I asked.

"Yeah, you can always find answers in a pub. Not always answers you like but… you know, answers."

"I think I'm a little young."

"Too young for the pub? Mate, I had my first tinny when I was still in the pouch. You'll be all right. Have a wander and find one. I'd best be on my merry way."

"I suppose we find a pub then," said Robyn. "Won't you join us?"

"You *want* me to come with you?" he replied.

"We could do with a local guide," I admitted. "We wouldn't have gotten this far without you. Besides, you said you wanted to Laurasia—that's where we're going."

A huge smile spread across our new companion's face.

"Oh, crikey. Sure thing, mates. I'd love to tag along."

His reaction to simply being wanted simultaneously warmed and broke my heart. I was glad we could make him feel that way but could only imagine what kind of life he led to be so excited by being welcome.

We wandered through the rustic town, looking for Benjamin's suggested pub. The whole settlement stank of fish, salt, and seaweed, but I liked it in a strange way. It was fairly busy as several large reptiles went about their business, roaming between the few small shops in the centre of town. I noticed several giving Benjamin some long, suspicious stares, while others glanced and then whispered to each other in urgent hisses.

Bells rang out from the fishing boats in the distance and the call of sea birds echoed off the stone walls. I looked up to see the source of those squawks, but they weren't the gulls I was expecting. They were large, black-and-white birds which sported eerily long, needle-like teeth protruding from their beaks.

"Those aren't normal seagulls, are they?" I mused.

Robyn glanced up.

"Oh, beach chickens," she chirped, that being her father's term for a gull. "Those are *Ichthyornis*. You know, there used to be a sea right down the middle of North America. That's where those guys lived—the Western Interior Seaway."

"What's with the teeth?" I asked.

"For catching fish. That's where the name comes from. *Ichthyornis* means 'fish bird.'"

"The place is chocker with them," observed Benjamin.

He was right. The more I looked, the more I saw. They perched on rooftops, nibbled scraps from waste bins, and squabbled with one another in the streets.

"Why are there so many?" I asked.

"For the free fish, of course," he explained. "This is Hangenberg—the main fishing port in Gondwana, or at least it used to be."

"Used to be?" asked Robyn.

"Fish stocks are pretty low these days. Most of the fish is brought in from Laurasia now."

Eventually, we found a little cottage with a wooden sign hanging above the door. The paint was faded, but it could still be read as "The Chisel & Brush Inn."

"I guess we found a pub," I said.

Robyn pushed open the old oak door and stepped into a quiet, smoke-filled bar. It stank of cigarettes and fish—not a combination I ever hoped to smell again. At first, our presence went largely unnoticed but slowly, the dozen or so occupants turned their collective gaze towards us. There were dinosaurs of various types, crocodilians, and even a giant salamander.

A small creature then leapt onto the bar. It was no larger than a pheasant, but it was armed with ferociously sharp, sickle-shaped claws on its feet. It was entirely covered in bluish-grey feathers which formed wings on its forelimbs and fanned out around its tail. It was like a shrunken and more delicate version of the large raptors from the forest.

"That one's a *Velociraptor*, right?" I whispered to Robyn.

She nodded in confirmation.

"Can I help you?" the barkeeper asked in a deep, confrontational tone.

"Uh, we're looking for someone," I answered.

"You won't find them here," she snapped. "Take your mammal and leave."

I realised that all the eyes in the bar weren't fixed on us as a group, but specifically on Benjamin.

"Maybe he should wait outside," I suggested, tilting my head towards him.

"What?" whispered Robyn. "He should be allowed in here like anyone else."

"Did I not make myself clear?" the *Velociraptor* continued. "Clear off!"

"Please, miss," said Robyn politely, slowly approaching the bar. "We… we just need to find Mother Mary."

"Mary doesn't do business with his kind, and neither do I. I don't know what kind of giant bobbit worm you are, but you think you can bring a furball into *my* inn? Get out of here, *all* of you. Be thankful I don't turn you in to the Guard."

"All right, lady," I interrupted. "Leaving is exactly what we're trying to do, but to do that we need directions. Tell us where to find Mother Mary, or we'll make a point of hanging around all day."

The *Velociraptor* didn't take kindly to this. She narrowed her eyes and snarled.

"Boys," she barked. "Show them the door. No need to be gentle."

Two far larger dinosaurs rose from their seats. They were huge, with long arms and narrow snouts—*Baryonyx*. They approached us, hands open and ready to grasp.

Robyn began to retreat towards the door, but I stood firm and growled loudly at the two looming theropods. Benjamin stood awkwardly between us, unsure of whether to retreat or stand his ground.

"Come on then," I challenged. "Throw us out all you want; we'll keep coming back until we have answers."

One of the *Baryonyx* smirked as he stared down at me.

"The little synapsid has spunk," he sneered.

"But the king said—" Robyn began.

"Wait!" ordered the raptor. "The king?"

"He sent us," I clarified. "We're to cross the sea to Laurasia."

The *Velociraptor* stood tapping a sickle claw on the bar, pondering her options. In the end, she seemed to decide that risking an upset king wasn't worth her pride. Through gritted teeth, she spoke.

"The pier. You'll find Mary at the pier. Now get out of here, and take that filthy milk drinker across the Tethys where he belongs."

I huffed in defiance before striding forwards and snatching a bowl of salted peanuts from the bar with my jaws. I tipped the entire bowl back into my mouth before dropping the ceramic bowl which smashed on the floor. I backed out slowly, maintaining eye contact with the *Velociraptor* all the way. She probably had plenty of peanuts with which to refill her bowl, but it felt like a small victory.

Despite succeeding in our venture into the bar, I was left with a bitter taste in my mouth. I felt for Benjamin, who hadn't said a word in his own defence—almost as though he accepted his lower standing. A wave of guilt then came over me upon realising I had said little to defend him.

"Awesome, I reckon that went pretty well," chirped Benjamin.

"It did?" asked Robyn.

"Nah, yeah, we didn't get beaten up or anything. That's a pretty successful trip into a reptile bar, if you ask me."

"That might be the most miserable thing I've ever heard," I said. "And I listened to an entire Lewis Capaldi album."

"Well, we have our directions," Robyn added. "That's what we needed."

"Good peanuts too. I think I like peanuts," I added. "Food in general, really. I had no idea what I was missing all these years."

At the far end of town, the sea wall was lined with rough, wooden fishing boats beside a rickety, old, wooden pier which extended out from the shore. The pier terminated in a large hut with two tall barn doors which lay wide open.

I found the creaky, wobbly boards of the pier rather disconcerting—the surface warped beneath my feet. A few steps later, one board snapped beneath my paw and fell into the sea below.

As we reached the hut at the end, I noticed that, curiously, it had no floor. Rather, there was a large square hole through which I could see the waves gently slapping the pier's support piles. On the far wall of the hut, at the other side of the gaping hole in the floor, was an assortment of seashells and fossils in large, wicker baskets.

"It doesn't look like anybody's home," noted Benjamin.

"Hello?" I called, wondering if Mary was a small species hiding within or behind the baskets.

"Do you think the innkeeper was lying?" Robyn asked.

"I can't say she seemed all that trustworthy."

We had almost given up when the surface of the water directly beneath the hut rippled and sloshed. A large, reptilian head breached and rose high atop a long yet thick neck. It was almost like looking at an enormous python with a slim, triangular-shaped skull and a mouth filled with long, pointed teeth. A plesiosaur, I noted. Indeed, the original plesiosaur—*Plesiosaurus*. What was striking was that I recognised this one from Robyn's recent drawing. It had a faint purple colouration to its smooth skin and darker, tiger-like stripes.

"Afternoon," the creature announced dryly, before attending to her collection of shells without so much as glancing at us.

"You… are you Mother Mary?" Robyn stuttered.

"That's right," she stated, still focusing solely on her shells.

We glanced at each other for a moment, unsure how to proceed.

"Well, are you going to buy a shell or not?" Mary snapped, breaking the silence.

On the shelf behind her, I could see dozens of beautiful shells and trilobites, some much like Robyn's, alongside ammonites, sea scorpion fossils, and a huge conical shell which could only have come from the giant, squid-like *Orthocone*.

"Oh, no, we're actually…" Robyn stammered.

"You could use a shell, little crustacean, it seems you've lost yours."

"Oh, I'm not a—"

Mary then shot a deathly stare at Benjamin.

"Have you brought a *mammal* onto my pier? Are you trying to get me *arrested*? Clear off, all of you."

"We're here for a boat," I stated. "The king sent us. He said you could arrange passage—for *all* of us. Are we to take one of these boats?"

"*All* of you, hmm?" Mary glared at Benjamin for a few long seconds before turning to Robyn. "Yes, of course, I've been expecting you. I suppose that would make you… the Architect."

"So I've been told," Robyn responded with a shrug.

"*Robyn!*" exclaimed Benjamin. "You didn't tell me you were the bloody Architect. Oh, boy, look at me, friends with a *celebrity*."

"I'd dare say the grand architect of our existence is a little more than a *celebrity*, wouldn't you say, *mammal*?" scolded Mary. "And I rather doubt she considers such a creature as a *friend*."

"Oh, well, I actually—" Robyn murmured.

"Benjamin *is* our friend," I pressed. "I think the king would expect you to treat a friend of the Architect with some respect."

Mary grumbled to herself for several seconds. "So be it," she conceded. "But he had better not cause any trouble."

"I'd really rather not have anyone make a fuss about the whole Architect thing," Robyn added. "I just need to get across the sea as quickly as possible."

"Quite," replied Mary. "As long as you're prepared—crossing the Tethys can be treacherous."

"Treacherous? How?"

"Let's just say that not all of the sea's inhabitants are as civilised as I am."

"That seems to be a low bar," I whispered to myself.

"Excuse me?"

"It's worth the risk," I said.

"But is there a safer way?" Robyn asked tentatively. "There isn't a way around?"

"Not unless you wish to walk for a month," Mary replied.

"We take the boat then," I concluded.

"Well, hang on," Robyn replied. "Maybe we could find a way to make that trip a little shorter. Ride a horse or something."

"Robyn, we don't have the time. Who knows how long Carol has left?"

"Okay, fine. We'll take the boat."

"Which boat is ours?" I asked, eager to get on our way.

"None," Mary replied with a reluctant sigh.

She grabbed a mouthful of stones from one of her baskets and tossed them down her throat. I knew that such reptiles ate stones to help them digest their food and to function as ballast, but seeing her actively swallow rocks was still fairly disturbing.

"A royal order demands a more personal touch than one of these old buckets," she said.

Mary's long neck retreated into the water until her head disappeared beneath the surface. I stared at the ripples she left behind for a few moments, somewhat bewildered as to where she had gone.

After a few moments, a huge swell of seawater burst upwards by the side of the pier, raining salt water on us. A vast, wooden structure revealed itself as the turbulent froth fell away. It rose higher and higher as waterfalls cascaded from its upper surfaces. A ship? It certainly appeared so. But as it raised itself higher, it became clear that, rather than being a ship in the traditional sense, it was built upon the blubbery back of Mother Mary herself. The *Plesiosaurus*'s front flipper slapped onto the pier like a huge, slippery, biological gangway.

"Quickly now," she commanded. "I don't have all day."

Voyage of the *Plesiosaurus*

The top deck of the *Plesiosaurus* vessel was remarkable. Firstly, for being something mounted on an actual animal, it was huge. But also, the ornate carvings on the outer railings were beautifully intricate and appeared to depict outdated, Victorian-style representations of marine reptiles. They were skinny and serpent-like sea monsters with gnarly teeth and blank, lifeless eyes. Unrealistic, sure, but wonderfully dramatic. To the stern was a long, pointed extrusion which overhung far beyond Mary's short, paddle tail.

Once at sea, it became painfully apparent that Benjamin wasn't at all fond of sailing. Only ten minutes or so after leaving the pier, he was violently sick overboard.

"Are you okay?" Robyn asked, placing a gentle hand on his shoulder.

"Nah, yeah, I'm—" Benjamin then paused to vomit once more. "I'll be right. At least it'll make me appreciate land more."

As I caught a whiff of vomit I stifled a gag reflex and clenched my lips together. "You really can see the good in every situation, can't you?"

"I try." He smiled with his teeth, but the sentiment didn't reach his eyes.

I staggered as the plesiosaur ship began to rock uncomfortably from side to side. As I peered overboard, I could see Mary attempting to shake some of Benjamin's greenish sick off her flipper. She then curled her long neck around to look the marsupial in the eye.

"Boy, I know life at sea isn't meant for you milk drinkers, but will you *please* head to the aft peak if you're going to be sick?"

"Oh, yeah, no worries. Sorry," Benjamin replied, his tail between his legs in embarrassment. "I'll head there now… aft… aft?"

"The *back*," Mary snapped impatiently.

As Benjamin stumbled towards the stern of the deck, Mary turned her attention to Robyn.

"Tell me, young lady, what business do you have across the Tethys?"

"I'm going to the Mausoleum of the Archean. The king tells me I can find something there."

"The *mausoleum*? And, pray tell, what do you expect to find there?"

"A cure. For my mum. She's sick."

"A noble quest. So, you're not here to fulfil the scripture?"

"Scripture? I don't know anything about any scripture."

"Curious..."

"Why?" I interjected. "What does the scripture say?"

"Well, it says the Architect will come to save Pangaea."

"Save it?" asked Robyn.

"What does it need saving from?" I asked.

Mary stopped and thought carefully.

"Never mind, I fear I've said too much already."

"What?" I asked. "I think it's fair we know what it says."

Mary sighed deeply. "You didn't hear it from me?"

Robyn mimed forming a cross over her heart, indicating her promise to keep it secret.

"Well, it's said..." Mary paused, turning her head sharply to the right, and stared intently into the distance.

"Uh, what's up, Nessie?" I queried.

"Get below deck," she whispered with some urgency.

"Huh?"

"Through the hatch. Get below the deck. *Now*."

Using her immensely strong flippers, Mary swerved to port—that's a left turn for you land lovers—and accelerated. Robyn was knocked off her feet by the sudden turn in pace. I scrambled towards the central hatch—a hinged square of iron grating which was heavy enough to require all my strength to heave open. Below was Mary's bare back.

"Robyn," I called. "Quickly!"

Robyn clambered back to her feet and staggered towards the hatch. She hopped down rather elegantly, a feat I failed to replicate as I tumbled after her. Mary's skin was smooth and rubbery, not especially reptilian but more reminiscent of whale or dolphin skin.

"Benjamin!" Robyn called out through the hatch.

There was no answer from him. Perhaps the stricken thylacine was simply too ill to take heed.

Mother Mary rocked violently, causing us to fall onto her back. Outside, a swift, black shape briefly blocked the sun, informing me that we were no longer alone. After regaining my footing, I rushed to the starboard—that's the right—side to peer out a porthole. To my horror, I witnessed an enormous, triangular dorsal fin, as tall as a full-grown man, rise from the depths. An even taller tail fin followed with a powerful swish which thrust a tall wave crashing into the side of the wooden structure. An explosion of salt water burst through the port hole, soaking Robyn and me.

"That..." I panted, shaking water from my sail. "That looked like a shark."

Robyn nodded, her eyes wide and skin pale.

"A *big* shark," I added. "Is it…"

"It has to be," she replied, confirming my fears.

"Megalodon."

You probably don't need much of an introduction to *Otodus megalodon*, but in case you do, it was a twenty-tonne shark which, until some three and a half million years ago, spent its days feasting upon whales. That's right, it ate *whales*. It was certainly not a creature I wished to encounter at sea.

The fins disappeared beneath the surface and, for a moment, all was quiet. I took the opportunity to scramble up the ladder and through the hatch to fetch Benjamin. He stood at the stern with his legs shaking. The poor beast was glued to the spot in a nauseated state. I figured there was a real risk of him being thrown overboard, so I scampered over to assist. I clamped my jaws around his tail, which caused him to whelp in fright, and I dragged him away from the edge.

"Come *on*," I yelled.

Mary, realising we were both on the deck, quickly echoed my sentiment. "You two do *not* want to be out in the open right now!"

Benjamin snapped out of his trance with a vigorous shake of his head before trundling across the deck and down the hatch. Before following him, I looked out to sea. The surface of the water seemed to bulge, building itself into a huge mound, the bow wave of a giant. It was coming straight for us.

"Oh, no," I gasped. "We're going to need a bigger plesiosaur."

I scrambled down the hatch as Mother Mary's side was met with a huge impact. I was hurled against a wooden support pillar before bouncing off the ceiling and slamming onto the plesiosaur's back. Dazed, I looked up to see that, thankfully, both Robyn and Benjamin had secured themselves well enough to avoid the same fate.

"*Ed!*" Robyn screamed. "Are you okay?"

"I'm fine," I said, raising a paw in confirmation.

I hauled myself to my feet. My ribs hurt, but I was otherwise fine. Suddenly, Mary's face appeared at my nearest porthole.

"You three *must* be quiet," she hissed.

"What's going on?" I whispered.

"Pirates. Sit tight and stay hidden."

Using her head, Mary then slid a large wooden crate over the metal hatch to hide it. Obediently, we sat silently and waited for whatever was to follow, praying that Mary knew what she was doing. Through the porthole I could see the vast *megalodon* rise once more, this time raising its body above the waves like a surfacing submarine. It floated there and drifted slowly alongside.

It didn't simply look like an oversized great white shark as is so often depicted. Its nose was more rounded and blunter, its body bulbous and whale-like. Upon the side of its head was a tiny, beady little eye from which we hid as it passed by the porthole.

Once the black, lifeless eye had passed, I peeked out again to see something curious—two creatures rode upon the great shark's back. They held onto long, barnacle-covered ropes which had been fixed to a wooden stake driven through the base of the *megalodon's* dorsal fin.

The first of the beasts was a *Megatherium americanum*—the great beast of America—an enormous ground sloth. From a distance, one might have mistaken it for some kind of grizzly bear. It had similar colouration and proportions, but it was as large as an elephant. Standing on its hind legs, it could have stared into the top windows of a double-decker bus without so much as rising onto its toes. Through its nose was a thick, metal ring, much like one you would expect to see on a bull. Its head was huge and muscular while its long arms sported terrifyingly long, curved claws. Curiously, on one arm the claws glinted metallic silver in the sunlight—it appeared as though this creature had lost a hand in the past and had it replaced with a fearsome, tri-bladed prosthetic.

In front of the sloth stood an even more formidable beast. A *Spinosaurus aegyptiacus*—the Egyptian spine lizard—stood at a similar height to its mammalian companion but was as long as an eighteen-wheeler truck. At the end of its long, S-shaped neck, it sported a narrow, crocodile-like snout from which long, sharp, conical teeth protruded.

Standing on two proportionally short legs, its forelimbs were free and, like the sloth, each possessed chilling claws. A huge row of tall spines supporting a membrane of skin, not entirely dissimilar to my own sail, ran along its back. This sail continued to the tip of its spectacularly long tail, forming a tall, paddle-shaped structure.

"Mother Mary," the spinosaur called out in a smooth, deep voice. "It's been too long. What brings you this far out to sea today?"

"I'm just passing through, Stromer," Mary responded. "There's nothing for you to steal here."

"So cynical," the dinosaur replied, feigning offence. "Can one seafarer not greet another without suspicion?"

"Does ramming other 'seafarers' with your overgrown goldfish usually work as a conversation starter?"

"Luckily for you, Louis here isn't going to take much offence to that goldfish jab, mostly because he's too dumb to notice. But still, old friend, maybe I should come aboard, and we can discuss this. For old times' sake."

"I suspect you'll do that with or without my permission," Mary retorted.

With that, the huge theropod dinosaur lowered himself into the water and began to swim towards Mary. Stromer, as Mary had called him, slithered elegantly from side to side, cutting through the water with ease, propelled by his large, flattened tail. The sloth followed and, while not as graceful with a clumsy, doggy-paddle style, it was a surprisingly capable swimmer too. After clambering up the plesiosaur's side, the pair's footsteps thumped ominously on the deck above us.

"And to think I just washed this deck," Mary sneered. "Is this all that's left of your low-life crew? I heard most were in prison."

"Wrongfully imprisoned, as I'm sure you know."

"So, they're not pirates?"

"We both know they were arrested for their fur coats as much as their actions."

"Or perhaps their kind are simply more inclined to break the laws of the seas."

I could hear the giant sloth growl under his breath.

"It is strange for someone to be sailing so far out with no cargo," Stromer said. "Wouldn't you agree, Cuvier?"

"*Oui*. Very strange," replied the sloth in a deep, gravelly tone and a strong French accent.

"Not even a box of shells for your little shack?"

"Sometimes one simply enjoys a sail," Mary replied.

"Well, I do understand how calming the ocean can be. But still, this is very far from port. It can be dangerous out here."

"Only because of the likes of you."

There was a tense silence for several long seconds. The three of us in hiding dared not breathe.

Finally, the sloth spoke up. "Do you think us idiots?" he snarled. "Where are the passengers?"

"You *dare* speak to me like that, *beast*?" replied Mary. "After all I did for you?"

"All you did for *me*?" the sloth snarled.

"What my ineloquent first mate is trying to say is that we heard a rumour you had some... *special* guests," Stromer interjected. "Courtesy of the king, no less. Now, I, for one, would be honoured to meet such important travellers."

"I'm afraid you've been misled," Mary stated coldly.

"Very well." Stromer sighed. "Cuvier, have a look around."

The hulking sloth began to thump around on the deck above. The wooden boards flexed under his immense weight and dust poured down with each step. Thudding and cracking sounds rang out from above as Cuvier presumably smashed barrels and crates to reveal their contents. He stormed around the deck with his footsteps edging closer to us. I looked up nervously at the crate which covered the hatch, praying it would remain in place. Soon, he was directly above our heads. The great brute smashed something against the deck and a dense plume of dust cascaded over us.

Robyn gasped in fright, inadvertently inhaling a huge lungful of dust in the process. She tried to stifle her inevitable cough, but the slight choke she emitted was loud enough.

The *Megatherium's* great, clawed fist smashed through the wooden deck in a hail of splinters and dust. The instant daylight illuminated the pirate's arm, covered in patchy brown hair and crisscrossed with scars. It also revealed, in horrifying detail, his vicious, black, steak-knife-like claws. With those claws, Cuvier grabbed Robyn and hauled her through the deck. She screamed as she disappeared out of sight.

"Robyn!" I cried.

Cuvier's hideously scarred face then appeared through the newly created hole in the deck. He bellowed a horrific roar as he laid his burning orange eyes on Benjamin and me. With a great crunch, he forced himself down through the deck in a cloud of splintering wood and scrambled after us. He didn't fit below deck, but he still moved quickly, with the wood above him cracking as his back ripped through it. The thick skin of such giant ground sloths was impregnated with a chainmail of bone, making Cuvier almost indestructible. Cornered, there was nowhere for us to go and, with a swipe of his vast hand, he thumped me in the head. In an instant, all was dark.

Haţeg Island

I awoke to find myself lying on a cold floor of cracked and dusty white tiles. After regaining a level of awareness, I raised my head to observe that I was inside a dimly lit building. Behind me was a large, stone fireplace with smouldering ashes which, from the look of things, had burnt out some hours ago. The white-painted walls were cracked with age and covered in stained, torn maps and frayed ropes.

It struck me that the ceiling was incredibly high. It had an odd, octagonal floor plan with a spiralling staircase looping around against the walls. I could see up through the centre of the staircase, the top of which was brightly illuminated by the sun. I thought it seemed like an enormous lighthouse. I could hear strong winds whistling and waves crashing outside, which seemed to add weight to this hypothesis.

Blearily, I tried to climb to my feet only to find them trapped beneath me. I rolled over onto my side and thrashed in an attempt to free my limbs, but it was useless. They had been bound tightly with damp, coarse rope which irritated my skin. I looked around and located both Robyn and Benjamin, who were also bound.

"Ed, are you *all right*?" Robyn asked with a whisper.

"Oh, grand." I groaned as my head started to spin. "You?"

"I've been better," she admitted.

"That was quite the knock you took, mate," said Benjamin. "You've been out for ages."

"I was getting worried," Robyn added.

"I'll live," I said, now feeling the side of my head throb.

"Abducted by pirates, though," gasped Benjamin. "Isn't it exciting?"

We both turned and stared at him in disbelief. *Exciting*? We were tied up and awaiting our fate at the hands of some cutthroat criminals.

"Are you broken?" I asked with narrowed eyes.

"You know where we are, right?" he continued. "It *has* to be—*Haţeg Island*. You know, the famous pirate hideout? Oh, just wait till my buddies hear about this."

"Benjamin, you have to be *alive* to tell your friends anything."

The tall, wooden door swung open, slamming against the wall, and blinding sunlight flooded the base of the lighthouse. As my eyes adjusted to the glare, the vast, looming silhouette of Stromer the *Spinosaurus* became clear.

"Are my guests comfortable?" he asked as he entered the shack.

Robyn and I simply glared at him in response.

"A cushion might be nice, but I'm all right," chimed Benjamin cheerily.

Stromer approached and towered over the top of Benjamin, looking down at him with narrowed eyes. He was clearly trying to decide if the little marsupial was sarcastic or mad—of course, I had already figured out that he was very much the latter.

"Would anyone *else* like a cushion?" he asked in a tuneful, sarcastic manner, wafting his faintly fishy breath in my direction.

"Shove your cushion up your cloaca," I retorted.

"Maybe a snack?" suggested Benjamin.

Stromer stared at him with heavy eyes and a frown, clearly unimpressed.

"We don't have snacks," he replied eventually with an exasperated sigh.

"Well then, get lost, danger duck," I said. "What do you want with us anyway?"

"Oh, don't worry," Stromer replied. "We've sent word to the king that we have you. He'll send us payment, and you'll be on your way. It's a simple transaction. Nice back sail, by the way."

"I had mine *before* it was trendy."

"What makes you think the king will pay for us?" Robyn asked.

"Now, *that* I don't know. But kings don't just arrange passage across the Tethys for anyone, kid. You're important somehow."

"And if he doesn't pay?" I queried.

"We *kill* you," replied the grumbling voice of Stromer's first mate Cuvier from the doorway. "We have to let the people know we are serious, *non*?"

He approached Robyn slowly and placed one of his formidable, metal claws against her throat. Up close, I could see how rudimentary his prosthetic was—it consisted of little more than three dagger blades buckled to his forearm with black leather straps.

"Of course," he continued with a wry smile. "If he does pay, I might cut you open anyway."

"Get your hands away from her, *sloth*," I snarled.

Cuvier turned and glared at me. He retracted his claw away from Robyn and began to walk towards me.

"Maybe we should kill this one to send a message, *Capitaine*."

"Stand down, Cuvier," replied Stromer with a sigh. "We don't know which of them is valuable. Given the king's views, it's unlikely to be the mammal, but it could be either the *Dimetrodon* or the... I want to say... salamander?"

"Oh, for heaven's sake... I'm a *human*," Robyn moaned.

"Sure, kid. Either way, let's keep them all alive... for now."

"Spoilsport," Cuvier grumbled.

"How did you know we were sent by the king?" I asked.

"A little bird told me. Almost literally, actually."

"This was a tip-off from Jynx?" replied Cuvier with a raised eyebrow.

"She's a reliable source, and you know it."

"She brings nothing but trouble."

"What business does a mammal have with the king anyway?" Stromer asked, turning towards Benjamin.

"Oh, I'm just along for the ride, really. I'm kind of a local guide. I guess I'm doing my bit for society by leaving Gondwana anyway, right?"

I was taken aback by the sincerity of Benjamin's words—he truly believed the people he was leaving behind were better off without him. Even Stromer seemed shocked. He widened his eyes and recoiled his head slightly.

"What do you mean?"

"Well, you know, fast metabolism and all that. Do you guys not get much news from the mainland out here?"

"Fast metabolism? Tell me you don't believe all that—it's propaganda. You think a thirty-tonne sauropod eats less than a little mammal just because of—"

A loud boom interrupted Stromer's train of thought. It sounded like an explosion of some kind and was powerful enough to shake the dust off the ceiling and rattle the picture frames. Cuvier and the captain looked at each other nervously. A second explosion soon followed.

"It sounds like we have some company," said Cuvier.

"Go and check," ordered Stromer. "I'll keep an eye on the hostages."

Cuvier dutifully headed outside. The hulking sloth pushed the door open and peered out before creeping through the doorframe. He was gone for several minutes and, in the interim, two more explosions thundered across the island. The rapid thudding of footsteps betrayed the urgency of Cuvier's return. He appeared in the doorway, panting.

"*Capitaine*, you must come and—"

A huge, dark mass ripped across the doorway, tearing the door off its rickety hinges and dragging Cuvier out of sight. There was the sound of a brief scuffle. Cuvier roared but, after a loud thud, he became silent.

"Cuvier!" yelled Captain Stromer. "Who's there?"

The intruder soon made himself known as an enormous *Tyrannosaurus* appeared in the doorway. It was the uglier of the two guards from the castle, the one covered in scruffy black feathers with the bald, lumpy head. Lord Gigas, they had called him. It seemed, rather than having sent a ransom, King Richard had sent a rescue.

"Well, well, Captain Stromer," the tyrant hissed. "I might have known."

"You should have stayed in the city, Gigas," Stromer retorted.

"I like to mix with the peasantry now and then. You look different—have you done something with your tail? How long has it been, Captain?"

"It hasn't been long enough," Stromer growled.

"I think you were a quadruped the last we had the pleasure of each other's company."

"You mean when you kidnapped my crew?"

"Arrested, Captain. I *arrested* your crew. Why not come and join them?"

"I'd like to see you make me."

Looking at the pair, I could tell neither was about to back down. They stood their ground and stared intently into one another's eyes. It wasn't clear to me who would win should they come to blows. Stromer, the spinosaur, certainly had reach. He was longer and taller with formidably clawed forelimbs. Gigas, on the other hand, had a clear weight advantage. His jaws were wide and powerful and more than compensated for his lack of other weaponry.

However, the fight between the two giants never came to be. As Stromer faced off with Gigas, a second assailant exploded through the aging wall of the lighthouse in a hail of brick and plaster, filling the space with dust and glaring daylight. It was Sir Barnum, the scaly, muscular rex. He clamped his enormous jaws around Stromer's neck and dragged him outside. I watched as Stromer was thrown down onto a pebble-covered beach.

Barnum had come dressed for the occasion. His back and flanks were protected by gleaming armour plating while chainmail sleeves covered his thighs and tail.

Stromer may have stood a chance against Lord Gigas, but Barnum seemed infinitely more ferocious and battle-hardened. He wasn't just strong; he was fast and, now, armoured. As Stromer tried to rise to his feet, the vast knight's jaws clamped onto his tail and swung him off balance once more.

Gigas had now emerged from the lighthouse, but he didn't join in the scuffle. Rather, he circled the battle ominously.

Stromer slashed at Barnum with his razor-sharp claws but found only steel, striking up sparks with every swipe. He dove to Barnum's side, hoping to find a weak spot, but the knight was clearly a seasoned fighter. He spotted the momentary opening as Stromer exposed his flank and barged the pirate over. As he landed, Stromer's side smashing onto the stones, Barnum slammed his huge, three-toed foot onto the spinosaur's face. He pressed an increasing amount of weight upon Stromer, who soon groaned out in pain.

It was then, as the captain was at his weakest, that Gigas joined the fray. He lunged and bit hard on Stromer's tall sail, pinning him to the ground at both ends.

"How did you think this would end?" barked Barnum. "Did you really think you would get away with kidnapping the *Architect*? You're a fool, pirate."

In that moment, Stromer's pupils widened as he stared through the gaping hole in the lighthouse and into Robyn's eyes.

"*Architect?*" he repeated. "Why would the king be helping the Architect?"

"Because he has some respect," Barnum replied. "Not that I would expect you to understand that."

Stromer's eyes closed, and he gritted his teeth. With a mighty roar and a surge of strength, he dragged his head out from underneath Barnum's foot. Gigas still had his jaws clamped around Stromer's sail and, as the pirate struggled, a huge chunk was ripped off. Stromer fled into the sea, scarred and beaten, a gaping gouge in his once magnificent sail. Far quicker than either tyrant could react, he had slipped into the waves and vanished from sight.

"Damn," Gigas hissed, after spitting a chunk of Stromer's sail onto the beach. "How could you let him get away?"

"Easy, Gigas," replied Barnum. "We didn't come for the pirate—we came for the girl."

"Hmm," Gigas grumbled, clearly disappointed that the captain had escaped his justice.

Barnum approached the lighthouse and entered through the destroyed wall.

"Are you hurt?" he asked Robyn.

"No," she replied with a nervous shake of her head.

With a surprisingly delicate snip of his forwardmost teeth, he severed the rope which bound her wrists and then did the same for that around her ankles. He turned his attention to my ropes and set me free in the same fashion. I stretched my limbs out before clambering to my feet.

"Thanks, Megazord," I said, standing in the shadow of the metal-laden behemoth.

"I'm just doing my duty, little one."

I had never been referred to as "little" before, but then I had never been in the company of anyone so huge until recently. Without further comment, Barnum walked across the shack to free Benjamin, who jumped to his feet in a typically excited fashion.

"A royal rescue," he exclaimed. "How awesome is *that*?"

I shook my head at his untameable positivity, yet I couldn't help but emit a relieved chuckle.

"A *mammal*?" sneered Gigas as he poked his head inside the lighthouse. "We should take him in."

"He's not in Gondwana," replied Barnum. "No law is being broken here."

"They shouldn't be allowed *anywhere*."

"Enough," Barnum barked. "This mammal has assisted our Architect. We owe him gratitude."

After a quick breather, we all stepped outside and gained our first glimpse of Hațeg Island. It was a luscious place with thick, palm forests. Along the beach, I could see a group of small, long-necked sauropod dinosaurs—small for a sauropod, that is; they were still larger than most cows. They glanced nervously over their shoulders at the two vast predators who had caused such a commotion. The enormous lighthouse dominated the view, but its white and red paint was faded and cracked, the plaster crumbling and, of course, it now had a gaping hole at the base.

"Wow, this place is—"

"Dangerous," retorted Gigas. "The home of feral, lawless, seafaring creatures. We would be wise to leave with haste."

My jaw dropped as I noticed the carcass of a vast shark beached further along the shore. This was surely the *megalodon* they had referred to as Louis. It wasn't hard to determine the cause of death—huge holes had been blasted in his side. I wondered what could have inflicted such damage.

I was pleased to see Mother Mary waiting for us at the shore. While she wasn't the friendliest of creatures, I felt as though she could be trusted—she had, albeit unsuccessfully, tried to protect us from the pirates. Upon boarding, she explained how she had gone back to port in search of help, only to find the tyrannosaurs already looking for us.

The remainder of the voyage was mercifully far less eventful. Mary's deck was a little more cluttered than before with additional crates and barrels, but most notable was the large cannon on the starboard side—I assumed this was how the *megalodon* had been dispatched. Lord Gigas lazed on the deck, but Sir Barnum paced vigilantly; keeping a constant eye on the horizon.

"How are you faring back there?" Mary asked.

"Not bad for having just been kidnapped," I remarked.

"Quite. You two are quickly becoming a bigger headache for those poor tyrants than even Jynx."

"Jynx?" Robyn asked.

"Yes, Jynx. You don't know of Jynx?"

"The pirates mentioned her, but I don't know much else. They said she told them we were coming."

"Well, that figures. She's little more than a terrorist. The rexes have been hunting her for years, but she always slips from their grasp. She set fire to the cable car tower in the capital last month. It ruined the pulleys—I hear the cable cars were down for weeks."

"Was everyone okay?"

"Yes. Thankfully, she seems to target property rather than people. It is perhaps her only redeeming trait. She thinks herself a revolutionary of some sort."

"Thanks for coming to help us," I said.

"That's quite all right, my dear. I couldn't let those vile pirates win."

***

Night fell and Robyn and I lay on Mary's deck gazing at the velvety black sky while the others slept, Benjamin snoring loudly.

"Mary?" I asked. "How can you see where you're going in this darkness?"

"I use the stars, dear."

"Huh, how does that work?"

"They make shapes," Robyn interjected. "The stars, that is. They form patterns in the sky that show what direction you're facing."

"That's right," Mary confirmed.

"Oh, yeah," I replied with a nod. "There's a name for those shapes."

"Constipations," Robyn stated confidently.

"Constipations," I mused. "Are you sure that's right?"

"Pretty sure. Although that might be when you can't—"

She was interrupted by a bright streak of white light as a shooting star flashed across the sky. "A shooting star," she cried. "I'll make a wish."

"Hush, child," Mary hissed. "A shooting star is not considered good fortune in these parts. May I remind you of our history with space rocks?"

"Oh, right," Robyn replied. "Sorry."

"Not at all. Just be mindful around the *tyrannosaurs*. Dinosaurs are especially touchy."

"Is there any food on-board?" I asked.

"I suppose you have had a long day. Check the crate in front of you, there should be some food in there. This is no luxury cruise though. Don't be expecting gourmet."

I padded over to the wooden crate on the forward end of the deck and pried the lid open with my front claws. Inside was a rather basic selection of tins and suspicious grey meats. Robyn peered over my shoulder into the crate and gritted her teeth in disgust.

"I'm not hungry," she decided.

Her loss. Food was still a novelty to me, and I was going to eat as much as I could while I could. I ripped open four tins of baked beans and happily consumed the strange meat which turned out to be salted beef. It was no king's banquet, but it was still only my second ever meal.

"Mary, how long until we arrive?" Robyn asked.

"Not until the morning," she responded. "Perhaps longer with this injured fin."

"What's wrong with your fin?" I queried, my words muffled by salted beef.

"Well, the... I'm sorry, *must* he snore so loudly?" she snapped, referring to Benjamin. "I can't even think with this racket. Wake *up*, milk drinker."

Benjamin was startled awake and the rest of us sat in awkward silence for a few moments after Mary's outburst. It was clear that Benjamin's mere presence was distasteful to her.

"You were telling us about your fin?" I said in an attempt to break the silence.

"Hmm, yes. The shark made the first strike," she explained.

"You took a bite from a *megalodon*?" chirped Benjamin, who had recovered from his abrupt awakening remarkably quickly.

I wasn't sure if Benjamin was entirely unaware of Mary's inherent disgust with him, or if he was simply used to such poor treatment. However, he chatted to her cheerfully as though she were his friend.

"More of a graze," she replied dryly. "Nothing more than a glancing blow."

I wandered over to the starboard side, beside the cannon, and peered down at Mary's front flipper. Sure enough, there was a huge gash running across the top surface. It looked like it had stopped bleeding, but it was still red and tender.

"That's got to smart," remarked Benjamin, who had followed me to the side of the deck.

"I'm not new to a little pain."

"I can help with that, you know."

"A *doctor*, are we?"

"Not quite, but my folks taught me a little trick. I always carry some of this around…"

Benjamin reached his head around and dug his snout into the pouch in his belly. From within, he extracted a large, yellow slab with tiny hexagonal structures—it looked to be honeycomb. He leapt over the side of the deck and onto Mary's injured flipper.

"*What* are you—" she protested.

"Trust me, sheila," he insisted as he began to spread the honey onto the wound. "How's that?"

"How dare you… you… you… well, hmm. Yes, that… that does feel a *little* better."

Mary seemed to almost choke on her words. Benjamin simply smiled and scrambled back onto the deck. Through an uncertain and forced smile, Mary turned to the little thylacine and thanked him.

Laurasia

As the sun rose, the northern coast of the Tethys came into view. The region ahead was somewhat less tropical than that to the south. Before us stretched a vast mountain range with evergreen forests around their lower slopes and gleaming, snow-covered peaks. There was a chill in the air and the scent of pine carried in the breeze.

"Welcome to Laurasia," announced Mother Mary as she began to drag her belly across the shallows. "I'm afraid you must now continue without me. I'm not much of a walker, you see."

"Thanks, sheila," chirped Benjamin as he scampered onto the beach.

Mary narrowed her eyes and opened her mouth to, presumably, scold the little marsupial. However, she froze for a second, before simply offering him a polite nod.

"It's good to see you found your sea legs."

"Thank you, Mary," replied Robyn sincerely.

"I hope you find the cure."

"You too."

Robyn dropped her gaze to the deck upon realising her embarrassing social faux pas. I decided to interject in an attempt to save her blushes.

"I'm sure we will, Mary. Thanks for the lift."

I plopped onto the damp, sandy beach and could feel every grain of sand beneath my feet. I could smell the salt from the sea and felt a faint drizzle of rain fall onto my back. It seemed so *real*. And yet, as I looked around at the magnificent landscape, as I gazed upon my impossible prehistoric accomplices, I still felt it was surely too fantastical to be true. I could tell Robyn shared this notion. She didn't say it out loud, she didn't let it show at all, but I could tell. That vacant stare into the distance—she was afraid this was all an illusion, a hallucination, a false hope. She was *terrified*—and, given the stakes, so was I.

The truth was, this entire adventure being fictional would be the easiest explanation. It was surely a dream, or a fantasy, or perhaps Robyn had simply gone mad. After all, having an imaginary friend, even one of the non-prehistoric variety, wasn't typically a sign of mental stability.

But how would one explain this being a reality? Would you call it magic? A miracle? Some tired sentiment about the power of a child's imagination? All of those seemed pretty farfetched. The hard fact was that the likelihood of failure was infinitely higher than that of success.

I had always had similar questions about my own existence. Was *I* real? What does it even mean to be real? If I did only exist in Robyn's head, if even my own consciousness was a delusion, what did that make me? Until now, I had always accepted this ambiguity. It didn't seem to matter. Now, though, the answer to that question was far more significant. Carol's life depended on it.

"We shouldn't waste any more time," announced Barnum. "The mausoleum is deep within those mountains."

"It would be wise to reach it before nightfall," concurred Gigas.

As Gigas spoke, I caught wind once again of his foul breath and wondered if Pangaeans had developed dental care.

The trek began slowly. After all, Robyn, Benjamin, and I had only relatively small legs. The tyrants soon grew impatient and, in a move which elated both Robyn and Benjamin, yet humiliated me to my bones, we were given a ride upon their backs. Robyn sat atop Barnum's neck while I lay further behind—gripping on as tightly as I could. Benjamin was, predictably, far more relaxed and stood proudly upon Gigas's back.

"Now *this* is the way to travel," Benjamin exclaimed. "You know, you guys could make a business out of this. You could call it *Tyrannosaurus* Rides, or *Rex* Tours… oh, *T-Treks*. I could be a tour guide—we could do safaris."

"Does this one ever shut up?" Gigas snapped.

"I think you have *wonderful* ideas, Benjamin," Robyn replied defensively. "This old dinosaur just has no imagination."

"I can imagine how he'd taste," the rex grunted.

"You know 'rex' means 'king,' right?'" Benjamin continued, unphased. "It's Latin. It's funny neither of you are the actual king, right? Oh, hang on. Sorry, mate, you're not insecure about that, are you?"

"No," Gigas grumbled unconvincingly.

"Do you like sports? I bet you'd be good at rugby because, mate, you are an absolute *unit*. The trouble with most sports is you need opposable thumbs—"

"I promise," the feathered tyrant grumbled, "if you don't stop talking, I'll *eat* you."

I wasn't sure if this was meant as a joke, but it certainly sounded sinister to me. However, Benjamin simply took it as an opportunity to discuss what kind of meal he would most aspire to become. In case you want to know, he settled on barbecue food. I guess you can take the marsupial out of Australia and such.

"Please, will you shut *up*?" Gigas snarled.

"Don't mind Lord Gigas," said Barnum. "He's just bitter at the world because he never achieved his artistic dreams."

Gigas growled quietly in response.

"What dreams?" asked Robyn politely.

"He wanted to play piano, but he never could. There's a reason there aren't any tyrannosaur pianists."

Benjamin started to giggle. "Because of the short arms, right?"

Both theropods halted in their tracks and snapped their necks around to face Benjamin. They narrowed their eyes and snarled, causing the poor marsupial to cower atop Gigas's back. Clearly, the short arm topic was a bone of contention.

"Because we can't pronate our *hands*," Barnum clarified in a deep growl.

"Oh."

Benjamin sat with his head drooped in embarrassment, having insulted both guides with a single careless comment. However, after some time, he raised his head and stared blankly upwards in thought.

"What does 'pronate' mean?" he asked.

Robyn snickered at Benjamin's persistence.

"It means they can't make their palms face downwards," I explained. "On TV, we always see theropods with limp hands facing down, but they couldn't actually turn their hands that way. They faced inwards."

"Huh," replied Benjamin. "Gigas, buddy, maybe you could take up the accordion instead?"

"The *accordion*? How dare you, mammal? I'm a *serious* musician."

The rain had progressed from a drizzle to a torrential downpour during the several hours we had been trekking up the forested mountain slopes. Other than Benjamin's cheerful humming, the party had been mostly silent for some time now. However, as we entered a steep, rocky valley, Sir Barnum spoke up.

"It's close," he said, his deep voice rumbling through his body and into mine.

The path snaked along the winding gorge, rising all the way. As we climbed higher still, the rain gave way to swirling snow and bitter cold. Robyn in particular was beginning to suffer from the cold. She shivered and wrapped her arms over her chest, gripping her shoulders. Of course, she was still dressed for the Dorset heatwave, with shorts and a t-shirt.

The path soon became a steep stairway, carved into the rock. However, part way up these stairs, we found the way impassable. A vast tree had collapsed and become wedged between the two valley walls.

"How are we supposed to get past that?" Robyn lamented.

"I'll shift it," I reassured her while gratefully scrambling down Barnum's huge, muscular leg.

Robyn was lowered rather more gracefully as the great tyrant crouched, allowing her to dismount from only a short distance above the ground. Gigas, however, simply shrugged Benjamin off, causing him to thump onto the snow. Not that the thylacine seemed fazed—he immediately sprang to his feet and bounded towards the tree.

"I don't know, mate. It looks pretty heavy."

I shoved my shoulder against the monstrous trunk, barging it several times. There was no movement at all—it didn't even creak.

"Stand aside," commanded Barnum.

Without actually waiting for me to stand aside, the knight smashed into the tree with the top of his head. The trunk cracked down the middle and, with a great thrust, Barnum shattered the tree in two, opening a wide path in the middle. Robyn and Benjamin stood with their jaws slack and eyes wide in awe of the beast's great strength.

"I loosened it for you," I grumbled.

I squinted through the whirling snow, unsure of what I was looking for, but I figured a mausoleum wouldn't be all that hard to spot. A faint, orange glow began to pierce the blizzard. As we pressed on, the source became clear. A flickering torch sat upon a pedestal of cobbled stones.

Robyn stepped ahead and placed a hand on the pedestal. The moment she made contact with the stone, a burst of wind rushed from beyond. In a near instant, the white-out was replaced by calm, clear air. We could now see tall towers and walls of grey stone, all in varying states of ruin and dappled with patches of green moss.

In the distance was an archway carved into the cliff face, the door within illuminated by an oil-burning torch.

The door was constructed of the same grey stone as the rest of the structure, but it was far more intricately carved, with elaborate spirals and strange runes around the doorframe.

"The Mausoleum of the Archean," Lord Gigas said in a low voice filled with awe.

"Wow," Robyn gasped. "What's inside?"

"They say it's the resting place of the Archean—the first lifeform in Pangaea. As the story goes, he was buried with his greatest treasure."

"The Heart," Gigas clarified.

"It's said to give life to all of Pangaea."

"How do we find it?" I asked.

"No one's ever entered to know," replied Barnum. "Only the Architect may open the door."

"I guess we'll find out then."

"Crikey, I hope this works," Benjamin chirped. "Can you imagine? *Inside* the mausoleum? That would be the best day of my life. Even better than when I won that eucalyptus eating competition."

"Isn't eucalyptus poisonous except to koalas?" asked Robyn.

"Nah, yeah, I got pretty sick, but a win's a win, right?"

"Uh, sure," I replied with a raised eyebrow.

We approached the door with a level of caution. It was almost perfectly sized for Robyn. Most animals in Pangaea wouldn't have fit—an adult human wouldn't have fit, for that matter. The runes dotted around the door frame were meaningless to me, but there were several rudimentary drawings carved into the door. I could see the citadel in Tanis painted in gold and, above it, a fiery comet. In the centre, there was a girl side by side with a *Dimetrodon*. It was odd to look upon what was clearly an ancient depiction of myself.

"A comet?" Robyn pondered.

"Do you think it has something to do with the scripture Mary spoke of?" I suggested. "She said Pangaea needed saving, but she never did say what from."

"How am I supposed to save Pangaea from a comet? Do I look like Superwoman?"

"I don't know, it could be metaphorical."

Robyn shrugged and gave the door a strong push. When it didn't budge, she turned and pushed her back against it with her legs, straining loudly. After applying all the force she could without success, she took a step back.

"How do you reckon it opens?" Benjamin asked.

"Maybe there's a secret passphrase of some kind," I replied. "You know, like in *Lord of the Rings*: 'Speak "friend" and enter.'"

"Could be," Robyn replied. "But how would we know the password?"

"Can any of you lot read these runes?" I asked the tyrannosaurs.

"No one can," replied Barnum.

"They're older than memory itself," added Gigas.

"Well," I continued, looking at Robyn, "this is all still, effectively, *your* creation—even if it's from your subconscious. So, it'll be something you like. Like, um… *ice cream*."

Predictably, nothing happened, but I didn't expect it to get it on my first try.

"*Ed*," said Robyn.

"What?"

"No, I was trying that as a password."

"Aww, sweet, but I guess that's a little obvious. What about… *ice cream*."

"*McFly*."

"*Eugh*, I'm an extension of your psyche and even I don't understand the McFly obsession."

This guessing game continued for some time, to no avail. We had to come up with a plan B.

"Maybe it's like a video game," I pondered. "You know, like in *Tomb Raider*. There could be an orb or a spear or a key lying around somewhere, and we could slot it into the door. Or we have one of the big guys bash it in. Maybe—"

"Many before us have tried brute force," Gigas interjected. "The magic which seals that door is beyond the physical. Don't waste my time with such idiotic suggestions."

"All right, murder turkey, way to stay positive," I retorted.

"Has anyone tried knocking?" asked Benjamin.

I stared at him incredulously for a moment. Did he really think the secret to unlocking such a profound, magical gateway was to *knock*? In contrast, however, Robyn's expression was one of intrigue. She looked at Benjamin and then me with a single eyebrow raised.

"Seems worth a shot," she said with a shrug.

She stepped up to the stone door and tapped three times with her knuckles. After a moment of silence, the carvings and runes began to glow a greenish-blue. I would have felt foolish for doubting Benjamin's idea had I not been so enthralled in the enchanting light show. It was oddly hypnotising.

A ghostly voice echoed throughout the gorge. It was grisly and aged, but definitely male.

"*Finally,*" it announced. "*I have waited many aeons for you, child.*"

The stone door swung inwards, grinding along the floor. Inside was initially an entirely dark void before rows of torches ignited into blue flame—illuminating a seemingly endless passage.

"I don't think I should go inside after all," said Benjamin, showing the first sign of nerves. "It feels like something for you."

"I agree, actually," I added. "I think it's clear only Robyn is supposed to enter."

Robyn's eyes widened in terror. "Go in by *myself*?" she squeaked.

"It's literally built for you. Look at the shape of the door. You'll be fine," I insisted.

"Your picture is carved into the door too, Ed. Where I go, you go. *Always*. Please, I need you."

I smiled. I'm not ashamed to admit I was fighting back some tears after that comment. I supposed it seemed right that we go together, and I was grateful she thought so too.

"I'd follow you anywhere, Robyn, though mostly out of morbid curiosity."

We stepped together towards the door before Robyn turned around to address the others.

"See you on the other side," she said.

"Good luck, little one," replied Barnum.

The Mausoleum of the Archean

I strode into the passageway. Robyn hesitated before following along the gloomy passage. The blue torchlight flickered and danced against the walls, but there were still no clues as to what lay at the end. It seemed to stretch into the depths of the mountain forever. The haunting voice of the mausoleum echoed out once more.

"Before the Architect can be bestowed with the Heart, she must prove she is ready. You must pass the three trials of the Archean."

"Trials?" I asked with a gulp.

"These trials will test the traits the Architect must possess to fulfil her destiny."

"What destiny?" Robyn replied.

"The scripture…" I mused.

"For your first trial, you must prove your haste."

I looked at Robyn with a sly smile.

"Hundred metre sprint champion four years in a row," I reminded her with a wink. "I think you can prove you're fast."

With the loud grinding of moving stone, a trapdoor opened before us. We walked towards this new hole in the floor and gazed into the abyss. As far as I could tell, the hole had no bottom. Who knew how far down it went or what lay below, but it was clear that this was where we needed to go.

"Architects first," I said, gesturing towards the hole.

"I'm not going down there," she replied, her eyes pinned wide with terror. "How deep is it? We could be jumping to our deaths."

"I don't think the disembodied voice of the mausoleum would have us leap to our demise. That seems a little convoluted."

"You don't know that, Ed. Oh, God, or we could get *stuck*, or there could be *spiders*, or—"

"Okay, I hear what you're saying, but…"

Without finishing that sentence, I gave her a gentle shove down the hole. She screamed for a couple seconds before thumping at the bottom. I dived after her, landing right by her feet in another long passageway.

"What was *that*, Ed?"

"You needed a push," I replied. "For your mum."

Robyn shook her head before sighing deeply.

"What's this trial of haste all about, then?"

Up ahead, at a distance which I reckoned might well have been exactly a hundred metres, two bright orange torches illuminated a wooden door.

"So, I guess you just run to the door as quickly as you can?" I suggested.

"Seems simple enough."

"Maybe too simple."

It was. From behind us came a dry, laboured gasping. I spun around to see a hulking mass covered in dark, patchy fur creeping out from the shadows.

The creature which emerged was hideous. Its jaws were vast and housed oversized teeth dripping with saliva. Dark, soulless eyes penetrated the torchlight. The beast's front limbs were much taller than its hind legs, creating a muscular, front-heavy body plan with an immense hump of muscle above its shoulder blades. Its matted fur was interrupted by seemingly random bald patches, scars, and warts.

"Is that…?"

"*Daeodon*," Robyn confirmed with a tremble in her voice.

I had feared as much, though I knew it better by its unofficial and well-earned title—the *Hell pig*. While not actually a pig, it was certainly hellish. Robyn and I spun and fled as the beast lunged for us. It seemed that failing the "trial of haste" would have fatal consequences.

Our feet pounded the ground with all the strength we could summon, but the heavy, dull hoofbeats of our beastly pursuer pounded ever closer. I focused on the salvation of the door ahead. We *had* to make it.

We were close, but I could feel the hot, wet breath of the Hell pig on my back. It was almost upon us. Robyn barged into the door which flew open. I dove through in time for her to slam it shut in the *Daeodon*'s face. It crashed repeatedly against it from the other side. The door appeared to have locked upon being shut, but it shook violently with each battering it took.

We now found ourselves in a small room dominated by a large, circular door of stone. It was adorned with an intricate carving of a great tree.

"You have proven your haste, Architect," announced the mausoleum voice. *"Now, you must prove your intellect. Answer me this riddle."*

As she rested her hands upon her thighs, I could hear Robyn's fearful panting subside. She stood and breathed in deeply before a sharp exhale.

"A riddle?" she chimed. "Oh, okay, I'm good at riddles. Is it a clock? Or the wind? Oh, *time*, I bet the answer is time."

"Robyn, I think you have to let him ask the riddle first."

"No, no. The... the answer was time."

"Yes," Robyn whispered to herself while performing a gentle fist pump.

"You may proceed to the next trial."

"That's it?" I asked. "That's the whole trial of intellect?"

"Indeed."

"It just seemed more like the trial of lucky guesses," I said with a shrug.

"Look, I had a more intricate trial planned, but the beta readers didn't like it."

"No?" Robyn replied.

"They said it was boring."

"Oh, had you worked on it for long?"

"Only since the dawn of existence."

"That's such a shame. Do you want to tell us about it? Maybe we could do it later."

"No, no, it's fine. Let's… let's just move on to the next one."

A crunching sound from the door behind us reminded me the *Daeodon* was still coming for us.

"Well, I'll not insist upon a harder trial," I added. "Let's get going."

The stone door clunked from within and began to roll to the side. As it opened fully, the wooden door behind finally gave way and the Hell pig burst through in a hail of splinters.

"Just in time," I yelped.

We leapt through the new opening and, to our relief, the stone door rolled back into place, locking the *Daeodon* out.

Robyn and I panted—that had been far too close. After a moment, I let a sly smile spread across my face.

"Speed and smarts?" I said. "These tests never stood a chance against you."

"*Well done, Architect,*" the mysterious voice announced. "*It is time for your final trial. The test of courage.*"

The Heart of Pangaea

Robyn glanced at me nervously and I immediately shared her concern. We already knew the girl was fast and clever, but—and I mean this with love—she was a scaredy-cat.

The torches illuminating our current room were snuffed out, plunging us into an all-consuming darkness. It was the deepest black I had ever experienced. I waved my paw in front of my eyes yet saw nothing.

"What do you think we have to be brave about?" asked Robyn with a tremble in her voice.

"The dark, I guess."

"I don't like the dark."

"No one *likes* the dark, but it's not so bad, right? We can handle this."

However, it soon became clear that we had much more than the dark to fear. I heard a hauntingly familiar wheezing sound, the laboured gasping of a monster.

"Ed, do you hear that?"

"I hear it."

"It's in here with us, isn't it?"

The torches burst back into life, revealing the Hell pig looming over us. We both screamed and scarpered, but the room was small. There was nowhere to run. We pressed ourselves against the wall with the *Daeodon* closing on us.

"Courage," I whispered. "Courage, Robyn. You have to be brave."

"And what?" she snapped. "*Fight* the Hell pig?"

"Just... stand up to it. Face it."

I could see Robyn's right leg shaking and her knuckles growing white as she gripped the wall. Her complexion had turned even paler than usual.

"I can't, Ed. I can't even move."

"Think of your mum," I insisted. "She *needs* this. You can face this big pork chop for *her*. I know you can do it."

Robyn shook her head in disagreement, her eyes pinned to the slobbering beast as it approached ever closer.

"Come *on*," I insisted. "For your mum."

She inhaled deeply and whispered, "For Mum."

"For *Mum*," I pressed.

Robyn nodded slowly, then again with a little more vigour. A tear began to swell and glisten in her eye.

"For Mum!" she yelled.

Still shaking uncontrollably, tears now streaming down her face, she pushed herself off the wall and took a stride towards the creature.

"I can stand up to you," she growled. "I *need* that cure, and you're in my way."

Even I was taken aback by this sudden burst of courage. I then noticed something odd: Not only had the Hell pig not eaten her yet, it had stopped and dropped its head in submission. On closer inspection, the creature had something lodged within its lower jaw.

"What's that?" I asked. "Robyn, between its teeth."

She leant in more closely. It looked like a large fish bone embedded in the monster's gum.

"I... I think it needs help," Robyn concluded.

She crept further towards the *Daeodon* and reached out a hand. It flinched at first and growled loudly, causing Robyn to snatch her hand back and retreat. With a deep breath, she regained her composure and stepped forwards once more. The animal growled again, but Robyn reached across regardless. She gripped the bone and pulled. It took more force than I expected, but the fish bone came loose into Robyn's hand. With that, the great beast vanished, bursting into a swarm of shimmering fireflies.

"Well, that was weird," I stated. "Good job, though."

Robyn nodded—panting with her hands on her knees. "What now?" she asked when she regained her breath.

"I don't know." I looked around in the darkness. "Surely you passed. You were brave and you took the moral high horse."

"Yeah, I guess—wait, you did it again."

"Did what?"

"Moral high horse. That's not the saying. You're mixing up two different—"

Her words were cut short as, with a loud *clunk*, the floor opened beneath our feet. My stomach lurched and my lungs refused to draw air as gravity took hold and we plummeted. The fall was short, though still entirely unpleasant. The landing, however, was simply bizarre. In truth, I don't even remember landing. Rather, shortly after falling, I realised I was standing on a pristine, blue rock pool. And I don't mean *in* the pool—I mean *on*. Standing *on top* of the surface, looking at the crystal-clear pool below, feeling the gentle ripples of the water beneath my feet. Anemones and various water plants danced slowly in the gentle currents.

It was impossibly bright, yet there were no obvious sources of light. Rather, all around us was simply an infinite, white expanse. I looked straight above to find no evidence of the room we had come from. There was no ceiling or walls—just an endless void.

"*Welcome,*" boomed the ghostly voice. "*You have passed the trials, including the most important one of all.*"

"Bravery?" Robyn replied.

"Was it truly a test of bravery? Or a test of compassion? For in the end, compassion will be the foundation of the new Pangaea."

"Who... who *are* you?" asked Robyn.

The was a slight shake in her voice—she was clearly intimidated by our bizarre new surroundings.

"I am the first. The Archean. I am Luca."

Looking around, I noticed that there was nothing much to see other than water and jagged rocks.

"I don't see anyone," I whispered to Robyn.

"I thought the Archean was dead," she mused. "This is a mausoleum, right?"

"Is that what they call it in the outside world? My dear, this is nothing so morbid. It is not a place of mourning, but a place of sanctuary."

I then perceived a small, black shadow scuttling across the rocks beneath my feet. I peered through the rippling surface to see what looked like a little scorpion. Its legs were short and at the end of its tail, where one might expect a stinger on a scorpion, was instead a flat paddle—not entirely unlike that on a lobster. It was unmistakably a eurypterid—better known as a sea scorpion—an ancient marine arthropod which was not, in fact, particularly closely related to actual scorpions. Was this the source of the eerie voice?

"Jækel, please guide our guests to me."

Upon that order, the sea scorpion gave a rapid flick of its tail fluke and propelled through the water with a surprising turn of pace. Robyn and I, still standing upon the water's surface, chased after. We didn't have to follow for long before the arthropod scuttled up a rock which protruded above the surface. This particular rock was tall and narrow and oddly flat on top. It was like a twisted, rocky pedestal standing to around chest height on Robyn. Sat upon this rock was, curiously, a microscope.

"Step forwards, child."

Robyn stopped for a second before edging cautiously towards the microscope. She glanced down at me before placing her eyes against the viewing ports. She gasped.

"Let me see," I demanded.

I stretched onto my hind legs and placed an eye against one of the lenses—the device was frustratingly only designed for the odd, closely spaced eyes of a human. Regardless, I could see well enough to make out a small, luminescent, blue blob with what appeared to be a poorly defined face. A single-celled organism of some kind.

"The original…" I pondered.

"Luca…" Robyn added.

"The last universal common ancestor," I continued, finishing our thought process.

"Indeed," Luca confirmed. *"I am the giver of life—the hand of the Architect. All that you have dreamt, I have birthed into reality."*

"'Giver of life,'" mused Robyn. "And so... also a protector of life? If you can grant life, then you can save one, surely?"

"The Architect is but a child," hissed the sea scorpion, who stood beside Luca's microscope. "She comes here with only personal gains in mind."

"Hush, Jækel," scorned Luca. *"The path of the Architect is not yours to question."*

"But she misunderstands your purpose," replied Jækel, before looking up at Robyn. "Luca will not do what you wish him to do. That is not the way of his power."

"You are too sure of yourself, Jækel. My power is not always so well defined, even to me. Child, what is it you wish of me?"

"My mum," Robyn replied. "She's dying."

"You wish me to save her from death?"

"You see?" snapped Jækel. "Pangaea suffers, yet she cares only for her own."

"Yet perhaps the mother is the key."

"The key to what?" I asked.

"The Architect's destiny, as the scripture says—she will save Pangaea."

"Save Pangaea from *what*?" replied Robyn, clearly exasperated by this yet unanswered question.

"From itself."

"Such ignorance," scorned Jækel. "Your quest is a foolish one, girl, and you will fail."

"Compassion? Love? This is not foolishness. Child, I will come to your aid, as I know you will one day come to ours. Our course is rarely linear, and so I will follow you on this winding path."

"Thank you," Robyn gushed. "Thank you *so* much."

"Take me to the mother of the Architect of Pangaea. I will restore her life force if I can."

Jækel growled quietly in protest but ultimately conceded to his master.

"The glass slide, child," Jækel barked. "Take it."

Robyn reached towards the fragile rectangle of glass which sat below the lens of the microscope. It consisted of two thin sheets of glass pressed together, and from between them came a faint, blue glow. Robyn held it up to the light and stared through it. Somewhere, within those layers of glass, amongst the small glowing smear, far smaller than the eye could see, was Luca.

"You know," she mused. "Not long ago, our pet goldfish died."

"Admiral Akbar," I replied with a smile, remembering the silly name Michael had given him.

"He was even older than me, which is super old for a fish. Dad loved that fish; he buried it in the garden. If you can create life, and if you can save a life—"

"*You wish to know if I can restore life?*" Luca concluded.

Robyn nodded.

"*Alas, I cannot. You must treasure the life you have, for it is finite, even for me.*"

As we began to walk away, the scorpion's claw clamped around Robyn's forearm.

"Luca has never left this sanctum," lectured Jækel. "He is the *Heart of Pangaea*—the very lifeblood of this world. He *must* be returned before the third sunrise, lest that to which he has given life perish. Do you understand the weight of this responsibility?"

Robyn nodded while gazing directly into his beady, black eyes. Jækel simply huffed—clearly not entirely convinced she did—and released her from his grasp.

"I'm sure Luca will keep us straight," I added in an attempt to reassure the guardian.

"*I am afraid it is the Sanctum itself which lends me a voice, young one,*" responded Luca. "*Once outside these walls, I can be of little assistance. But fear not, I have faith in you both. You have demonstrated all the required virtues.*"

"I cannot assist you either," Jækel added. "The sanctum binds me for as long as Luca's power remains. But allow me to provide a simple warning—beware of the Bishop."

"The Bishop?" I asked.

"One of the first to be created, a beast of immeasurable strength. He resides in the shadows, but he *will* seek the Heart. You must not allow Luca to fall into his hands."

"Okay. Bishop. Evil shadow beast," I replied. "Got it."

"One more thing," Jækel hissed. "Should you betray our trust, should Luca's power wane from this place, I will have no purpose left in life. I will find purpose in your *torment*, Architect. That I promise."

Robyn nodded with a slight tremble.

"Then let us depart, young one," said Luca.

The Gobi Reaper

In 1948, deep in the barren expanse of Mongolia's Gobi Desert, a rather remarkable set of fossils was discovered: three enormous claws, as long as machetes. These claws lent the animal its name—Therizinosaurus, the scythe lizard.

But what was this animal? Well, at first it was assumed to be some form of giant turtle relative. Then, several decades later, it was considered to be a theropod dinosaur—the family which includes tyrannosaurs and raptors. Those vicious claws, combined with their fearsome relatives, surely meant this animal was a formidable predator.

And yet, future research and discoveries of related animals eventually revealed a surprising twist. Rather than being a blood-thirsty carnivore, Therizinosaurus was of the vegetarian variety, using its impressive claws to harvest plant material and defend itself.

Natural history teaches us much, and the case of the Mongolian scythe lizard shows us that things aren't always as they seem. An apparent predator could turn out to be a herbivore. An enemy could transpire to be a friend. And an ally could, in fact, be a traitor.

Betrayal

In a blink, I found myself outside once more with no idea how I had gotten there. I wasn't sure how long we had been gone. It felt like less than an hour, but the sunrise over the frosty forest indicated that we had been in the mausoleum all night. It had snowed overnight, and a thick layer of white powder carpeted the forest floor. I looked to my right to see Robyn standing by my side, cradling the glass slide on her outstretched palms. Her breath condensed into clouds in the air, but she seemed not to notice the cold now. She focused only on the precious artefact in her hands.

I could smell something unpleasant, a musty odour—and soon realised it was Robyn's clothes. We had been in Pangaea for too long. That girl needed a shower.

Our companions lay asleep on the ground around a smouldering campfire, and I immediately felt guilty for leaving them so long. It was bitterly cold, and I could only imagine how spending the night outside must have been. Benjamin was the first to notice our return. His eyes flickered open before he sprang to his feet.

"You're back!" he yelled before leaping to his feet and bounding over. "Did you find it?"

"We did," Robyn replied, gesturing at the slide in her hands.

"Crikey, it's so *small*."

Benjamin stretched his front legs forwards and yawned loudly, his mouth opening remarkably wide—his jaws almost becoming parallel. Only then did I notice the small chip in his upper canine tooth. Awoken by the commotion, Barnum and Gigas rose high onto their feet and strode over.

"*This* is the heart?" Gigas asked with an eyebrow raised, clearly unconvinced.

"That's what he said," I responded.

"He?"

"The Heart," explained Robyn. "This is Luca. The Archean *is* the heart."

"But that's little more than a sheet of glass," said Barnum.

"No, he's just very small," Robyn corrected. "A microbe."

"I see," Barnum replied. "Well, let us return to the king."

"The king?" I asked. "We don't have time for that, we have to get back to Carol."

"Carol?" asked Gigas.

"My mum," insisted Robyn.

"Ah, yes, the mother."

"How do we get back to the real world?" I asked, turning to Robyn.

"I have no idea," she replied. "Last time, we just fell asleep. Perhaps I can imagine up another door."

"Maybe Luca knows how. *Luca*? Are we still close enough to the sanctum for you to speak to us?"

"Child, a door will present itself when you will it to," he replied, faintly now that we were outside. *"Clear your mind of all distractions, focus only on the door. But you must now make haste."*

"Okay, clear my mind, clear my mind. Wait, why do I have to be quick?"

"I do apologise, little one," interrupted Barnum. "But I can't let you leave yet."

"What?" she gawped.

"The king needs the Heart. We're to bring it to the citadel."

"But I need it. You *knew* I needed it. My mum, she... you *lied* to me?"

"I'm sorry, but it's for the good of the kingdom."

"To hell with the kingdom," I scolded the beast. "Everything here looks fine to me—*Carol* needs that cure."

"Hand over the Heart, little girl," hissed Gigas as he stepped towards Robyn.

"*Run!*" boomed Luca.

Robyn gripped the slide, ducked her head, and dashed between Gigas's legs. Benjamin and I followed suit, scampering around the great beasts and fleeing through the snow. As we reached the stone stairway, I could see it had frozen overnight and was covered in a thick sheet of ice. Robyn ceased her mad run, staring at the treacherous descent, but we didn't have time to perform a risk assessment. I barged into her back, bowling us all over into an uncontrollable slide down the stairway. The stairs were solid and the corners sharp, making the descent entirely unpleasant and leaving more than a few bruises.

The great tyrants behind were even less elegant on the slippery stairway, tumbling after us, roaring and snarling in frustration.

Reaching the bottom of the stairs, we regained some grip as the ice gave way to snow once more. With such great momentum, the two pursuing henchmen bowled past us before colliding with the rock walls of the gorge. We skipped past as they were attempting to rise to their feet, Benjamin only narrowly bounding away from the snapping jaws of Lord Gigas.

As we sprinted further, my heart pounding in my chest, the gorge gave way to coniferous forest. The previous night's snowfall had extended beyond the mountains and into the surrounding woods, the thick layer of powder making our escape more difficult still. Behind me, I could hear the steady padding of Benjamin's footsteps followed by the beating thumps of the tyrants. Benjamin, being a nimble-footed creature, quickly pulled ahead. Curiously, he didn't run at all, but rather he bounded on his back legs like a kangaroo. I could tell he could go faster, but I suspected he was pacing himself so as not to leave us behind.

For a few minutes, we scampered through the forest, dodging trees, leaping over logs, and beating undergrowth away where we could. I looked behind to see that, while Gigas was losing ground, Barnum was still very much on top of us. I feared that the difficulty in navigating such dense woodland, something far more difficult for the pursuing giant, was the only thing keeping him behind. For now, he was hampered by his need to manoeuvre through the gaps between the trees and smash through trunks and hanging branches, but I had no idea how much further the thick vegetation would extend.

The forest wasn't only an obstacle to the chasing tyrant, however. At full sprint, Robyn caught her foot on a tree root hidden by the snow and tumbled to the ground. I arrived by her side after she completed several barrel-rolls and a long slide on her belly and heaved her to her feet with my head. I turned to see Barnum's jaws wide open and lunging for the kill.

We both dived to the side as the great beast's jaws snapped shut with a deep, sickening thud. We scrambled behind the trunk of a huge evergreen tree in a bid to protect ourselves. Barnum initially tried to round the tree to find us, but we scuttled around just as quickly as he did.

In response, he tilted his head to the side and clamped his jaws on the trunk. With impossible strength, he heaved the entire tree out of the ground, roots and all. A shower of dirt and snow rained from the exposed, tangled roots. The tree thumped onto the ground behind us as he tossed it from his gaping maw. With us backed against the trunk with nowhere to go, he stepped forwards and prepared to strike.

Before Barnum could unleash his brutal bite, a small object of tan fur slapped against his face. Benjamin, the diminutive marsupial, had, in an incredible act of either bravery or idiocy, attacked the monstrous reptile. Of course, the impact of his ambitious fly-kick was negligible; he may as well have kicked a brick wall. Barnum didn't even move, but he was briefly distracted. It was only for a fraction of a second, but that was enough for Robyn and me to dash away from the trap we found ourselves in.

Barnum roared with rage as he turned back to find us running off. In his fury, he swiped at Benjamin with his powerful tail. The little thylacine whelped as he was launched through the trees, far into the frozen forest and out of sight.

"*Benjamin!*" Robyn screamed.

But there was no time for notions of retrieving our new friend as Barnum was immediately bearing down on us again. Worse still, Gigas had now caught up and the two tyrannosaurs were once again barrelling through the forest after us. We had to flee. I only hoped we could return for Benjamin soon.

To my dismay, the treeline approached. We burst out of the forest and onto the damp, sandy beach. Here, the snow had partially melted into a wet slush. With nowhere to go, we ran along the coastline, hoping for an escape route to present itself. However, as I had feared, Barnum was much faster across open ground. Being the slowest of us, I was caught first. I felt the great, crushing weight of his foot land on my tail, bringing me to an immediate and jarring halt. It felt as though my tail was almost pulled off as I transitioned from a full sprint to a dead stop within a fraction of a second. The pain jolted along my spine and into my neck, and it felt as though my brain slapped the front of my skull. Dazed, I could only watch as he then shoved Robyn hard with his snout, sending her tumbling forwards and Luca within his little glass slide flying out of her hand.

Barnum stepped over Robyn and scanned the beach, searching for the glass slide. Once this was located, he crouched and lay on the sand to reach with his tiny arms. He scooped Luca up along with a two-fingered handful of damp sand.

"No!" I yelled as I saw Carol's only hope fall into the tyrant's hand.

"Do you have it?" Gigas demanded.

"I have it," Barnum replied.

Barnum's response was direct and professional—there was no sense of celebration. He seemed almost ashamed.

"Then let's finish the job."

"What do you mean 'finish' it?" I yelled, more than a little concerned by the implications.

"Do you know the scripture, synapsid?" replied Gigas.

"It says Robyn will save Pangaea," I replied. "Don't you *want* to be saved?"

"That's not all though, is it? 'The Architect will save Pangaea, and assume her place upon the throne.'"

"The *throne*?" Robyn demanded, baulking. "I don't *want* any *throne*."

"Be that as it may," Barnum elaborated. "The king can't take that risk. We must protect what King Richard has built. You have my apologies for what we must do."

Gigas stepped forwards menacingly and opened his jaws wide, preparing to strike down Robyn. I immediately sprang to my feet and launched myself at Gigas. I knew I was no match for the murderous behemoth, but I had to try. Before I had the chance, however, a huge, reptilian mass swept across the beach and knocked Gigas to the ground. I dug my feet into the sand and brought myself to an abrupt halt, gazing at the newcomer to assess our apparent saviour: a massive, hulking reptile with a tall sail upon its back—a sail with a substantial chunk missing from it.

It was the *Spinosaurus*—Captain Stromer. He had launched himself from the sea and rammed his head into Gigas's side. I wasn't sure if this was a rescue or if he was simply kidnapping us again, but at this moment, I fancied my chances as a hostage as opposed to rex fodder.

Sir Barnum emitted a deep, booming call from his chest and launched himself at the pirate. The tyrant's enormous jaws slammed around our rescuer's neck and threatened to pull him down. Stromer grimaced as the immense strength of Barnum's jaws crushed his throat.

However, the cunning pirate twisted his head underneath to inflict a bite of his own on his attacker's arm. Barnum roared as the spinosaur's sharp teeth pierced through his chainmail and into his arm, forcing him to release Stromer from his grasp. In his shock, the rex slipped in the slush and toppled, thudding into the cold sand.

But now Gigas had regained his footing and lunged for the kill. Globules of spit sprayed from his mouth as his black, wart-covered head closed on our rescuer. Stromer swiped a forelimb at Gigas's face, sinking a long claw deep into the tyrannosaur's eye socket. Lord Gigas howled in pain.

Sensing his opportunity, Stromer turned and dashed for the sea.

"Grab onto me!" the captain yelled.

Robyn and I quickly did as instructed and grabbed onto Stromer's tail. I took a quick, sharp breath before being plunged into the salty spray of the breaking waves. I clambered forwards onto Stromer's back as his powerful tail began to paddle with enormous force.

Once we had cleared the breakwater, I regained some composure. Robyn stood and gripped onto Stromer's great, though damaged, sail. I turned to see the two tyrants standing defeated on the beach. I had no doubt that they were capable of swimming, but they must have known they would never catch Stromer at sea. This was the spinosaur's element. Here, he had the advantage.

"Luca! Benjamin!" yelled Robyn, looking around frantically.

"We *have* to go back," I cried.

"Are you crazy? We can't go back there," Stromer replied. "I'm sorry about your friends, but those two will kill us. The king doesn't send them just to rough people up."

"The *king*," I snarled. "I can't *believe* we trusted that Crystal Palace reject."

"Luca! Oh, *God*, they have Luca." Robyn was near tears.

"It's you they want. They might be vicious, but they're professional—I doubt they'll hurt your friend."

"You don't understand. Luca is the *Heart*."

"The heart?"

"The Heart of Pangaea."

Stromer swivelled his head around to look at Robyn.

"The *king* has the *Heart of Pangaea*?"

Robyn nodded and Stromer sighed.

"Then we're all doomed, kid."

A Royal Plot

King Richard emerged from his luxurious living quarters and onto his ornate, golden balcony. Without his cloak, yellow, weeping sores were visible upon the king's back.

The vast lizard breathed in the cool, evening air. From here, he could see the entire city of Tanis lit by torches. In the daylight, he could see most of Gondwana—all the way to the Tethys coast.

A loud knock sounded from the door of his bed chambers.

"Good morning, sire," came a smooth, well-spoken voice from outside.

Richard recognised this as the voice of Doctor Boggs, his most trusted advisor.

"Come, Doctor," he instructed.

The large mahogany door opened slowly and the giant *Therizinosaurus* ambled through, his glossy, blue feathers glinting in the torchlight. He was followed by his assistant, Oskar the *Boverisuchus*.

"Who's this?" Richard asked, glaring at Oskar.

"Oskar, sire," the crocodilian replied with a gentle bow of his head.

"Oskar is my new assistant," Boggs clarified, his sword-like claws intertwined across his portly belly.

"What happened to the old one?" the king queried.

"You killed him, sire."

"Ah, yes, of course. Anyway, you're just the one I hoped to speak with."

"How so?"

"I wish to name Etheldred my heir, and I need you to organise the ceremony."

"The *general*, sire?"

"Indeed."

"Your Grace, may I speak freely?"

"You may not."

"Well, I shall regardless. The general is a fine warrior, but as the monarch? I fear she is too—"

"I've made my decision, Boggs."

"So be it. I trust you slept well, Your Grace?"

"Not for a moment," Richard replied with an honest sigh.

"The girl?"

"*Yes*, the girl." he snapped.

"She seems unaware of her apparent purpose, my lord. Besides, the scripture is little more than superstition—you've never believed it to be true."

"That was before she appeared in my city—now, I'm not so sure. Do you think she is truly the Architect?"

"I do, but I believe she speaks the truth. She is simply here to help her mother. Besides, Pangaea was built by you—the people know that. They're loyal to you."

"In the city, perhaps, but what of the peasants? What treasures she could promise them."

"She's just a girl—I've seen no indication she can offer any such promises."

"How do we know she is who she says? You could… test her blood, perhaps? To be sure. Since you are an esteemed doctor of science."

"I'm not that kind of doctor, sire."

"What kind of doctor *are* you, again? I don't think you've ever specified."

"I'm a doctor of—"

"Never mind that," the king rasped as he began to wheeze. "How do we know she is the Architect for sure?"

"If she is, she will enter the mausoleum and retrieve what she needs. No one else but the Architect can enter."

"Was I foolish to send her there?"

"She is too young to fulfil the scripture. Even if she discovers her rumoured purpose, she lacks the maturity to make it happen. The child simply wishes to help her mother and go home."

"Nevertheless, the people might believe. Belief is powerful; we *must* keep this quiet. The sooner she leaves Pangaea, the better. Once she has the Heart, she will be gone."

"I have given that some thought."

"How so?" the king replied, his breathing increasingly laboured.

"Well, *if* we assume the Heart is real and that the girl *can* retrieve it—perhaps there is an opportunity."

"I—"

The king interrupted himself with a harsh, gritty coughing fit which lasted for several seconds. Once finished, he looked onto the floor of his balcony at the pool of phlegm he had expelled. It was a timely illustration of the point Boggs was about to make.

"If the stories are true, it could cure your illness," he suggested.

"I don't believe in magic, Doctor," gasped the king, somewhat out of breath from his violent coughing.

"I think magic might be all we have left. We have exhausted all medical options."

"I cannot have a fated usurper kicking up a fuss—" The king twitched his head from side to side before an intense muscle spasm caused him to wrench his head upwards, staring at the ceiling. He grimaced as his neck muscles cramped and seized, locking his jaw shut and forcing his teeth to grind.

"The stargazing is getting worse?"

With a groan, the king slowly lowered his head level once more.

"It's been more frequent the past few days."

"Why is it so important for the girl to leave so soon?"

"Because I built this city from the dirt!" he roared. "Before me, the citizens lived in the mud, scraping a living from the land, barely surviving. I will *not* give it up to a *child*."

"And when the illness takes you? Do you really believe the general is ready to rule?"

"I'm old, Boggs—older than you'll ever know. If my time is coming, then so be it."

"And what of the kingdom? You can name an heir all you like, but you know there are others with a claim."

"Nonsense. The Bishop hasn't been seen in aeons."

"Biding his time in the shadows, sire. He *is* still alive; of that, I have no doubt."

The king stood in silence for a moment, growling to himself.

"Perhaps you have a point," he grumbled reluctantly. "So be it. Send word to Barnum and Gigas. Retrieve the Heart."

"I already have. They tracked down the girl."

"You what?"

"They are escorting her to the Mausoleum."

"How *dare* you issue such an order without my knowledge? Do not forget who is king, Doctor."

"Your Majesty, the good doctor simply did what *you* must do," interrupted Oskar.

"Oskar, be *silent*," Boggs hissed, but it was too late.

The king growled and turned to face the crocodilian, who was but a fraction of Richard's size.

"What are you suggesting? That I, the *king*, cannot make decisions for myself?"

"*Nein.* I just thought—"

Oskar didn't get the chance to articulate his thought process. Richard's vast jaws opened and clamped around the croc with a crunch. He fell limp, hanging from the king's great maw. With a swing of his powerful neck, Richard launched Oskar's body off the balcony, from where he fell for some time. He bounced off the sloped, golden walls once before slamming into the lake with a profound *splash*.

The king breathed heavily, rage still pulsing through his veins. "I did not care for your new assistant, Doctor."

"Please," Boggs croaked nervously. "Understand I sent the orders for you, for *Pangaea*. The people need you alive, as do I. How long have I been by your side? I couldn't bear to watch you succumb to this cruel sickness."

Richard nodded slowly for a moment, absorbing the words of his feathered advisor.

"You have never let me down, Boggs. Do what must be done."

"And what of the girl?"

Richard, still panting, glanced at his old friend.

"Kill her."

"Sire?"

"*Kill her!*"

"So be it," Boggs replied with a heavy sigh.

The king nodded gently in approval. He approached and placed his lizard-like mouth by Boggs's ear.

"Do not ever betray my trust again, Doctor," he snarled. "It will be the last thing you do."

Romer's Town

We drifted through the waves for some time. Barnum and Gigas were long out of sight, but we kept within range of the Laurasian coastline, and the snow-covered mountains still dominated the horizon. The three of us maintained a sombre silence. I couldn't believe how close we had come. We'd had the Heart. We *had* it. All we had to do was get it to Carol, but that hope was gone.

"What do we do now?" I finally asked Robyn.

"I have no idea," she replied with a shake of her head. "I guess we go home."

"So, this was all for nothing?"

She nodded, fighting back tears.

"Where are we going?" I called to Stromer.

"Nowhere," he replied with an odd calmness.

"Nowhere?"

"There isn't anywhere safe to go, pal. The king wants you dead and he'll be hunting you. I can't exactly go back to Hațeg, that's the first place those boneheads will look."

"Why did you save us?" asked Robyn. "You were going to trade us for a ransom not so long ago."

"That's before I knew you were the Architect."

"Why does that make a difference?" I asked. "I'd say kidnapping is wrong either way."

"I do what I have to—it's a tough world—but I'll make an exception for our creator."

"In the mausoleum, the guardian mentioned something about a 'Bishop.' Ever heard of him?"

"The Bishop?" Stromer replied. "Only stories. They say that in the beginning, the Heart created three—the triad. The Knight, the Rook, and the Bishop. They were the protectors of Pangaea, ruling together."

"Hmm, I wonder why Jækel felt the need to warn us about protectors," I pondered. "That sounds like a good thing."

"Well, they *were* the protectors. Eventually, they became greedy. Each wanted complete power, so they waged war on one another. No one knows who won. Some say they destroyed each other, some say they went into hiding. Some say it's all just superstition."

"What do *you* say?" Robyn asked.

"I say I'm willing to believe a lot more now that the saviour has arrived."

"'Saviour,'" Robyn replied with a roll of her eyes. "You sound like some kind of cult leader. People keep telling me I'm supposed to save Pangaea, but I'm not even sure what it needs saving from. A comet? The Bishop? What am I supposed to do about a space rock or some kind of shadow-demon?"

Stromer was silent for a few moments, seeming deep in contemplation.

"Let me show you something."

***

Stromer quietly sailed back to shore, and we soon arrived at the mouth of a great river. For some time, he swam upstream until the current became too fast. He ambled onto dry land before letting us onto the ground. From there, we walked along the river's edge.

"Tell me, kid," said Stromer, finally breaking the long silence. "What does a spinosaur like me eat?"

"You're a piscivore," Robyn replied confidently. "You eat fish."

"Right. Do you see any fish in that river?"

Robyn and I gazed into the murky water as it washed past. There was nothing visible within the cloudy, brown current. Robyn shook her head to confirm that she, too, saw no fish.

"I can't see any," she said. "I can't see much of anything, though."

"Then you'll just have to trust me; there aren't any fish."

"So, it's a bad fishing spot?" I replied.

"Trouble is, there aren't any *good* fishing spots anymore."

It hadn't been snowing here, but the ground was frozen solid, and frost covered the landscape like a carpet of glitter. We climbed a low hill, still walking upstream and, beyond the crest, a small town came into sight. It was filled with simple wooden buildings gathered around the riverbank, none more than two stories tall. Black smoke poured upwards from chimneys, and I could smell the burning wood fires from here.

After trudging across the tundra, we wandered through the town. The ground was less frozen here and was instead thick with sticky mud. Many of the buildings had long balconies which wrapped around the upper floor and provided shelter beneath. Large, wooden signs adorned several: "BANK," "SHERIFF," "SALOON." It felt like a frontier town from an old western movie, just... *colder*. I spotted a large woolly rhinoceros equipped with a saddle upon which rode a feathered theropod dinosaur. The raptor gave us a subtle nod as his hulking steed thumped past.

"Welcome to Romer's Town," announced Stromer.

I looked around at the inhabitants of Romer's Town. A *Triceratops* ambled past—typically a vast and impressive creature, yet it looked painfully thin. Its ribs and hipbones were showing through its lumpy skin. The same seemed to ring true for almost everyone here—they all looked dirty, emaciated, and generally unwell. They wandered aimlessly along the roads in an eerie silence.

Rolling hills covered in tall, green grass and moss stretched out for miles around us, but the nearest, the hill across the river, had a huge, gaping wound. It was as though half the hill was missing, and dark, grey shadows had taken its place. The town appeared to be centred around this anomaly.

As we ventured closer to the river and gazed over at the opposite bank, I could see shabby woolly mammoths dragging enormous carts out of the scarred hill and towards wooden barges tied to a pier in the river. These carts trundled along rickety rails, their wheels screeching as if in pain with every rotation. Even for creatures as great as the mammoths, the carts were cumbersome. The vast beasts strained with every step. Their fur looked matted and patchy, their feet caked in old, dry mud. Where great, curling tusks should have swept from their jaws, there merely stumps where they had been cut.

"You asked what Pangaea needed saving from," said Stromer softly. "I don't know anything about a comet or the Bishop, but this is what's *really* killing Pangaea. Everything in this world used to have a balance. We took what we needed from the land, and it replenished itself. But not anymore."

"What is this place?" Robyn asked.

"It's a mining town, kid. And that over there is the third biggest gold mine in Laurasia."

"Only the third? How many are there?"

"Dozens. And it's all shipped to the citadel."

"Why do they need so much gold?" I asked.

"No one *needs* gold, they *want* it. The king wants it. At any cost."

"It's unsightly, I'll admit, but is it really that high of a cost?"

"You see how filthy the water is? It's been poisoned from the silt and metals washed out of the mine. That's why there aren't any fish. And that's why the people here all look so hungry."

"That's awful," Robyn said with a sigh.

"If it's killing the fish, why don't the people just stop mining?" I asked.

"The crown gives them food for their service. It's a pitiful amount, just about enough to keep them alive. They won't bite the hand that feeds, even if it barely feeds them. Look around: they're kept so underfed, they'd starve before the river recovered."

"Surely they could leave this dreadful town?"

"To where? The next river to the west? Filled with boats which scoop up every last fish? They'll be taken back across the Tethys too. The king, the lords and ladies, the dukes and duchesses, they'll feast until they feel sick. But here, we go hungry. It's the same story with meat, fruits, and vegetables. Food isn't rare in Pangaea, it just all ends up on one table."

"There *was* a lot of food when we were at the citadel," Robyn admitted. "More than we could ever eat."

"And every scrap of that food would cost a bounty of gold here."

"Is that why you kidnapped us?" I asked. "To buy food?"

"A guy has to eat. You know, in the old days, Pangaea didn't even have currency, and now you need to hand over gold for everything."

"That just sounds like money," Robyn replied. "We have money back home. Is it really so bad?"

"It is when it's all in the one place—there isn't much gold outside the city walls. I'm sorry for what I put you through, kid, but these are desperate times. No one wants to be a pirate. No one *likes* being a pirate."

"Cuvier seemed to kind of like being a pirate," I remarked.

"Cuvier *does* like being a pirate," Stromer conceded with a wry smile. "But Cuvier is crazy."

"You don't seem so unhinged," I continued. "Why keep him around?"

"Cuvier's troubled, I'll give you that, but you would be too, pal. When the king outlawed mammals in Gondwana, General Etheldred rounded up all she could find."

"Etheldred," said Robyn with a nod. "We met her, in the woods. The white *Dilophosaurus*."

"Then be glad you're still breathing, kid."

"How did Cuvier get out?" I asked.

"Mother Mary and I sprang the mammals from the citadel, but... let's just say it went bad. Only Cuvier survived the night. We took him in."

"You and Mary?" Robyn asked.

Stromer nodded.

"She didn't seem too fond of mammals to me," I added.

Stromer nodded again with a sad glint of reminiscence in his eyes.

"Over time, she bought into the propaganda. One day, she sold him out. The general tortured him for months. She did things to that sloth no sane creature would do to their worst enemy. Etheldred the *Bloodthirsty*—they got that right."

"Why is she like that?"

"The rumour is she never imprinted at birth. That can do terrible things to the mind of a dinosaur."

"So, Pangaea needs to be saved from the general?" asked Robyn.

"Etheldred's a piece of work, all right, but she's just a weapon. Who wields the weapon?"

"The king," concluded Robyn.

"You got it."

"I'm not sure I know how to do anything about the king," she replied.

"That makes both of us, kid."

"Why are you so afraid of the king having the Heart?" I asked. "I thought Luca gave life. How could that be dangerous?"

"Jækel said his power would fail if he wasn't returned before tonight," said Robyn. "What happens then?"

"Everything you see here will die," Stromer replied.

"Wouldn't the king suffer too?" asked Robyn. "If Pangaea died? He wouldn't get all his gold or food."

"If he has the Heart, he can grow all the food he needs right in his courtyard. The city will be fine, but everywhere else…"

The trumpeting call of a mammoth rang out across the river. I looked over to see that one had collapsed, presumably from exhaustion. A gang of feathered raptors charged out of the mine, armed with long whips, and began to thrash the stricken creature. The fellow mammoths trumpeted in protest, but the whipping continued. The fallen beast tried to rise, only to collapse under its weight once more.

"We should help them," I said.

"What?" asked Robyn. "How?"

"You've got heart, I'll give you that," Stromer interjected. "But you two should be keeping a low profile."

"No," Robyn protested. "Ed's right. We can't just stand by and watch. Luca made me prove I had courage. Maybe this is why."

From the muddy riverbank, I looked around for a way to cross. I noticed a stone bridge upstream, but it was a considerable distance away. A long, floating pontoon then caught my eye. It was a rudimentary structure made from wooden logs and large, wooden barrels which extended out into the river. I trotted over and took a tentative step onto the pontoon. It wobbled under my weight, but ultimately stabilised.

"This seems okay," I announced.

"I don't think it looks very safe, Ed," Robyn protested. "Look, there's a bridge."

"Robyn, come on. We don't have time."

Robyn took a deep breath, nodded, and stepped out onto the pontoon. While Stromer was forced to stay on the bank due to his immense weight, Robyn and I walked out into the river.

As I reached the middle of the pontoon bridge, the water swelled beneath and began to froth. I turned to see Robyn following behind as an immense mass burst through the surface. It was tall, covered in scales… and *teeth*. A similar tower of meat and bone rose on the other side of the pontoon—a colossal set of crocodile-like jaws had opened wide around Robyn.

They snapped shut with ferocious speed and power, shattering the pontoon into splinters. Robyn disappeared within the creature's maw as it disappeared beneath the river once more.

"*Robyn!*" I screamed.

The Belly of the Beast

On a small square of the pontoon which had miraculously remained intact, I now floated adrift. I dove into the water and paddled downwards in search of my best friend. I wouldn't let her go, not like that. I swam and swam, but I could see nothing in the murky depths—until a dark shadow emerged before me. The water rushed towards me as the monstrous reptile lunged. At the last second, just as it was too late, those great jaws appeared once more—enveloping me in its fleshy, muscular throat.

To my surprise, after plunging through that monstrous mouth, my feet found solid ground. At least, fairly solid—it was somewhat mushy. I looked down to see dark, sodden grass and mud squishing between my toes.

I was soaking wet, but I soon realised the pouring rain may have explained that. The swelling current and vast river monster had disappeared and, after a brief look around, I grasped that we were in Robyn's back garden. Somehow, we were in Lyme Regis once more.

Robyn stood beside me, dripping wet also. Behind us was a hole in the garden wall, through which was what appeared to be the inside of a mouth of sharp, conical teeth.

"*How?*" I gasped.

"I think…" Robyn paused for a few long, shaky breaths. "I think I made a doorway back home inside its throat."

"Jeez," I replied, pausing to pant for a second. "Good thinking."

"I didn't mean to. It was just instinct, I guess."

"Well, that instinct saved both our cloacas. Was that a *Sarcosuchus*?"

"*Deinosuchus*, I think. Though I can't say I had a great view from inside its mouth."

"A massive bloody crocodile either way. Maybe imagine up a safer fantasy world next time?

"*Robyn!*"

Michael Talbot rushed through the downpour towards Robyn, his face twisted in panic, before scooping her into his arms and squeezing tightly.

"Robyn, where have you *been?*" he sobbed. "Don't you *ever* run off like that again, don't you *ever*…"

"I… I'm sorry, Dad. I didn't think I had…"

"Oh, my pumpkin, I thought I'd *lost* you," he continued, tears of relief streaming down his face and merging with the pounding rain.

After quickly ushering her inside, Michael draped a warm blanket over Robyn and turned the thermostat higher than I had ever seen. Normally, he was fairly militant about saving energy, but tonight he made an exception. To be fair, it was bitterly cold, and we were soaked to the bone.

After having a much-needed shower and a change of clothes, Robyn returned to the living room to find a steaming mug of hot chocolate waiting for her. Michael had topped it with a mound of whipped cream and marshmallows just as he always did—though there was definitely some extra topping tonight.

"Here you go," he whispered, handing her the mug.

"Thanks," Robyn replied with a smile.

"So, where have you been?"

"I'm so sorry, Dad. I had to..." Robyn trailed off, quickly realizing the truth would sound insane.

"I just needed some space," she lied. "You know, with Mum—"

"It's been three *days*."

Robyn's face dropped. I shared her surprise. I'm not sure why—we had seen the nights come and go—but the notion that we had been absent from the real world for that time had never crossed my mind. It felt oddly dreamlike while in Pangaea, as though time didn't pass the same. Clearly, it did.

"I stayed with Abigail for a couple nights."

"Abigail?"

"My friend, from school."

There was no such person as Abigail, and Michael was visibly surprised at the revelation of this friend. However, he was blinded by his hopeful optimism and believed, because he wanted to believe, that Robyn had a friend called Abigail. It felt cruel to deceive him so, but I saw little choice for Robyn.

"You should have let me know where you were. Why didn't you take your phone? It's in your room—not even charged. That's why we bought it for you."

That wasn't entirely true. Carol had insisted Robyn have a phone in the hope she would use it to communicate with her peers online and make friends. Long gone were the days when her mother would worry about social media; she worried far more about social isolation. But, like most things people her age were obsessed with, Robyn had no interest in such things.

"I know, I'm sorry. I should have called. I... my head has just been all over the place."

Michael offered a gentle smile, but his eyes betrayed a sadness as he placed a hand on her shoulder.

"Me too, pumpkin, me too. But we'll get through this, we've got each other."

Robyn hugged her father tightly in response and, before long, she began to weep.

"I'm scared," she sobbed. "I don't want to lose her."

Michael pulled back slightly from their embrace and gazed into her eyes.

"Robyn, listen…"

I don't know what Michael discussed with Robyn after that, and I suspect she didn't either. It was as though she had fully zoned out—enough so that even I didn't take much notice of him. I could understand why she would be distracted. With the mention of Carol, it seemed we had been refocused—reminded of the real world and the pressing matter at hand. Yes, what we saw in Romer's Town was tragic, and we *would* help them, but Carol's situation was time-sensitive. We *had* to prioritise.

***

"So, what do we do now?" I asked as I lay on Robyn's bed later that evening.

"I don't know," she replied while pacing back and forth across her bedroom floor. "We can't go off for that long again, I can't do that to Dad."

"True, but Luca is still out there somewhere. He could still help your mum."

"I know, I know. But *how*?"

The bedroom door swung open and, as she had done on so many occasions, Carol Talbot strode confidently into Robyn's room.

"*Mum!*" Robyn yelled before running over and hugging her mother tightly.

I was surprised to see that Carol looked rather well. Her previously pale, sickly skin had been restored to its usual shade of peachy-pink. She looked a little thinner than before, but it was hardly dramatic. She was dressed in a red, floral, summer dress and a smart, navy-blue head scarf which was finished with a delightful, off-centre bow.

"I didn't know you were coming home," Robyn squealed. "You look *so* much better—I was so *worried*."

"Well, I feel much better," Carol replied with a smile. "I'm just glad to be back home with my little sweet pea." She squished Robyn's cheek between her thumb and forefinger before planting a kiss on her forehead.

"*Are* you better?" Robyn asked. "Like, *really* better? Is the cancer gone?"

Carol offered a sad sort of smile in return.

"Let's take things one step at a time."

"So… no."

"I'm afraid not, but… oh, my *God!*"

It took me a moment to realise what Carol was so surprised by. Something over Robyn's shoulder had caught her attention, something behind me. I twisted my head around to see, but there was nothing there.

"Robyn," she whispered.

"Mum?"

Carol took a step back towards the door, clearly frightened. I realised she hadn't seen anything *behind* me at all.

"I see him."

"What?"

"That *thing*."

Robyn looked at me and her eyes widened in realisation. I had no idea what had changed while she was in the hospital but, like she had done for a brief moment mid-seizure, Carol stared directly at me.

"Jesus, it's *real*," she gasped with a shake in her voice. "Robyn, get out of here."

"But Mum—"

"Go!"

Carol took off her shoe and launched it across the room at me before hustling Robyn out of the bedroom and into the landing. I scuttled off the bed and chased after them, the shoe bouncing off my head.

"Wait, Robyn," I called.

"Mum, please," Robyn pleaded. "Look at him again. He's not dangerous, he's not frightening. He's my friend. My *best* friend."

Reluctantly, Carol turned once more and looked at me as I peered out of the bedroom doorway.

"I don't mean any harm, Carol," I said, which was fairly unimaginative on my part, but it seemed to be what she needed to hear.

"It can talk? How does it know my name?" Carol whispered to Robyn.

I ducked back into the bedroom as Carol's other shoe hurtled towards my face.

***

It took some time for Robyn to calm Carol down. I understood, to be honest. As far as she was concerned, a giant lizard had appeared in her daughter's bedroom, chased her into the landing, and begun to speak. I think most people would have been shocked. I waited in the bedroom, resuming my comfortable position on the bed, while Robyn spoke to her mother downstairs.

It must have been an hour or so later when Robyn returned. Carol crept cautiously through the door behind her, poking her head through. She flinched slightly upon laying eyes on me once more—clearly, she had hoped I might have disappeared or been a hallucination. Regardless, she entered, sitting on Robyn's desk chair, making sure to keep her distance from me.

"So," she began with a shake in her voice. "You're… Ed?"

I nodded.

"And you are a…"

"*Dimetrodon*," I confirmed.

"Which is *not* a dinosaur."

"Definitely not."

"But an imaginary not-dinosaur."

"Yes, well, I suppose."

"But you're also, somehow, *real*?"

"I don't really get it either."

"And you're Robyn's friend?"

"Her *best* friend," I replied with a smile.

"You wouldn't harm her, would you?"

"I'd never dream of it, Carol."

"See?" Robyn chimed. "He's a perfect gentleman. And he's not new, he's been here all along, for years. He's only ever looked out for me."

"How can I see him if he's imaginary?" Carol asked.

"I don't know," Robyn replied honestly. "But maybe it's not that simple. There's more to tell."

She then proceeded to tell her mother everything—about Hannah, Pangaea, and Luca. Despite how obviously ridiculous the story was, Carol seemed open to it. Perhaps my presence was enough for her to now consider anything to be possible.

"So, how do we get him back?" Carol asked.

"What do you mean?" Robyn replied.

"Luca. We have to get him back, right? If I'm not hallucinating—which, given all the drugs I've had to take, is a real possibility—then we have to get him back."

"We?" I asked.

"This Luca chap... If he can cure me, then it'll buy me years with my baby girl. Robyn, I don't know if this is all true or if I've gone mad, but I don't want to see the other side just yet. Even if there's a heaven, even if it's the most wonderful paradise I can imagine, it would be missing the thing that matters to me most—*you*. Now, how do we get him back?"

"I... I guess we need to get back to Pangaea f-for a start," Robyn stammered.

"Well, first you'd better come up with a good story for your father. The poor man was worried sick last time."

"Good idea."

Robyn skipped out of the room and made it halfway down the stairs before bumping into Michael.

"Dad, would you mind if I went to Abigail's for a few more nights?"

"You're just back."

"I know, but I—"

"It's okay," he replied with a gentle nod. "I understand."

"Great, thanks, Dad. You're the best!"

She spun around and burst back into the room, slamming the door behind her.

"Okay, how do we get there?" asked Carol.

"I don't know," admitted Robyn. "It just kind of happens."

"No," I said. "I think you can make it happen. It's *your* world. They call you the Architect, don't they? You built it in your mind. Just concentrate."

Robyn took a deep breath and nodded. She closed her eyes and stood quietly for some time. Carol and I remained deathly silent in anticipation but, after a few long minutes, nothing had happened. Robyn strained, furrowing her brow in frustration.

"It's not working." She sighed in exasperation.

Before any more thought could be given to the matter, the ceiling began to crack above our heads. Plaster dust showered us as the cracks spread into a jagged web. The disintegration intensified and accelerated. The floor shook and the windows rattled before the ceiling finally gave way entirely. Lumps of wood, concrete, and plaster came crashing down on top of us.

I attempted to make a break for the door, only for a huge, wooden beam to come bearing down onto my back. I was crushed into the floor, the weight upon me unbearable. I tried to call out for Robyn, but so heavy was the growing mound of rubble that I couldn't even breathe, never mind speak. In no more than a few seconds, I was completely buried. I took some final, shallow gasps before the avalanche concluded.

The Wrong Hands

The giant doors of the golden citadel's throne room burst open, revealing the great tyrants Barnum and Gigas. The latter dragged a long, heavy, steel chain along the ground behind him. King Richard had anxiously awaited their return as they had taken much longer than expected. His apprehension wasn't entirely abated by their return—blood trickled from Gigas's eye, which betrayed that not everything had gone to plan.

"Sir Barnum, Lord Gigas," the king boomed. "Welcome home. I trust you were successful?"

"Yes, sire," replied Barnum, who strode up the stairs to the throne and placed a small glass slide upon the throne's golden armrest.

"What's this?"

"The Heart of Pangaea, Your Majesty."

"How curious…" replied the king as he examined the slide. "And the other task?"

Barnum glanced at Gigas and then fixed his gaze to the floor. "I'm afraid the Architect escaped."

"What!?"

Richard exploded into a fit of rage. He marched away from his throne and smashed his muscular tail into the marble wall, which cracked and crumbled.

"Idiots!" he roared. "How can two tyrants fail to slay a little girl?"

"We *will* find her," Gigas insisted.

"*Will* you now? You have delusions of adequacy, Gigas. I should mount both of your heads upon my wall."

"Please, accept my humblest apologies, Your Grace," grovelled Barnum. "The girl had assistance."

"Assistance? From *whom*?"

"The pirate captain, Stromer," replied Gigas.

"That bandit," Richard seethed. "He's always fancied himself a revolutionary. I suppose he is to blame for the condition of your eye?"

"Yes, sire."

"Pathetic," Richard lamented, now pacing back and forth. "I want everyone looking for her. The raptors, the pterosaurs, *everyone*."

"Perhaps I can help narrow the search," offered Gigas.

"And how might you do that?"

Gigas yanked on the chain he had dragged in until a diminutive mammal skulked through the door. Benjamin the Tasmanian tiger gazed up at the king. His eyes were wide with fear.

"Who is this mammal?" demanded the king.

"The girl's travel companion," Gigas explained.

"I see. Mammal, you know where the Architect is now?"

"I don't, mate," Benjamin replied, shaking his head. "Though I don't reckon I'd tell you if I did."

Richard scrunched his lip and licked his front teeth as he considered his options.

"Take him to the fortress," he ordered at last. "Send the general—she'll make him talk."

"Etheldred?" asked Barnum.

"Did I mumble?" Richard snapped.

"My apologies, Your Highness. I merely find her methods… distasteful."

"I find *failure* distasteful, Barnum. Perhaps if you were more like the general, there would be no need for her intervention."

Barnum nodded, his eyes pinned to the floor once more in shame.

"And what of the Heart?" asked Gigas.

"I'll have that taken to the fortress later. Doctor Boggs will study it before taking it to the vault."

"Study it?" asked Barnum.

"I don't think Boggs is that kind of doctor, sire," said Gigas.

"What would you know of it? Now, both of you get out of my sight."

The tyrannosaurs skulked out of the citadel, Benjamin being dragged unceremoniously behind. Once the doors shut, Richard turned his attention to the little plate of glass sitting upon his throne. He approached slowly and stared into the blue-green smudge pressed between the tiny slides.

"So small," he muttered to himself.

With some hesitation, he raised his front paw and placed it atop the Heart. A blinding blue light burst out from the glass and the king's veins began to glow. He felt a rush of energy, of invigoration.

His illness was healed—of that he was sure, he could feel it. But not only was he no longer sick, he felt stronger than he had ever been. In an instant, he felt half his age. A sharp-toothed grin spread across his face, and he began to cackle.

"Magnificent." He gazed down at the Heart. "I wonder… what else can you do?"

The Induan Sand Sea

I tried to inhale but didn't have the strength to expand my lungs under the crushing weight. But then came the sound of Robyn crying for help. I couldn't just lie there. I don't know how, but I found a sudden and remarkable burst of strength and, to my surprise, the rubble shifted with relative ease. The great slabs of plaster and wood disintegrated into fine, coarse dust. I heaved my head upwards and burst through into clear air. My lungs filled, bringing relief like none other.

Once I had caught my breath, I looked up to see an immaculate, sapphire sky dominated by a blazing sun. Around me was mile upon mile of bleached, hazy dunes — a scorching desert as far as the horizon.

Robyn's hand exploded through the sand beside me. I scrambled out of the ground and gripped my paw around her wrist. With all my strength, I heaved. Robyn's face soon pierced through the surface as she, too, took a grateful gasp of the hot, dry air. My eyes then darted around the desert — where was Carol?

"*Mum?*" Robyn called.

A faint muffle sounded from directly beneath our feet. Together, we dug through the sand until we unearthed Carol's head.

"What was *that*?" she cried.

"Sorry," Robyn replied. "That was a little more violent than before."

"A little?" I baulked.

"I'm still trying to get the hang of this. I guess I forced it too hard."

After extracting Carol from the sand, we took a moment to settle our nerves after fearing death from what seemed to be a collapsing building. I assumed the house hadn't actually collapsed, but I wasn't exactly certain of that.

"So, this is Pangaea?" asked Carol, still brushing sand from herself.

"I guess so," Robyn replied. "I don't recognise this place, though."

"I suppose this is a different part of Pangaea," I concluded. "I did get the impression it's a pretty big place."

"What now?" Robyn asked. "I don't see anything but sand."

"I suppose we find someone to ask for directions to the citadel?"

Robyn raised an eyebrow. I looked around at the blatantly barren environment and immediately realised how silly a suggestion that had been. The forests might have been teeming with life, but there was nothing here whatsoever.

"Shall we at least get some shade by that cactus?" Carol suggested.

I turned and was surprised to see an enormous cactus on the next dune. How had I not seen that before? Carol was right, though—we needed the shade. It was unbearably hot—even with my sail parallel to the sun's rays, I was struggling to stay cool.

When we arrived at the lone desert plant, I found it towered over even Carol's head. Oddly, it appeared that someone had placed a huge sombrero hat atop the cactus, the large spines protruding through the rim. It had vibrant red and yellow, zig-zagging stripes all around the rim. It was a magnificent piece of headgear.

We gathered in its shadow and basked in the slightly cooler air. The short walk in the heat of the desert had been exhausting, and we stood panting for several minutes.

"Oh, *hola*," announced a mysterious voice from somewhere ahead.

Collectively, we flinched in fright. We peered around the cactus to see where it had originated, but saw nothing but dunes.

"Who..." Robyn began.

We stood back in confusion. Then, to my surprise, a large pair of black, beady eyes opened on the cactus.

"*Hola, amigos,*" the cactus continued.

All three of us shrieked in surprise at the talking plant.

"Oh, I am sorry," it continued in a Spanish accent. "I did not mean to startle you. I do not get many visitors."

"Robyn, the cactus is apologising," I said without breaking eye contact with it.

"It is," she confirmed.

"Cactuses don't usually do that."

"Cacti," Robyn corrected.

"Actually, either is fine," confirmed Carol. "And, no, they don't."

"They don't usually talk at all."

"My name is Felipe," the cactus announced.

"Uh, hi, Felipe," replied Robyn. "I'm Robyn. I like your hat."

"Oh, thank you, *señorita*. So nice to meet you."

"Robyn, your subconscious is an odd place," I observed.

"Talking dinosaurs you can handle, but this is too much?" mused Carol.

"Fair point."

"Uh, I don't suppose you know where we are?" Robyn asked Felipe.

"*Sí, señorita.* This is the Induan Sand Sea. It is very hot here."

"You don't say," I said.

"Do you know the way to the citadel?" Robyn asked.

"To the capital? To get there you walk that way..."

Felipe indicated to his left with a shake of his arm-like stalk.

"Oh, thank you," she chirped.

"... for about nine days," he finished.

"Nine *days*?" I cringed at the thought.

"*Sí*, it is very far."

"We can't leave your father for nine whole days," said Carol. "He'll be worried sick."

"Why must you go to the citadel?" asked Felipe.

"Something was stolen from us," replied Robyn. "We're going to get it back."

"Stolen by the king?"

Robyn nodded. "How did you—"

"It happens a lot. If it is valuable, he will not keep it in the citadel."

The three of us looked at each other in surprise.

"Where would he keep it?" I asked.

"The fortress."

"Fortress?"

"Where is the fortress?" asked Carol.

"It could be anywhere, *amigo*," he replied with a shrug.

"I don't understand," Robyn replied.

"It moves. It is a *very* secret place. No one ever knows where it is or what is inside."

"So, how do we find it?" asked Carol.

"You must speak… with the *outcast*."

"The outcast?"

"*Sí*, he lives in *el*… swampo."

"El swampo?" replied Carol with an eyebrow raised. "Robyn, if you must imagine up Spanish-speaking cactuses, please do at least learn some more Spanish. This poor creature barely knows his native tongue. No offence, Felipe, you seem very sweet, dear."

"*Merci*," he replied.

"That's Fr— never mind. Where is the swamp?"

"You could follow the migration."

"Migration?" I asked.

Felipe didn't have to answer. I felt the sand tremble beneath my feet. I turned around to see a vast swarm of robust creatures appearing over a row of dunes. Great clouds of dust were churned up by the roaming herd. As they approached, it became more apparent what they were. Stocky creatures, around the same height as Robyn, with four chunky legs and short, stumpy tails. Their heads were short and squat with flat faces and two blunt tusks protruding down below their jaws. They had smooth, sand-coloured skin with a light, fuzzy coating of sparse fur.

"What are they?" Carol asked.

"*Lystrosaurus*," replied Robyn with a gasp of awe.

"A list of what?"

"*Lystrosaurus*," I clarified. "The toughest animal of all time."

"How so?"

"They survived the Great Dying," Robyn explained.

"The asteroid?"

"No, no, long before that. The Permian extinction. It killed off almost all life on Earth, especially big animals. But not these guys."

With some frantic hand waving, Robyn and Carol flagged down the herd of therapsids which soon flocked in our direction. They closed the distance quickly and slowed as they approached. I was taken aback by how brightly coloured they appeared, and I soon recognised that they were all draped in red, green, and orange beads, and blankets of intricate geometric patterns. Most carried large packs upon their backs which were equally ornate. One particularly large specimen at the front approached—this one was set apart from the others not only by her size, but by her red fabric headdress with a single, huge, white feather protruding from the top.

"Greetings, travellers," announced the lystrosaur, in a husky but eloquent voice. "I am Cleo, chieftess of the Curvatus tribe. How may we offer assistance?"

"Hello, Cleo," replied Carol. "I suppose we need to get to the swamp."

"The Carnian Swamps? You are in luck, my lady, our migration passes the swamps. Please, join us, we have food and water."

"Thank you," replied Carol. "That's very kind of you."

"It is the way of the nomad, my friend. The desert is unforgiving, and so we must all look after one another. However, we cannot stall for long. Let us leave."

Before heading off, we turned and waved to Felipe.

"Thank you, Felipe," Robyn called.

"Good luck, *señorita*."

***

The trek through the desert was long and hot, and keeping up with the industrious lystrosaurs was no simple task. None of them were especially talkative, but their sense of direction was invaluable. Every way looked the same to me, but they seemed to know exactly where they were going.

"I don't know how much more of this heat I can take," I groaned.

"At least the Pangaean sun doesn't seem to affect my skin," Robyn replied. "Look at me, white as a sheet. I'd usually look like a cooked lobster by now."

"Yes, you have your father to blame for that complexion of yours," said Carol. "You ought to bring him here, let him enjoy some sunshine without cooking for once."

"I'll have to figure out how I managed to bring you here first."

"That's true. I'm sure we can figure it out before the end of the summer."

I could see Robyn purse her lips and flinch at the mention of summer's end. She knew that meant beginning high school. Carol, however, seemed oblivious to this.

"And then high school time. That's exciting, right?"

"Sure."

"I loved my time there. You should join the drama club; they have such a wonderful drama department."

"I don't think drama is for me."

"No?"

"Standing in front of all those people and speaking? I'd rather hang from my eyelashes."

"Fair enough. Well, what *would* you like to do?"

"Some kind of science club, maybe. Do you think they have athletics?"

"Probably. You might meet some friends there."

"I doubt it."

"Why would you say that?"

"I don't know, I'm just not good with people. Besides, I have Ed."

"As sweet as Ed is, some real friends would do you good, Robyn. No offence, Ed."

"None taken," I lied.

"I'll try, Mum," Robyn replied, which I suspected was also a lie.

After many hours, deep green foliage became visible in the distance. As we approached, the treeline grew large until it loomed over us. The shade was welcome, but the dense vegetation made the swamp itself dark and foreboding, not to mention hot and humid.

"My lady, the Carnian Swamps," announced Cleo.

"Thank you, Chieftess," replied Robyn.

"Might I ask why you wish to venture into the swamp? It's a place most choose to avoid."

"We were told to look for an outcast."

"You *seek* the outcast?" she replied, with an eyebrow raised.

"Yes, why? What do you know about him?"

"Only stories, but he's the reason most avoid the swamp. Dare I ask *why* you seek him?"

"We need to find the king's fortress. He has stolen the Heart of Pangaea, and we're going to take it back."

"My *lady!*" Cleo hissed. "You are fortunate in the company you keep. We are a nomadic people and hold no allegiance to the king, but he has eyes *everywhere*—you *must* be more careful how you speak. I shouldn't have asked."

"Oh, I'm sorry. I'll be more careful."

"But the Heart, you say. He stole it from you?"

Robyn nodded.

"How did such a strange octopus come to have the Heart of Pangaea?"

"She's a human, man," I interjected.

"Those brown things on your head, they are not tentacles?"

"My hair doesn't really look like octopus tentacles, does it?" she moaned, clutching at her head in embarrassment.

"Arms," I clarified. "Octopuses don't have tentacles. Common misconception."

Robyn scowled at both my pedantry and lack of reassurance that her hair did not, in fact, look like octopus arms.

"A young *human* in possession of the Heart—well, that makes much more sense now. You're sure you can trust he who resides in this swamp?"

"That depends," I interjected. "Can we trust the cactus?"

"Cactus?"

"You know, Felipe," replied Robyn. "The cactus who was with us when we met you."

Cleo narrowed her eyes in confusion. "I saw no cactus," she said.

"He was a pretty huge cactus," I argued. "There's no way you didn't see the massive talking cactus. It wore a giant hat and everything."

"A quite lovely hat," Robyn added.

"It sounds to me like you were visited by the desert spirit," Cleo concluded with a smile. "He is said to reveal himself to those in need in any number of physical forms. If that's the case, and this is where his guidance has led you, then I have faith in your quest. Go forth, my lady. You have the support of the Curvatus, should you ever require it."

Robyn nodded in approval.

"Thank you, Cleo. I hope we see each other again."

"It would be an honour," she replied with a smile.

With that, the chieftess bellowed to her clan and the huge herd began to trundle through the desert once more.

The Outcast

The swamp somehow felt even hotter than the desert. The temperature itself was similar, despite the sunlight being mostly blocked out by the thick canopy above, but the air was thick and heavy with humidity. Flies buzzed around by the thousand as if in a single dense cloud.

Underfoot, the ground could barely be described as ground at all. Rather, we were now wading through shallow water which was sufficiently covered in floating vegetation as to make whatever lay below an unnerving mystery. Occasionally, something would brush past my feet and cause me to flinch. It took some effort to stay cool and not thrash around, but I figured causing such a commotion was likely to attract the wrong kind of attention.

After some time wading through the marshy undergrowth, a large, wooden cabin came into view. It was old and in a serious state of disrepair. The boards of timber which made up the walls were cracked and covered in sporadic patches of green moss.

"Do you think he's in there?" asked Carol.

"I don't know," Robyn replied.

"It looks deserted to me," I added.

We took several steps forwards before something else began to move beneath my feet. I flinched again at the thought of strange beasts swimming unseen around my legs, but I soon realised this was different. The movement wasn't *around* my feet, but *beneath* them. The ground itself was shifting. Then, rising out of the murky water, a huge net, covered in black sludge and mushy vegetation, wrapped around us. As the net tightened, all three of us were crushed together and lifted off the ground. The thick, coarse rope scratched and irritated my skin as it squeezed.

"Who goes there?" boomed a coarse and elderly voice from within the cabin. "*Spies*, I presume?"

"What? We're not spies," I objected.

"That's *just* what a spy would say," he roared back. "I thought Richard would've given up by now."

"*King* Richard? We don't work for the king," I insisted.

"He's telling the truth," Carol added. "We need your help to find the king. He's stolen something from us."

After a moment of silence, a great beast paced slowly out of the wooden hut and through several narrow sunbeams. He was huge, easily the size of an elephant, but he looked more akin to a giant rhinoceros with green, lumpy, reptilian skin. His legs were thick and sturdy and his head similar to that of a monitor lizard, but with a small horn upon the end of his nose. I recognised it as an *Iguanodon*, or rather, an old Victorian depiction of an *Iguanodon*. It reminded me somewhat of the king himself, who appeared as an outdated *Megalosaurus*. This creature appeared to be similarly old.

"Stolen?" he replied solemnly. "What has he stolen?"

"The Heart," replied Robyn. "The Heart of Pangaea."

The great reptile growled and stepped forwards into the shallow water to examine his three captives.

"Who are you?"

"My name is Robyn. This is Ed, and my mum, Carol. We're just looking for some help."

"And how did you come to be in possession of the Heart?" he snarled. "Unless…"

He raised a huge paw towards Robyn's face, before curling a claw around the underside of her jaw.

"It *can't* be," he continued. "Human?"

"Oh, thank *God* for that. Yes, I'm *human*."

"The Architect," he whispered.

Robyn nodded hesitantly. The *Iguanodon* turned away and waded towards an old mangrove tree to which the net was secured by a single rope. He slashed the rope with his claw, causing the net to drop and for us to splash into the swamp.

"Come inside," he instructed as we picked ourselves out of the muck.

***

Inside the cabin, the air was warm and dusty. The sun was beginning to set, and the *Iguanodon* responded by lighting a fire. While my reptilian skin dried fairly quickly, my human accomplices seemed relieved to stand beside the fire to dry their clothes. Above the fire was a large cauldron, the contents of which simmered gently and gave off an oddly fishy smell.

As the flames danced and crackled in the crooked, stone fireplace, the three of us sat in silence, waiting for the giant to address us. He was an intimidating beast, and none of us dared break the silence.

"You should eat," he said finally. "Though I'm afraid I don't have any cuisine fit for guests. This will have to do."

Using his great clawed paw, he plunged a ladle into the cauldron and decanted the liquid contents into three bowls.

"Please, eat," he insisted, after lifting the bowls onto a large, wooden table in the centre of the cabin.

"What is it?" Carol asked, recoiling slightly from the fishy odour.

"Primordial soup," the vast beast replied.

"Uh, I'm not hungry," Robyn said.

"You're sure?" he insisted. "It's full of amino acids. You must recoup your strength."

"We're sure," said Carol with a nod.

"Suit yourselves," I said. "That means more for me."

I reared up to the tall table and began to slurp the fishy soup directly from the bowl.

"I never thought I'd see the day," the *Iguanodon* said after a long pause. "The Architect has come to us. Tell me, do you intend to fulfil your destiny? To take the throne?"

"Throne?" asked Carol.

"We might have left that part out," I admitted. "Apparently, Robyn's destined to be queen."

Carol stared at her daughter with raised eyebrows. "That's a fairly major detail to omit."

"It's not like I actually want a throne anyway," Robyn replied. "That's not going to happen."

"How disappointing," the great reptile replied. "Pangaea needs you."

"So we keep hearing," I said. "But we have more immediate concerns."

"Ah, yes, the Heart."

"It's in the fortress," added Robyn. "We were told by a cactus that you'd know where to find it."

"A cactus?"

"Apparently it was a spirit," I clarified.

The reptile nodded slowly, acknowledging that he understood.

"The desert spirit is wise. I can indeed lead you to the fortress, but you'll not get inside so easily. It's a vast castle, mounted upon the back of the largest sauropod in the land. It's defended by a legion of raptors and a squadron of pterosaurs. No one has ever breached its walls."

"How do you know so much about it?" I asked. "Isn't it secret?"

"I have my sources," he replied. "Forgive me, I have not yet introduced myself. My name is Gideon, formerly *King Gideon of Pangaea*."

"You were the *king*?" Robyn replied with a gasp. "What happened?"

"*Richard* happened," Gideon snarled. "You're not the only one he has stolen from."

"He took your crown?" I asked.

"He took more than that."

"How?" asked Carol.

"He was clever," Gideon began. "Richard convinced the people my ways were keeping them down, stopping them from reaching their potential."

"Were they?" asked Robyn.

"Of course not. I simply understood the delicate balance of our world. But Richard? He wanted to strip the land for himself. He said as he grew richer, the people would too. He promised glittering cities and great feasts. With his deception, he raised an army. He didn't just steal my throne; he stole my *people* from me."

"Did he do what he promised?" I asked. "Did he make the people rich?"

"He made himself rich, he made his friends rich, but the people? He cut down their forests, dug up their lands, poisoned their rivers, and then blamed the inevitable famine on the mammals."

"Why don't you take it back?"

"I'm an old dinosaur now. Most don't even remember my time as king, never mind recognise my claim."

"So, you need Robyn," I concluded. "You can't retake the throne yourself—you need Robyn to ascend and remove Richard. But why would they accept Robyn any more than they would you?"

"She is the *Architect*—the mother of all. She transcends all royalty. Robyn, you can restore the natural order with the blessing of all of Pangaea, because we are each your children."

"I'm *far* too young to be a grandmother to a million dinosaurs," said Carol with a frown.

"Why couldn't I reinstate *you* to the throne?" asked Robyn. "You'd restore Pangaea. If I blessed the appointment, would the people not accept it? It sounds to me like you were a good king."

"Perhaps," conceded Gideon. "I confess I have long dreamt of restoring my kingdom. But for now, we must discuss the return of the Heart. Without it, there will be little left of Pangaea for either of us."

"How do we do it?" I asked.

"First, we will require a *team*."

An Abomination

A hulking frame of shimmering blue and green feathers strode through a vast, disorganised mass of gold and other treasures. Jewels, precious metals, and priceless artefacts were all around, most cast carelessly onto the floor. There was so much wealth here that each piece had lost any sense of value—except for one.

Doctor Boggs approached a white marble pedestal adorned with golden leaves which glinted in the bright light of a hundred flaming torches. Upon the pedestal sat a small piece of glass. Boggs thought it looked far less impressive than anything else in the vault, but he also knew it was the most precious by far: the Heart of Pangaea.

While the Heart itself was kept safe in the vault, the doctor had arranged for its power to be redirected elsewhere. A thick web of copper cables sprawled out from the pedestal, suspended in the air and disappearing through the ceiling. The glass slide glowed a dim shade of blue, but that light was flickering—which explained some problems Boggs had been facing in the laboratory above.

The doctor sighed as he gazed at the failing magic. He had hoped that the cabling had come loose or even melted, but it seemed it was the Heart itself which faltered.

Once upstairs in the laboratory, he was greeted by the unsightly, pale *Dilophosaurus* known as General Etheldred. He was not a fan. This creature had been plucked from the forest as little more than a common bandit. She was dirty and ill-mannered—even now she drooled on his floor. And yet, somehow, he found himself being outranked by this vile creature.

"Have you fixed it?" she barked.

She referred to the shining, stainless-steel box in the centre of the room—it looked somewhat like a phone box without any windows. The cables from the vault below rose from the floor and into the machine, but it hadn't been functioning as intended.

"Fixed it?" he replied. "I don't even understand how it worked to begin with. It's just a metal box with some cables welded on."

"You designed it, doctor. The science is your area."

"The design was a fluke. I simply thought I'd see what would happen if I plugged it in. I'm not that kind of doctor."

"I don't care, Boggs. Fix it."

"I'm not even sure it's broken," Boggs argued. "I've checked the cables three times—the problem is the Heart itself."

"So, fix the Heart."

"General, this is a magical being we're talking about. It can't just be glued back together."

Etheldred snarled and strode towards him.

"Believe me when I say you don't want to discover the consequences of failing me, Doctor."

Boggs sighed. If she couldn't see the obvious solution for herself, he would have to spell it out to her.

"Perhaps His Majesty would consider a brief pause in operations. The machine has been running at full capacity for days—it's possible the Heart simply needs to recover its strength."

"Forget it. This needs to be churning out soldiers night and day until the girl is found."

"But the Heart is *dying*, General. We have no idea of the potential consequences. Have you spoken with the king today?"

"This morning."

"And did he seem well?"

Etheldred paused and narrowed her eyes.

"I thought not," Boggs continued. "He was stargazing again, yes? With the Heart waning, his illness is returning."

"No matter," Etheldred insisted. "You *will* follow my command."

When the king had approached Boggs to investigate the potential of the Heart, the doctor had been thrilled, if a little baffled. What wonderous potential it had—after all, they said it created life itself. Sure enough, with remarkably little effort, Boggs had birthed new life right on his workbench. With just a tiny sample of a living creature, he was able to quickly replicate it by the Heart's magic. It was fortunate the task proved so easy, since cloning wasn't in his field of study at all.

Sadly, the king had a somewhat limited imagination. This discovery could have grown enough crops to feed the entire realm or cured all diseases, but Richard simply wanted to grow his raptor army. Just batch after batch of huge, feathered *Utahraptors*—each one exactly like the last.

It had been effective, though. Despite having no idea how the Heart functioned, Boggs had successfully grown an entire new legion of raptors. The fortress was more heavily guarded than ever, but still Richard wanted more. Sadly, as time went on, the quality of the new replicas declined.

"But with even a short reprieve, I think the results would be of a *much* higher quality. The first specimens were magnificent. Look here. Guard!"

Obediently, a guard paced into the laboratory. It was a large dromaeosaur or raptor, as they are often known. Standing taller than any man, it was covered in a luscious coat of glossy, mahogany-coloured feathers from the end of its tail to the tip of its snout. The palms of its hands faced each other, and its arms sported magnificent wing feathers which were brilliantly white at the tip. It was as though a giant, toothed land-eagle had stridden in.

"*Look* at her," Boggs explained. "She was one of the first replicas. She's magnificent—a perfect *Utahraptor* specimen in every way. Not only is she beautiful and healthy, but almost unnaturally fast, strong, and intelligent—surely important qualities in a soldier."

The steel box then hissed loudly, and two metal doors began to swing open. The capsule was filled with smoke which slowly seeped out into the lab.

"The gate," Boggs hissed to himself.

He dashed over to the capsule and dragged down a barred shutter door with his long, scythe-like claws.

"*This*, on the other hand…" he lamented.

As the steam cleared, the hideous creature within came into view. Its basic body plan was much like the first *Utahraptor*, but it was entirely without feathers, barring a few ragged quills dotted unevenly across its body. Its palms faced the floor, and its arms took on a broken, limp-wristed posture. Its pale grey skin was dry and lumpy, and its eyes seemed glazed. With an awful, unnatural shriek, it launched itself at the shutter gate and began to chew frantically at the bars.

"What's wrong with it?" asked Etheldred.

"I don't know, they're just coming out… *wrong*. It's not just how they look, either; they have no real cognitive ability."

"So, they're ugly *and* stupid?"

Boggs imagined Etheldred knew both of those qualities well.

"Precisely," he concluded.

"Do they follow orders?"

"Simple orders, but they're savage and difficult to control."

"Savage can be useful," Etheldred stated as she approached the deformed dromaeosaur. "Soldier, will you track down the girl they call the Architect?"

Rather than answer, the raptor simply unleashed an ear-splitting scream.

"Is that a yes?" she asked.

"I think that gives too much credit to its vocabulary," Boggs replied with a slight eye roll.

"Well, let's find out."

Etheldred gripped the bottom of the shutter and threw it upwards. After taking a step back to acknowledge its new freedom, the *Utahraptor* screamed before sprinting out of the laboratory. Boggs flinched as the demented beast raced past.

"Where's it going?" Etheldred asked.

"To find the girl," confirmed Boggs.

"Just like that? I'm not sure these things are so broken after all, Doctor. *That* is motivation."

"That *thing* is an abomination. I won't create any more of them."

"Abomination. I *hate* that word," she growled. "There is a place for these creatures. You *will* keep the machine running. We'll have the girl soon, then you can worry about how attractive your clones are."

General Etheldred marched out of the laboratory. Barely a second later, a small pterosaur swooped in through the window, dropping a rolled piece of parchment by Boggs's feet. He crouched and collected the parchment, careful not to tear it with his fearsome claws. A wry but cautious smile spread across his face.

"So, it's time."

Three Renegades

After discussing the possibility of retrieving Luca, Gideon attached several pieces of parchment paper to a little pterosaur and sent it off into the swamp. I wasn't sure exactly where it was going; all Gideon said was that he was summoning his associates. For several hours, we heard nothing other than the heavy, beating rain on the thatched roof. Soon, however, came a single knock on the door followed by a pause and three more knocks in quick succession. It was clearly a code, as Gideon froze tensely after the first knock only to relax upon hearing the remainder. He paced to the door before easing it open.

"Thank you both for coming so soon," he greeted whoever stood outside. "Please, come inside."

The first to step into the shack was a small creature which, at first glance, looked like a large magpie. It walked on two legs and was covered in black and white feathers. However, on closer inspection, I saw that this animal had a snout filled with teeth, and protruding from the leading face of its wings were long, clawed fingers. It was a dinosaur, specifically an *Archaeopteryx*—an animal which beautifully demonstrated the evolutionary connection between birds and other theropod dinosaurs.

The second guest was considerably larger—a giant, feathered, pot-bellied creature with scythe-like claws. It was the same *Therizinosaurus* who had first taken us to the citadel. Doctor Boggs, they had called him.

"Good evening, old friend," Boggs announced.

"Hey, Gideon. So, is it true?" asked the *Archaeopteryx* with a high, tuneful voice as she shook the rainwater off her feathers. "Richard has the Heart?"

"I'm afraid so, Jynx," replied the *Therizinosaurus*. "I've seen it myself."

"Then we don't have time to be wasting."

"Indeed. We—"

"Please," Gideon interrupted. "Allow me to introduce you to the Architect and her companions."

"Well, render me extinct and call me a fossil," gasped Jynx. "It's *true*."

"Of course, it's true," retorted Boggs. "I escorted them to the citadel myself."

He bowed his head slightly as a mark of respect while Jynx simply stared, wide-eyed.

"Whoa, hold on Edward Scissorhands. Don't you work for the king?" I asked Boggs.

"Indeed, I've been the king's most trusted adviser for an age."

"Of course, he has been *my* most trusted advisor for even longer," Gideon added. "Boggs has been my inside man for as long as Richard has been in power. You can trust him."

"I work undercover," confirmed Boggs, "while Jynx here undermines the system. All in preparation for this day."

"Wait, *Jynx*?" Robyn asked. "You told Stromer to kidnap us!"

"Those pea-brains were supposed to help you, not hold you hostage," Jynx explained. "I guess my message wasn't idiot-proof. Those boys have two brain cells between them—both fighting for third place."

"Didn't you also set a fire in the cable car tower?" I added.

"Yes, yes, Jynx has set a lot of fires in a lot of places," Boggs clarified. "I don't condone her methods, but you can trust her."

"Condone my methods?" Jynx retorted. "Buddy, just because you don't get your hands dirty doesn't mean you aren't—"

"Please, both of you," Gideon said. "We have work to do. We need a plan."

I nodded. "We should get all our ducks on the same page."

Robyn narrowed her eyes and stared at me.

"Are you doing that just to annoy me?"

"Doing what?"

"It's ducks in one basket."

"If you say so," I replied with a shrug.

The six of us soon found ourselves gathered around the old, rough wooden table. I began to slurp Robyn's untouched bowl of soup.

"Didn't you already have a bowl?" asked Robyn.

"Objection; relevance," I countered.

"Sustained," she conceded with a smirk.

"Careful," added Carol. "You'll get the crapulence."

I spit out a little soup as I tried to stifle a laugh.

"Do you have them?" asked Gideon.

"I do," replied Boggs before reaching his long claws deep into his blue plumage and extracting a large roll of parchment.

He rolled the parchment out gently to reveal a set of blueprints for what, effectively, appeared to be a castle.

"Why do we need all of this?" asked Jynx.

"The complex is labyrinthine, Jynx," replied Gideon. "Without these plans, it would be like looking for a needle in a haystack."

"More like finding a straw of hay in a stack of needles," Boggs added.

"But we have the *Architect*, don't we?"

"What do you mean?" asked Robyn.

"It would appear the Architect has not yet unlocked her full potential," explained Gideon.

"What potential?" Robyn pressed.

"Well, Pangaea is your creation, silly," Jynx continued. "You built it, so you can change it however you like."

"I don't think it works that way," Robyn said with a slight shake of her head.

"Jynx is correct," said Gideon. "You *do* have the power to alter this world, but it's not a skill one would expect you to have mastered after such a short spell here."

"Well, why not wait it out?" asked Jynx. "Let's train the Architect and then tear the fortress apart brick by brick."

"Alas, it's not so simple," countered Boggs. "Richard is not merely biding his time. He has discovered the Heart can be used to replicate his *Utahraptors*. Regrettably, my curiosity may have accelerated this process."

"How many raptors does he have now?" asked Gideon.

"An additional legion and a half already. It will be thousands by the end of the week—*if* the Heart survives."

"If?"

"Its power is fading—it's being pushed too hard. We *must* retrieve it quickly."

"So, where's he keeping it?" asked Jynx.

"Richard is taking no chances," replied Boggs. "The Heart is locked in the main vault, deep in the bowels of the fortress and far above the ground. It won't be easy to retrieve."

"The vault won't be too much trouble," Jynx countered. "I've worked myself up a little toy for breaking in."

"I do hope it works better than the shark launcher," Boggs countered.

"Hey, I just needed to work out some kinks on that one."

"I *still* have tooth marks in my hind quarters."

"That proves it worked, if you ask me."

"The vault aside," Boggs continued. "There's an entire legion of raptors between the gate and the vault. Not even you could sneak past them without detection."

"You could work up some sleeping gas or something, couldn't you? A little chemistry shouldn't be a problem for you."

Boggs sighed deeply. "I'm not that kind of doctor," he replied, closing his eyes in weary frustration.

"Then I'll come in from above and sneak down from the roof."

"Past the pterosaur squadron?" Boggs scoffed. "That's suicidal."

"So, what *do* you propose, Doctor?" asked Gideon.

"It's simple, isn't it? I already have access; I'll simply enter and remove the Heart quietly."

"And how long before they notice it's gone?" asked Gideon.

"Ten minutes at the most; the guards are constantly checking on it."

"You'll be lucky to be out of the courtyard after ten minutes, big guy," said Jynx. "You'd never get out in time. I can fly it out much quicker."

"And then you'll be torn apart by the squadron," protested Boggs.

"We need a distraction," suggested Robyn. "To draw all the guards and the pterosaurs away."

"That's not a bad idea," said Jynx, pointing at Robyn with a snap of her clawed fingers. "What are you thinking? Explosion? I can get on board with a bomb plot. Dynamite? C-4? I'm also partial to a good, old-fashioned Molotov cocktail."

"You know fine well you can't be trusted with explosives anymore," Boggs scolded. "Remember what happened at the La Brea Tar Pits? What a mess. There was bitumen in my feathers for weeks."

"I'll draw them out," I suggested. "They're looking for us, right?"

"No," replied Boggs. "Neither of you should be anywhere near the fortress."

"Why not?" Robyn asked.

"Because the king wants you dead," the doctor explained. "You being there is *exactly* what he wants, that's why he took him. If he has Ed too, he will lure you out."

"I think he's right," agreed Carol. "It sounds too dangerous."

"Yeah, but… wait, what do you mean 'took him'?" asked Robyn. "Took who?"

The three renegades glanced at each other.

"You don't know?" Boggs asked.

"You know, maybe that's for the best," added Jynx.

"She deserves to know," argued Gideon.

"Know *what*?" Robyn demanded.

"I think it's risky, Gideon." insisted Jynx. "It's better she doesn't know. She might go all crazy on us."

"The thylacine," Boggs explained. "Richard has him."

"Benjamin?" Robyn whispered. "He's in the fortress?"

"Yes, in the dungeon."

"We're going to break him out then, right?" I replied. "We'll be there anyway."

"I think that would be unwise," argued Boggs. "We shouldn't walk straight into an obvious trap. The dungeon will be well guarded."

"Luca is the *only* priority," insisted Gideon.

"We can't leave him in there," I protested.

"Gideon's right, fellas," interjected Jynx.

"We can't allow ourselves to be distracted," Gideon pressed. "We must focus on the goal at hand. The marsupial can be rescued after we restore the Heart to the mausoleum. I will *not* risk the primary objective."

"So, we let him rot in there until then?" I remonstrated.

"Please," pleaded Boggs. "We *will* save him, but Gideon's right. If we lose the Heart, then we lose everything—we *all* do. Your friend included. We must take as few risks as possible."

I scowled to show my discontent, but I was outvoted.

"How about this distraction then?" asked Carol. "If not Ed, then who?"

"I'm a banished enemy of the crown," mused Gideon. "I could be the distraction."

"Very noble, Gideon," replied Boggs, "but you won't exactly draw out a whole legion, will you?"

"I suppose not," conceded Gideon. "It would appear we may need some more allies if we are to draw out *all* of the fortress's defences."

"Stromer?" suggested Robyn.

"*Captain* Stromer?" baulked Boggs. "You can't be serious. He's a *pirate,* a scoundrel. We couldn't possibly trust such a character."

"He fought off two *T. rexes* to save us."

"He did?" asked Jynx, clearly impressed. "He's got guts, I'll give him that. Stromer and I go way back. I trust him. And he is pretty dashing, if you ask me."

"We *didn't,*" the doctor retorted with a scowl.

"He didn't seem to have much love for the king either," I added.

"That's all well and good," replied Gideon. "But I don't see how one pirate could draw out the entire defences."

"Actually," Boggs interjected. "While I doubt the beast's honour, the king despises Stromer. He would throw everything at him."

"Perhaps the captain could be of use then," concluded Gideon. "I will send a messenger to find him. As for the rest of you, try to get some sleep."

"Good idea," I replied, stretching my front legs out and yawning. "I think that's been quite enough exposition for one night. Let's kick some butt tomorrow."

Mending Bridges

Waves rolled gently onto the pebble-covered beach, the sun shining brightly and a gentle breeze carrying the sweet smell of coconut milk in the air. Huge, furry feet beat down upon the pebbles as the giant ground sloth stomped along the coast. Cuvier hadn't had the best of times recently. He still limped slightly from the wounds he received at the hands of Lord Gigas. Despite this, he was beginning to appreciate his current circumstance.

He had heard rumours from across the sea, rumours of a brewing war. The young captive he and Captain Stromer had taken transpired to be the Architect of Pangaea, and the word was that she was after the throne. Cuvier had no love for the king, so the prospect of a regime change didn't concern him. He was simply grateful to have the eyes of the authorities drawn away from Hațeg.

Piracy had been profitable of late—profitable enough for him to soon purchase a new means of transportation. Since the untimely demise of Louis the *Megalodon*, Cuvier had relied upon Stromer's swimming ability. Being a *Spinosaurus*, Stromer was a capable swimmer for sure, but

Cuvier needed something with more space for loot—an *actual* ship. Besides, he wasn't sure for how much longer the good *capitaine* would be in the game—his heart didn't seem to be in it anymore.

As he returned to the lighthouse, he saw a small pterosaur flutter out the door. He knew a messenger *Pterodactylus* when he saw one, and they rarely brought good news. He trudged inside to find Captain Stromer caressing his long lower jaw deep in thought.

"Well?" he asked. "What was the message?"

"She's *alive*," Stromer replied.

He was wide-eyed with surprise and a grin began to spread across his face. Cuvier hadn't seen him smile for some days, though he hadn't alluded as to why.

"Who?"

"Robyn."

Cuvier shrugged and raised his brow to indicate that he had no idea who that was.

"The *Architect*," Stromer clarified. "I saw her die or, at least, I thought I did. Taken by a *Deinosuchus*."

"She was eaten by the terror croc?"

"I saw it with my own eyes, pal. I guess it takes more than that to kill the Architect."

"That was all that was in the message?"

"She's with Jynx."

"Oh, that *girl*, she is bad news. She always gets you into trouble. Filling your head with… *des idées*."

"I didn't realise ideas were such a bad thing."

"Her ideas are bad ideas."

"She's making moves. The message was a call for aid."

Cuvier grunted and shook his head.

"We should not get involved in this, *Capitaine*. Let the royalty and the gods fight amongst themselves."

"You don't want to see the king fall? After they took our whole crew? Not even after what they did to you?"

Cuvier looked down at his prosthetic claws where his left hand used to be.

"*Oui, bien sûr*, but we finally have everything we need here, *Capitaine*. The king will win. He *always* wins. But for now, we have freedom."

"Things won't ever change if no one stands up to him."

"So, let someone else stand up to him."

"Why not *us*?"

"We would not even stand a chance without Louis—"

"Don't worry about that," Stromer replied with a smirk. "I have a fine vessel in mind."

"Oh, *non, non*. You don't mean…"

***

Stromer, with Cuvier upon his back, swam through the jumble of fishing boats to the seafront wall. It had been a long time since he had set foot in Hangenberg—a place he had once called home. He placed his clawed forelimbs upon the top of the wall and heaved himself out of the water before hauling Cuvier out by the scruff of his neck. The town hadn't changed in the slightest.

As the pirates approached the floorless hut at the end of the old, rickety pier, the snake-like head of Mother Mary erupted out in a froth of white spray.

"What are you two doing here?" she spat.

"Good to see you too, Mary," replied Stromer with a smirk.

"You've got some nerve. Last time I saw you, you were *robbing* me."

"And you were blowing my transport to bits with a cannon."

"He was our *friend*," added Cuvier.

Stromer shrugged.

"More like an acquaintance. He had taken a few too many concussions, I reckon. That shark was *mean*. But it did leave us without a vessel. Very inconsiderate, if you ask me."

"What do you want, Stromer?"

"Well, I'm in need of a new vessel, aren't I?"

"*Ha*! You do have quite the audacity."

"Come on, it'll be like old times. Besides, a mutual friend needs our help."

"We have no mutual friends."

"I mean the Architect."

"The Architect you kidnapped?"

"And then *saved*, I'll have you know. Those two buffoons you led to us tried to kill her."

"The tyrants? But they were working for the king."

"It seems King Dicky wants little Robyn dead."

"I'm not sailing off to help you commit treason," Mary concluded sharply. "Now, leave this place."

"Oh, come on, Mary. Just—"

"I said *leave*," she yelled, slapping the pier with her flipper in frustration.

Being such a large and powerful creature, the slap against the pier caused several of the seashell-filled baskets behind her to rock and topple. However, as they fell, it became clear that shells and fossils weren't all she had stashed inside. As one of the wicker baskets fell off the shelf, a small, furry creature rolled out onto the wooden pier. It looked somewhat like a badger—stocky, with a pointed snout.

"What the…" Stromer began.

"Uh, oh my," Mary stammered. "Vermin, vermin. Shoo."

Stromer smirked—Mary had never been a good liar. From behind her, he could see several other small, hairy faces peeping above the basket rims.

"Are... are you harbouring *mammals*, Mary?"

"Of *course* not," she retorted. "How dare..."

Mary paused as it became clear from Stromer's raised eyebrow that he wasn't buying it.

"Fine," she admitted. "Just a couple."

"Just like old times. That's quite the turnaround—why the change of heart?"

She huffed.

"The little marsupial, the one who accompanied the Architect."

"Ah, *oui*, the irritating one," added Cuvier.

"He surprised me," Mary continued. "I was unkind to him, and yet he helped me. It made me think perhaps they aren't all like... you know."

"Like him," Stromer replied, nodding towards his first mate.

"What?" Cuvier barked.

"Exactly," replied Mary. "After everything he put us through—the lies, the theft, the violence—I believed the king was right about them. But perhaps Cuvier is just a bad egg."

"Hang on a minute—" began Cuvier.

"No, no," interrupted Stromer. "She's right, pal, you're the worst." He turned to Mary. "You have to admit though, it's sort of understandable. You know, with what the general did to him."

"I suppose." Mary took a long pause before turning to Cuvier. "I was too harsh on you. I should never have turned you in. I'm sorry."

"I..." Cuvier muttered. "I am also sorry. *Je m'excuse.* For everything."

Slowly, a deeply reflective glint formed in Cuvier's eye.

"Is that a *tear* in your eye?" Stromer asked with a gasp.

"*Bien sûr que non,*" Cuvier replied calmly.

"The stone-cold killer has a soft centre after all. Who knew?"

"It is *not* a tear," he insisted. "I have dust in my eye."

"You have *emotions* in your eye," Stromer responded with a smirk. "Well, now we've all made friends, how about we go and balance our karma?"

A mischievous grin spread across Mary's face.

"For the Architect?"

"And the annoying marsupial," Cuvier added with a smirk.

"And the little guy with the sail, of course," said Stromer. "I liked his style."

"Just one thing," Mary added. "My cannon was damaged at Hațeg."

"Oh, don't worry," replied Stromer with a smirk. "I have something *much* better. A gift from an old friend."

Valley of the Husks

Dawn was breaking, creating near-horizontal beams of orange light which cut through the swamp. After a restless night on Gideon's damp, wooden floor, Robyn, Carol, and I emerged from the cabin. Jynx was already outside testing her safe-cracking device. It took the shape of a small, metallic tripod which she had placed near a tree. Atop the tripod was a large suction cup along with several razor-sharp, rotating blades.

"Oh, you've come to see my new toy in action, folks?" she chirped as we arrived by her side. "I built this puppy all by myself for this very job—I've been *dying* to get into that vault for years."

"Why? What else is in the vault?" I asked.

"You don't know? Why, it's the Pangaean treasury. Every single piece of blood-stained loot and plunder is in that place—I reckon I could put it to better use than the king could. Now, let me just plug these two brown wires in... shoot, which one is which?"

I watched on as she fumbled with two wires.

"Those wires are red and green," I said.

"They are?"

"Jynx, are you colour blind?"

"Oh, only a little. I'm pretty sure they go this way round."

Jynx stabbed the wire connectors into their respective sockets.

"What happens if that was the wrong way around?" I asked.

"Trust me, kid."

"How does your machine work?" Robyn asked.

"Ain't I glad you asked."

She pulled a small lever on the base and scampered to a safe distance—gesturing with a flap of her wings for us to do the same.

"First of all, it suckers itself to the door," she explained as the suction cup extended forwards and fastened itself onto the tree trunk. "Then those wicked, obsidian-tipped blades quietly slice a hole through the door that's *just* big enough for me to fit through."

As the blades began to spin, the machine sparked and vibrated violently. It made a squealing sound which, while quiet at first, grew to be deafening within only a few seconds.

"You did say 'quietly,' didn't you?" I yelled.

"Uh, that's not good," stated Jynx. "You guys might want to hit the deck."

"Why—" I began, but it was too late.

The machine exploded, throwing chunks of metal and splinters of wood and bark in all directions. One of the saw blades whizzed through the air like a frisbee and came terrifyingly close to slicing off half my sail.

"Huh, that didn't *quite* go to plan," Jynx said in a surprisingly calm tone. "I guess those wires *were* the wrong way around. Maybe I should wire it with colours I can tell apart."

"You *think*?" I yelled.

"All right, keep your sail on. I can fix it," she insisted.

"I have kept my sail on—*just*. No thanks to that thing."

"Maybe if it exploded a *little* less?" suggested Robyn in a vain attempt to be supportive.

Jynx stopped for a moment, with a claw to her chin in consideration.

"Or maybe… what if I made it explode *more*?"

"Aren't we trying to be subtle?" I asked.

"That was before I knew we were creating a distraction. Subtlety doesn't seem so important now." Jynx clasped her hands together and hopped slightly in excitement at the prospect of getting to create another explosion.

"You can't just go around blowing stuff up," I protested.

"Not with that attitude, you can't. Just don't tell the fellas, yeah? They don't like me using explosives."

"Why not?" I asked.

"Boggs says I'm a pyromaniac with sociopathic tendencies, but what does he know? He's not even that kind of doctor."

"My lips are sealed," replied Robyn with a nervous smile.

"One more thing," added Jynx. "Gideon asked me to give you this."

She held up a brown leather vest which looked about Robyn's size.

"What's this?" Robyn asked.

"Armour, silly," Jynx replied, handing the vest over.

Robyn and I glanced at each other with our eyebrows raised.

"It doesn't look all that protective," I said. "Will it really help?"

"Oh, yeah," Jynx insisted. "It's *plot* armour, the strongest in Pangaea. Trust me."

Robyn slipped the vest on. It was a perfect fit, but it did look rather ridiculous over her yellow and green sportswear.

"Looks like we have the king's army *and* the fashion police to watch out for," I teased.

***

Our party of six—Boggs had returned to the fortress the night before to avoid the king's suspicions—left the swamp soon after and trudged for several hours across a wide, grassy plain. Occasionally, Robyn, Carol, and I were ushered to hide beneath Gideon's great belly as a bird or pterosaur flew overhead. Clearly, our new companions considered each of them to be potential spies.

We eventually found ourselves trekking through a wide, sandstone canyon with cliffs on either side. The valley's river had long since dried up, leaving only dust and rock where it once flowed. The sun was high in the sky and blazed down upon us—only the odd, cooling shadow swept over us as flying creatures soared above. Gideon was initially nervous, believing them to be royal pterosaurs, but the flying critters were soon identified as *Argentavis*—the giant teratorn.

They resembled huge, black condors with a wingspan which could cover a bus from bumper to bumper. This seemed to relax Gideon—apparently, the king didn't tend to employ such creatures—but I didn't feel quite so relieved. They were the vultures of the Miocene Epoch, and they circled us as though they knew something we didn't.

Robyn flinched as a rock tumbled down the cliff face, clattering off outcrops on the way in a series of echoing cracks. Gideon froze and stared towards the cliff top, his eyes narrowing as he gazed into the sun. It was clear he was trying to determine whether the rock had fallen of its own accord or had been disturbed by something more sinister.

"Everything okay, boss?" asked Jynx.

"I'm not sure," Gideon replied quietly.

"We can't wait here all day," I pointed out. "We need to get there before nightfall, right? We should keep moving."

Gideon grunted and reluctantly began to press on. Nevertheless, he now kept watch on the clifftops. We trudged on further, the dry heat beginning to take its toll. I knew we still had a long way to go, but I was exhausted.

"Does anyone else hear that?" asked Carol.

We stopped and listened. I could hear a gentle breeze and the occasional far-off bird call, but nothing of any real note.

"I can't hear anything," I replied.

"No, hold on, now," added Jynx. "I hear it too."

I listened once more, this time holding my breath to be as quiet as possible. Faintly, there was a distant, repetitive padding sound, like something slapping against the rocky ground over and over in quick succession. It was difficult to pinpoint from which direction it originated. Above, perhaps? No, *behind*.

I turned back to have a look. At the far end of the valley was a small dust cloud with a faint figure moving ahead of it. It was moving towards us—quickly—*frighteningly* quickly.

"What *is* that?" Carol asked, squinting into the distance.

"I don't know," Gideon responded. "Jynx, you have fine vision—what do you see?"

"I can't be too sure," she replied, her head tilted slightly to the side as she tried to interpret what was before her. "It's strange, kind of like a..." Her face dropped and her eyes widened in fright. "Oh, my word—it's a *raptor*."

"A royal assassin," Gideon boomed. "Everyone, move!"

Obediently, we turned and fled. However, Jynx aside, none of us were especially fast. I turned back to see the creature much closer than before; it wouldn't be long before it caught us. From my glance backwards I was horrified by what I saw. It looked broadly like a large raptor, Jynx was right about that much, but it was hideous. Where it should have had feathers it had only grey, lumpy, cracked skin and its arms flopped loosely beneath its body as if they were hopelessly broken. It was a monstrous sight.

"It's catching us," I called out.

Gideon glanced behind before turning around and halting in a dust cloud of his own making.

"Run, *all* of you!" he roared.

It seemed the logical action. While the raptor was enormous for a dromaeosaur, it was still dwarfed by the vast *Iguanodon*. Gideon could surely hold it off with little effort. He roared at our pursuer as he dropped behind. I looked over my shoulder once more to see Gideon raise a huge foot and stomp the raptor into the ground. It was a short battle—if it could even be described as such. With the danger seemingly gone, I began to slow.

"Keep going, fella," Jynx scolded. "That won't be the only one."

Sure enough, more rocks began to rain from the valley walls, crashing and exploding onto the dusty riverbed. I could only make out silhouettes against the sun, but it was clear that there were dozens of raptors along the clifftops. They began to leap down, which was incredible given the height of the cliffs. Indeed, some landed with a crunch, breaking legs and ribs in the process. Yet despite their obvious injuries, they began to drag themselves across the ground by their forelimbs. Others bounced off the rocky walls, spinning violently and landing hard before scrambling to their feet.

We picked up the pace once more, fleeing the incoming horde. Gideon followed and continued to crush an impressive number of assassins. Even with their great numbers, they appeared to be little match for him, but he couldn't fight all of them. He couldn't be everywhere.

Jynx launched herself high into the air to avoid an incoming attack from ahead. With the sickly beast careering towards us, I thrust my head forwards, butting it away. It fell to the rocky ground, rolling over a few times, before leaping back to its feet and hurtling at us once more.

This time, I waited for it to approach, dodged to the side, and clamped my jaws around its neck. I hauled it to the ground and bit hard. My sharp teeth sank into its rubbery flesh before my powerful jaws crushed the beast's throat. It made me feel sick to do so, but I had to kill it. It was the only way to protect Robyn.

I bit harder still, and I could feel something crunching and separating. Once convinced I had inflicted a fatal wound, I released my grip.

To my horror, the deformed raptor made a haunting, gargling call and flailed its legs, kicking up the dust. With an ungainly twist, the beast rose to its feet. Its head hung loose on its floppy, broken neck, yet it *lived*. As I looked back to the trailing pursuers, I saw even Gideon was struggling to finish them off. They were mostly crushed, some with visibly broken legs and jaws, some crawling along the ground. It was as though they felt no pain and knew no death.

"In here!" called Jynx.

I could see the little *Archaeopteryx* had flown under a web of old, dead tree roots which formed a sort of cage. It did look as though the roots were spaced too close together for the large raptors to fit through—indeed, it looked like a squeeze for me. We made a break for it with the bobble-headed raptor snapping at our heels. Robyn was the first to scuttle to safety, followed by Carol. I made the dive for sanctuary only to become stuck halfway through, my hind legs not quite fitting between the old roots.

The sickly dromaeosaur took its opportunity to bite hard on my hind leg. Naturally, this was an unpleasant experience and one I wish to never relive. The creature's blade-like teeth sliced through my skin with ease and my flesh burned with pain. I kicked hard, knocking the raptor to the side, where it tumbled over.

Robyn and Carol gripped my forelimbs and pulled hard until I slipped through the tightly spaced roots. I turned to see the crazed theropod leap at the rotting wood. The huge, horrifying, sickle-shaped claws on its feet pierced the roots while the raptor repeatedly smashed its flopping head into the wood. The bars of our makeshift cage began to splinter and crack—it would break through in very little time at all. We needed an escape plan.

Behind us was the solid rock of the cliff face, and to the other side the roots were far too tightly packed to fit through. What *idiots* we had been. This wasn't a sanctuary—it was a *trap*. With every strike of its face against the wood the roots deteriorated, but so, too, did the raptor. Some teeth fell from its mouth and its eyes grew bloodshot and wept, yet it pounded on regardless.

Our options were limited. This savage creature seemed impossible to stop—yet stop it did. It took one last strike at the roots before retracting its claws, stepping back, and collapsing. It appeared to gasp desperately for air, taking three long, laboured breaths before stopping altogether.

"What the..?" I began.

"Is it... is it dead?" asked Carol, panting heavily.

Jynx hopped out from under the old tree and crept towards the fallen monster. She held a wing out in front of its snout for several seconds.

"It ain't breathing," she announced before kicking it in the head in an attempt to provoke a reaction. "It looks pretty darn dead to me."

We crawled out from our ill-advised bunker and gazed down at the odd creature. I looked back along the valley to see that most of the others had fallen to a similar fate, with only one or two still crawling, injured, along the ground.

"What's wrong with them?" Robyn asked.

"What's not wrong with them?" I replied. "And the way they moved, as though they had no thoughts, just empty shells. *Husks.*"

"They look like the raptors from Jura—"

"Shush, Robyn! Are you trying to get us sued?"

"I'm just saying there's a similarity—"

"Of course, there is. That's sort of the point, but you can't just say it out loud."

"Eugh, I hate dromaeosaurs at the best of times," exclaimed Jynx.

"Really?" asked Robyn. "*Archaeopteryx* are pretty closely related to them."

"Only by marriage," Jynx insisted.

"They are products of the Heart," announced Gideon, arriving behind Robyn.

"*Luca* created these things?" Robyn gawped.

"Not by choice. It's like Boggs said—its power is failing. He's forcing it to make too many."

"So, the king's getting greedy," replied Jynx. "No surprises there."

"We must hurry," insisted Gideon.

Pebbles began to dance along the dry ground as the earth vibrated beneath our feet. It was like an earthquake, but a look back along the narrow valley revealed the source. A second wave of husks was tearing through towards us, this time many hundreds of the beasts.

"Get out of here!" Gideon snarled.

"Gideon," Jynx protested. "You can't hold off that many."

"Not for long," he replied with a gentle nod. "So, move *quickly*."

"Come with us, we can outrun them."

"You know we can't, Jynx. We must protect Robyn. I will do my duty. Now, do yours. *Run!*"

Jynx stared at her leader for a long moment before huffing reluctantly. "Give 'em hell, big guy," she whispered.

She turned and spread her wings wide, flapping them to usher us onwards

"Let's go, folks. No lollygagging."

At her command, we began to run.

"Wait, what about Gideon?" Robyn asked.

"He's doing what he has to. Let's make sure it isn't for nothing."

After a few moments, I turned to see Gideon battling the front of the pursuing swarm. The valley narrowed, and so he seemed to be keeping them at bay. However, as we put more distance between us, I glanced back once more to see the wave of monstrous raptors swarm over him. He writhed for several seconds as the numbers built on top of him, weighing him down and crushing him into the ground. Soon, there was no more movement to be seen. Already he was overrun; they wouldn't be long in catching us.

With a mighty roar, Gideon burst upwards from the swarm of husks and thrust his head into the cliff face over and over. Small rocks cascaded from the top, soon followed by large boulders. He looked towards us for a final time before ramming into the cliff once more. The valley walls began to collapse, raining tonnes of rock onto the husk swarm—and onto Gideon. Within seconds, he was out of sight, buried beneath the rubble.

"Jynx, shouldn't we—"

"We keep going!" Jynx snapped, her eyes glistening as tears fought to escape. "We do as he asked."

Footprints of a Leviathan

There is a wondrous place in the north of Africa, deep in the Atlas Mountains, where evidence of a remarkable creature can be found. There are no fossils of the animal itself, but merely traces of its presence—footprints. Footprints made over a hundred and twenty million years ago by an animal of impossible proportions.

Science knows next to nothing about the beast which left these prints, only that it was a long-necked, sauropod dinosaur and that it was vast. Provisionally named Breviparopus, it may well have been the largest animal to ever walk on planet Earth.

It's strange how something so incredibly large could leave no evidence other than a few footprints. How something which shook the very ground is remembered by nothing but the ground itself—a whisper in the winds of history. Yet even the most powerful are not immune from the relentless ticking of the clock—time catches up with us all.

The Fortress

Some things in life are easier than they look. Riding a bicycle, for example, looks like a pretty difficult feat, but most children can do so before they start school. Other things are much harder than they look, like collecting a pile of wet laundry from the washer. It looks as though it can just be scooped into your arms, and so that's what you do. But then a single sock falls to the floor. You bend down to pick up the sock and three more fall. Rinse and repeat until most of the clothing is on the floor, and you finally admit this task may need several trips.

Burgling a high-security fortress is not like riding a bike. Nor is it like collecting laundry from the floor. Rather, it's like trying to collect a mountain of laundry from the floor using only a pair of chopsticks held between your teeth. It never looked easy, but it was much harder than it looked nonetheless.

***

By the time we arrived at our destination, the sun was low and dusk approached. Exhausted, we found ourselves at the edge of a huge, brilliantly white cliff face. Below was a stony beach battered by a restless, swelling tide of turbulent, grey water. Given that we were only a day's walk from the sweltering desert, it was remarkably cold with a vicious wind whipping at our faces.

"The Burgess Coast," announced Jynx as we stared out towards the sea. "It's the edge of the world. Out there is the Panthalassa Ocean, which some folks reckon goes on forever."

None of us replied; we simply stared out in wonder. It was a vehement expanse of water. The waves grew to immense heights, restlessly rising and falling along the horizon.

Jynx had been clear in her wish for Robyn and me not to be present, but I insisted. We should at least *be* here, even if we had been relegated to mere lookouts. I understood that Robyn was important, and they needed to keep her safe, but I still had the urge to have a more proactive role in the mission. We had failed Luca and Benjamin too. It was surely our duty to set that right.

It didn't take long before we felt a faint tremble in the earth. It was almost imperceptible at first, but soon it became a deeply unnerving rumble beneath our feet. It was accompanied by a faint *boom, boom, boom*. Dust and small stones began to crumble off the white cliffs and trickle towards the beach. This was the signal Gideon had told us of.

We stood and looked along the coast to see a vast leviathan approaching, its massive footsteps the source of the tremors. It was an enormous, long-necked, sauropod dinosaur—a colossus of impossible magnitude. Upon its back stood a mighty stone castle with walls around the perimeter and a tall tower in the centre.

"Well butter my butt and call me a biscuit," exclaimed Jynx.

"Look at the *size* of that thing," mused Carol.

"Is that…" I began.

"*Breviparopus*," Robyn confirmed. "It *has* to be. I bet it could make a huge vomit crater."

"I'm sorry," interrupted Carol. "A *what?*"

I giggled at the prospect of explaining one of Robyn's favourite pieces of obscure dinosaur trivia.

"There's this theory," I began. "With sauropod heads being so high off the ground, some people think they might have used vomit as a defence."

"The vomit would be so heavy and would fall from so high," Robyn continued, bringing her fist down and slapping it into her palm, "it would crush any predators."

"Death by puke?" Carol replied.

"Yup," I confirmed. "A homicidal hurl."

"Murder by chunder," Robyn concluded.

Jynx pointed towards the top of the tower.

"All right, folks," she stated. "That there is my entry point. All going well, I'll be back here in a hot second."

She looked above the fortress at two dozen pterosaurs which trailed it. They ranged from powerful giants as large as small aeroplanes to creatures barely larger than a pigeon, but extremely agile. With their high vantage point, there was no way they wouldn't see us approach.

"Hide," Jynx instructed.

We took heed and ducked behind a nearby bush to avoid the gaze of this reptilian air force.

"Let's hope your friend comes through," whispered Carol. "We need that distraction."

"He will," replied Robyn with a nod. "I trust him."

"I guess we'll soon find out if trusting a pirate was a smart move."

The sauropod moved ever closer until its head passed by us, its eyes just above the cliff top. From here, I could see the huge chains which wrapped around its long neck towards its face. They were attached to either side of a giant metal bar loaded with sharp spikes, which was clamped within the creature's mouth. It looked incredibly painful, and it seemed clear the sauropod wasn't the foundation of the king's fortress by choice. Its eyes were glazed and motionless as though it were in a trance.

Jynx's window of opportunity was closing fast, but the promised aid hadn't arrived.

"What do we do?" asked Carol.

"I'll distract them," I stated coolly.

"Don't be an idiot," Jynx scolded. "Those pterosaurs'll tear you to pieces."

"Maybe they'll let me in the gate," Robyn suggested. "I'm the Architect, after all. Maybe they'll bring me in instead of killing me."

"Sweetie, I thought you were the smart one. You're no good to anyone dead."

"It's *my* choice…"

"No," Jynx hissed. "No, it's *not*. *This* is why you should've stayed in the swamp. Everything and everyone you see around, it's all *you*… and it's all *gone* without you. You're not being brave; you're being a knucklehead. Now, get *down*."

After her stern telling off from the little feathered dinosaur, Robyn slumped back down.

"So, what now, then?" Carol whispered.

"We go back," Jynx admitted glumly.

"Give up?" asked Carol.

"I'm not leaving here without Luca," I insisted.

"It's not giving up," Jynx replied. "We retreat and we come up with a new plan—we have to be smart about…"

She stopped and looked out towards the sea. Her head twitched from side to side as if she could hear something. In the distance, the surface of the water seemed to swell into a huge dome before exploding into a ball of white foam.

From beneath the depths, the *Plesiosaurus* Mother Mary exploded into view. Aboard her main deck, I could see Captain Stromer and his first mate Cuvier. Between them was what appeared to be a catapult of some description. Even from the top of the cliff, I could hear Stromer's great roar.

"*Fire!*"

The catapult arm launched upwards and a glistening, slender, grey object flew through the sky.

"Is that…" I began.

"Shark launcher!" Jynx squealed with a broad grin.

The first shark crashed against the stone fortress and ploughed through the wall. Shrieks of panic ensued from within as the shark writhed around the courtyard, snapping its jaws. The pterosaurs turned towards the sea and swooped in the direction of Mother Mary and her crew. The top of the tower was now right below us and, with the pterosaurs gone, this was Jynx's chance.

"I guess we've got our distraction after all," said Jynx with a smile.

"Good luck," said Carol.

With that, Jynx spread her wings and leapt off the top of the cliff. We ran to the edge to gaze down as she soared onto the tower with wonderful elegance.

"We should go," I stated.

"What?" replied Robyn.

"Down there, it's not that far. Look, Jynx will get Luca, we can run in and get Benjamin. How hard can it be? The guards will all be distracted."

"Jynx said—"

"This is *your* world, not hers. Do you want to leave Benjamin down there?"

"Ed, I don't think that's a good idea," warned Carol.

"No, Ed's right," Robyn said with a nervous nod. "Benjamin's our friend. He helped us before; we owe him. Benjamin wouldn't leave us in a dungeon. Luca made me show courage—I can't let them down."

"No time like the present," I called before leaping off the cliff onto the top of the stone tower.

It was a longer fall than I had anticipated, and I began to pitch forwards as I dropped. I hit the roof face-first before toppling onto my side. I groaned as a dull pain pulsed through my brain.

"What are you doing?" Jynx lamented.

"Are you all right, Ed?" called Carol from above.

"Yep," I grunted unconvincingly. "Yep, all good. My skull broke my fall."

"That would have done some damage if you had a brain in there," remarked Jynx with a roll of her eyes.

I looked up to see Robyn staring at me, eyes wide in terror. She had never been great with heights, something which I had, somehow, not given any thought to. The tower itself wasn't all that far below the cliff top, but the courtyard beneath was a long way down indeed. Missing the tower would surely be a fatal error.

"Oh, come on," Jynx pleaded. "Don't do it, Robyn."

Before the small, feathered dinosaur could protest any further, Robyn and Carol linked arms and leapt—but they had misjudged. Since the fortress was still moving, their trajectory drifted away from their targeted landing zone. Robyn was going to miss the tower by no more than a hair's width, but miss nonetheless.

Carol landed hard onto the outer wall of the tower and Robyn plummeted past. With their arms still linked, Carol was yanked towards the edge after her daughter—they were both about to plunge onto the stone courtyard.

I bounded towards Carol and clamped my jaws onto her dress. I clenched my eyes shut, planted all four feet firmly onto the floor, and held on tightly. As I opened my eyes, I saw Carol precariously teetering on the edge of the wall and Robyn clinging to her arm, dangling high over the courtyard, almost hyperventilating with fear. Robyn's arm slipped out of her mother's and she began to drop, only for Carol to grab a hold of her leather vest.

With a great lurch, I heaved backwards. It was only a few steps, but it was enough to pull the pair safely onto the roof.

"Let's never do that again," Robyn gasped as she slumped onto the stone roof.

"Agreed," Carol huffed. "Thank you, Ed."

"Don't mention it," I replied, trying to disguise how shaken I was—that had been *way* too close.

Carol then wrapped her arms around me and squeezed.

"Now I see why you're Robyn's favourite lizard-dog," she said with a cheeky smile.

Jynx looked unimpressed, tapping her foot with her wings crossed over her chest.

"Ya'll are really testing the limits of that plot armour already," she said. "Well, you're here now, I guess. You might as well make yourselves useful."

I hauled Robyn to her feet.

"I think we're skating on thin eggshells with Jynx," I said.

"Oh, there's no way you think that's the right saying," Robyn bemoaned.

"What do you mean?"

"I know you're just trying to wind me up."

"You're looking into it too much," I argued. "Let's get going."

Together, we paced by Jynx's side towards the wooden trapdoor.

Robyn screamed as a huge hammerhead shark slapped onto the trap door. After a small bounce, it writhed and snapped its jaws towards her leg. I gripped it by the tail and dragged it away before dodging another of its strikes.

"Were the sharks really necessary?" Carol asked.

"Necessary?" replied Jynx. "Heck no, but they're cool, right?"

"She has a point," I conceded.

Carol grabbed the iron ring handle and heaved the trapdoor open. Beneath was a dark, spiralling staircase of stone. After collectively taking a deep breath, we began our descent. The dull, sloppy sound of sharks impacting the fortress walls continued to thump nearby—some with enough force to shake the floor and cause dust to rain from the ceiling.

The gloomy stairway was only illuminated by the occasional glassless window, through which we could see the ensuing battle between Mother Mary's crew and the pterosaur air force. Given how agile the aerial attackers were, it didn't look like an easy task. To make matters worse, they were also being barraged with returning cannon fire from the fortress, the surface of the water exploding all around the plesiosaur. Mary appeared to be trying to head for shore, but she was being repelled as she evaded a barrage of attacks.

Halfway down the tower, we reached an open doorway through which we could see the shadows of two large *Utahraptors*. Jynx raised her clawed finger to her snout, indicating that we should be quiet. We could hear the guards, who were preoccupied with watching the attack unfold, conversing inside.

"Bloody pirates, they get bolder all the time," one said.

"What makes them think one plesiosaur could take on the whole fortress?" another replied.

"They'll try anything, the desperate wretches. They'll learn their lesson soon enough."

"If only we could get out there. We'd show them what a mistake they've made face to face."

I glanced inside to see the tall, stocky creatures covered from snout to tail in a puffy coat of dappled hazel plumage and armed with horrifying, curved sickle claws on each foot. They were rather less disturbing to look at than the deformed husks we had met in the valley, but these specimens were obviously stronger, faster, and more intelligent creatures. We snuck past the doorway and continued down the steps. Once I was confident we were out of earshot of the guards, I whispered to the others.

"That raptor made a good point: the guards can't get out to Mother Mary."

"Well, isn't that good?" asked Robyn.

"The whole point was to distract the guards too, not just the pterosaurs."

"The fella has a point," Jynx agreed. "We have to wait for Stromer to reach the beach."

We shuffled along further to the next window and peered out to view the crew's progress. They fended off wave after wave of swooping pterosaur attacks and avoided the barrage of cannon fire, but I wasn't sure they could hold out much longer.

Fury of the Panthalassa

"Fire!" screamed Captain Stromer.

The giant ground sloth Cuvier responded by triggering the shark launcher once more. Throughout his life as a pirate of the high seas, he had become adept at reloading the catapult with remarkable speed. It was quite the contraption. At the end of its long, wooden arm was a net which he filled with chum and tossed overboard. The shark-infested seas of Pangaea never failed to catch a shark within a few seconds, after which the spring-loaded mechanism was released, launching the poor fish for hundreds of feet.

Cuvier never hid his pleasure in piracy—he openly admitted his love for intimidation, murder, and plunder. Perhaps inflicting suffering upon others made his own seem less acute. Perhaps it allowed him to regain the power he had been robbed of all those years ago. He was under no illusions about what kind of sloth he was but, still, firing upon a worthy target for once felt strangely fulfilling.

With every flabbergasted shark which flew through the air and pummelled the fortress, he grew happier still. There was no denying that he got a thrill from such destruction, but it somehow tasted sweeter to know his target *deserved* it. He pulled the lever for each release with his prosthetic claw as a reminder to himself of why he was there. He would never regrow his hand, nor would he lose the memories of years of captivity and torture, but a little vengeance might stop the nightmares.

"Here they come!" yelled the great *Plesiosaurus* Mother Mary.

Stromer, the bold *Spinosaurus* captain, looked upwards to see the squadron of pterosaurs swarming the fortress—a flurry of shadows against the darkening sky. The captain swiped at them with huge claws as they swooped low.

Unlike his first mate, Stromer didn't take pleasure from his profession. For him, it was a dirty necessity. He dreamed of redemption—to be the hero he wished he had always been. He relished this opportunity. He swiped once more, spearing a low-flying *Pteranodon* through the wing. It squawked and barrel-rolled violently before pitching into the waves.

"How do you like *that?*" he yelled triumphantly.

But one *Pteranodon* was merely a dent in the vast squadron. The tiny *Pterodactylus* were impossibly agile and darted around every defensive strike with ease. Equally troubling were the bulky *Hatzegopteryx*—vast pterosaurs with the wingspan of a light aircraft and a beak as long as a city car. They were slow flyers which barely flapped a wing, but they had incredible strength.

The diminutive *Pterodactylus* were the first to cause real damage to the crew. They swooped low across the deck, repeatedly swiping at the pirates' ankles with their sharp beaks and needle-like teeth. Cuvier caught one with his prosthetic blades—slicing its wing off entirely—but, for the most part, they were untouchably swift. The bombardment seemed unending. The cuts were small, but they were mounting and both pirates began to falter.

"Mary," Stromer called. "I'm not sure how much more we can take. We *have* to reach the beach quickly."

With the pair weakened, the masters of the skies closed in. A *Hatzegopteryx* slammed onto Mother Mary's deck, splintering the planks with the force of its landing. It stood as tall as a giraffe and was incredibly robust. Under normal circumstances, either one of the pirates would have taken his chances against even the biggest of pterosaurs—despite their size they were still fragile creatures. But such was the punishment they had taken, they could now barely stand.

The giant azhdarchid reeled its head back before striking forwards with its razor-sharp beak. Stromer was punctured in the shoulder, receiving a deep wound. Cuvier lunged with his gleaming claws, but the beast vaulted off the deck and circled back around. Several more of these monsters swooped in, soaring along the surface and stabbing their beaks into Mother Mary's flippers. She lurched violently to starboard as her injured flippers struggled to maintain an upright condition.

"We have to retreat!" Mary called out. "I can't hold them off."

"No," insisted Stromer. "This will all be for nothing if we don't reach the beach. We have to draw out those raptors."

"We'll never make it, Captain, not with—" Mary groaned as another of her flippers was speared.

The broiling water of the Panthalassa began to turn red as Mary bled into the brine. She sank lower into the water, low enough that the waves now washed over the deck.

"She is right, *Capitaine*," Cuvier concurred. "We have done all we can."

"We can't fail, Cuvier," snarled Stromer. "The king *has* to fall today. For the good of Pangaea."

"To hell with *Pangaea*," roared Cuvier, swatting off another *Pterodactylus*. "It has never done anything for me. *Rien!*"

"What about the king? Robyn can bring him to justice if we can just buy her a little time."

Cuvier's expression hardened. He didn't care for Pangaea, that much was true, but he cared deeply about revenge.

Mary twisted her neck around to look the pair in the eye.

"Gentlemen, I'm not proud of my allegiance to the king. Perhaps this is a chance to restore some dignity. Pangaea needs change—I'm here until the end if you are."

Stromer and Cuvier looked at each other and nodded slowly.

"To the end," agreed Cuvier.

The flurry of tiny pterosaurs continued, as did the attacks on Mary's flippers. Nevertheless, the great plesiosaur accelerated towards the shore. Teeth raked. Claws slashed. Cuvier even managed to take out a *Hatzegopteryx* with a particularly lucky shark launch.

Despite their efforts, Mary was now listing severely to starboard, and half her deck was underwater. Through the flurry of wings, a huge *Hatzegopteryx* swooped and speared her in the head with its beak. It was a decisive attack. After a brief pause, her long neck flopped into the sea.

"Mary!" Stromer called.

She rolled to her side, submerging the whole deck. Stromer and Cuvier gasped as a wall of frigid water washed over the deck. Mother Mary's great mass slipped beneath the waves, dropping away beneath their feet. While ordinarily powerful swimmers, neither captain nor first mate had any fight left in them. Their muscles tightened until their limbs were paralysed. Stromer opened his mouth to mutter a final farewell to his first mate, but no sound came. Instead, they offered each other only a shivering nod.

Stromer turned to face the beach he would never reach. He had been so close, but it hadn't been enough.

The turbulence of the sinking plesiosaur dragged Stromer and Cuvier with her into the black, crushing depths of the Panthalassa.

The Heist

"*No!*" Robyn screamed as we watched Mother Mary and her crew slip beneath the waves.

"Oh no," whispered Jynx. "Stromer."

We stared out at the churning sea for some time, expecting the hardy pirates to resurface, but they never did. I glanced towards Jynx, conscious that she had described Stromer as a friend.

Carol had seemingly also recalled this detail. "I'm so sorry," she said, placing a gentle hand on Jynx's back.

Robyn followed suit, a tear running down her face. "He was a hero," she added.

"We all make sacrifices," Jynx stated, patting Robyn on the head. "I'll mourn him when we're done. Chins up, we still have a job to do."

I wasn't sure whether to be impressed or troubled by how quickly Jynx recovered from the death of an old friend. Perhaps it was merely a coping mechanism.

"What now?" asked Robyn.

"The courtyard will still be swarming with raptors," replied Jynx.

"And we can't exactly get out the way we came," I added.

"*I* could have," snapped Jynx. "Maybe you three should have stayed put like I *told* you to."

"You're right," said Carol. "But that doesn't help us now. Let's see how busy it is down there."

Sure enough, when we reached the base of the tower and peered out through the slightly open wooden door, we saw a courtyard swarming with feathered raptors, the killing claws on their feet held high at the ready.

"We have to get rid of those clowns somehow," whispered Jynx. "We'll need

to make a distraction of our own."

"But how?" asked Robyn.

As if to answer, a horrifying shriek erupted from behind us, echoing through the tower. I turned to see a set of iron bars. Behind those, the stairwell continued into the bowels of the fortress. The high-pitched screams coming from beneath were hauntingly familiar.

"The raptors," I said. "The... the *wrong* ones."

"This must be where they keep the husks," Robyn reasoned.

Robyn and I gave each other a knowing look.

"You two can't be serious?" Carol scolded. "No, those things nearly *killed* us."

"They did seem pretty rabid to me," added Jynx. "They'd make a big old mess."

"A mess could be exactly what we need," I replied with a smirk.

With a deep breath, Robyn reached out a hand and grabbed the sliding bolt which held the barred door closed. She slid it slowly over, unlocking the enclosure. I rattled the bars with my tail a few times to let the creatures below know of our presence, and then we crept back up the stairs, just enough to be out of sight. Within only a second or two, dozens of the deformed dromaeosaurs came tearing through from the stairway, clattering the metal door open. The mob poured out into the courtyard.

"What now?" asked Carol, her brow furrowed with concern.

A reply wasn't required. Soon came the sound of glass smashing, the shrieks of the husks, and the frightened yells of the guards. Bells began to ring out across the fortress. We could hear the guards from the tower above scamper down the stairs, their sharp claws clicking on the stone steps. Instinctively, we all slunk into the shadows beneath the stairway and waited for them to pass.

All four of us then crept out into the courtyard, which was now in chaos. The feathered raptors were outnumbered and each battling several of their deformed brethren. Using the mayhem as cover, we followed Jynx through the courtyard and towards a large arch at the forward end—near the base of the *Breviparopus*'s neck.

Inside, we found a large, circular room with a wooden floor. Six chains were strung from the floor to the ceiling, where they coiled around huge reels. Our feathered companion confidently pulled a lever by the door. With a loud creak, the floor gave way. The great, chain-driven elevator lowered slowly with a clunky, unstable motion. We delved into the depths of the fortress.

The elevator ground to a halt with a metallic squeal as we reached the bowels of the fortress. Before us was a giant, steel door with a rotating, spoked handle. Jynx skipped out of the elevator with supreme confidence. She reached a clawed hand under her opposite wing and retrieved a tiny stick of pink clay with a fuse embedded in one end.

"Those idiots," she said with a wry smile as she examined the door. "They put so much trust in their fancy fortress, they barely even made an effort on the vault."

"Where did you get *dynamite* from?" I asked.

"It fell off the back of a Laurasian mining wagon, which I definitely did *not* run off the road and set fire to. Don't listen to what Boggs says."

"Boggs never mentioned anything about a wagon," Robyn replied.

"Oh, well, forget I said anything then."

She slapped the stick onto the vault door's hinge before scampering back into the elevator.

"Oh, maybe don't tell the doc I used explosives, he doesn't like that sort of thing," she said, placing her hands over her ears. After a moment, she turned to us. "You guys might want to cover your ears."

I was sceptical that such a small stick of explosives could require me to protect my ears, but Robyn, Carol, and I acquiesced, nonetheless. It was a good thing we did as the resultant explosion was powerful—the noise of the blast was almost deafening. My chest reverberated like a drum and my ears rang. The shockwave knocked Robyn and me to the floor and raised a cloud of thick, white dust.

Jynx emitted a shriek of joy and clapped her wings together gleefully.

"What the...?" I groaned.

"Some folks just don't appreciate a good explosion," Jynx said with a shake of her head.

As the dust settled, I could see the vault door still in place. Jynx skipped towards it, giggling to herself and, with only the slightest of tugs, pulled the door off its hinges. She dodged to the side as it tipped over and slammed into the floor with enough force to shake the ground.

"Don't you think someone will have heard that?" I asked.

"Half the fortress, surely," Carol concurred.

"We'd better hustle then, folks," Jynx replied.

***

Against the wishes of the king, Boggs had disconnected the cloning machine. He had to let the Heart recover. Besides, after tonight, he would likely have to go into hiding—there was no way Richard wouldn't suspect him.

He gave the machine a final inspection, brushing away a spindly white feather from inside before locking it up. As he closed the shutter, a resounding blast rang out beneath his feet, shaking the floor.

"What was *that*?" yelled one of the guards from outside.

Boggs sighed. He knew all too well. "That wasn't the plan, Jynx," he whispered to himself.

He then marched outside, intercepting a small group of guards as they headed for the stairway down to the vault.

"Nothing to worry about, folks," he stated. "Just a little experiment of mine gone awry. Return to your posts, I'll deal with this."

"Yes, sir," their sergeant replied smartly and turned to leave.

***

The inside of the vault seemed to glow from the huge mounds of gold held within. As we walked in, almost in a trance, I could see most of it was in the form of coins and jewellery, but there were also several magnificent statues and a ruby-encrusted throne which, oddly, seemed far too small for the king. There were also piles of silver cutlery and glittering jewels of all colours. The vault stretched for an incredible distance and was filled from floor to ceiling with riches. It was a hoard of wealth the likes of which I could never have imagined—and yet it had all been tossed carelessly into huge mounds as if worthless. At the far end stood a marble pedestal upon which sat a small glass slide connected to a web of thick, black cables.

"*Luca!*" Robyn cried.

She ran over to the pedestal and lifted the slide, holding it up to the light to see a familiar, bluish-green smear. A glow pulsed from within, but it was extremely faint.

"So, this is the Heart," remarked Carol.

"It's so *little*," Jynx added. "Let me see."

Robyn obliged and handed Luca to Jynx.

"You should go," I said. "Fly the Heart out of here. That way, we can break out Benjamin without risking Luca."

"Wait, do it *without* her?" asked Robyn in a panicked whisper.

"Don't you worry, sweetie," Jynx said," I'm not going anywhere. If I don't protect you, this little piece of glass won't be no good to anyone. And I don't suppose I can convince you to leave your friend behind. The dungeon's the next level down."

Robyn offered a grateful smile in response. Carol stopped for a moment and gazed at the mounds of treasure.

"That's a lot of gold," she said in admiration.

"A mountain of gold while the people starve," Jynx replied. "It don't seem right, does it?"

"No, it doesn't. Not in the least."

Even I was initially in awe of the king's riches. The great feast in the citadel was one of the best evenings of my life but, when painted in contrast with the struggle we had seen in Romer's Town, it seemed somewhat obscene. I felt like I could relate to those miners as much as any other creature in this world. As a creation of Robyn's, they were like me—those were my people.

"*The vault has been breached!*" came a booming call from outside.

"Dang it," hissed Jynx. "We've got company."

Robyn's leg began to shake as the sound of footsteps approached. Each step was accompanied by the tell-tale *click* of a sickle claw on stone. Raptors. I whipped my head from side to side in search of a hiding place.

"We should *bury* ourselves," Robyn whispered.

It was a pretty good idea. We all plunged into separate piles of gold, digging into them as quickly as we could. The gold clattered and jangled as I dug my forepaws in and tossed it behind me. Once inside the golden mound, I froze, barely daring to breathe.

Through the slightest of gaps between the coins, bars, and goblets, I could make out two feathered raptors as they entered the vault.

"The Heart," one barked. "It's *gone*."

"Damn," replied the other. "We should have been here."

"The general's going to gut us like pigs."

"Not if we gut the thief first. They can't have gone far; the lift is still here."

"You think the thief's still in the vault?"

He took a deep inhale through his nose before baring his teeth in a wicked grin.

"*Thieves*. And they're still here, all right."

"In the gold?"

"In the gold."

Using their clawed hands, they began slashing at the piles of treasure, tearing through them with frightening speed. They wouldn't take long to find us at this rate. In my haste, I hadn't noticed where the others had hidden. They could have been anywhere, and they could be uncovered at any moment.

Then, a scream. Robyn was the first to be unearthed from beneath the gold. The raptor gripped her by the forearm and launched her across the vault. She whelped as she thumped onto the floor.

"Where is the Heart?" the raptor snarled.

"I-I don't know what you mean," she squeaked.

In a hail of treasure, I burst from my hiding place and roared at the guards.

"Get away from her!"

Carol followed suit, erupting from behind the raptors and lobbing a heavy silver cup at a guard's head. He didn't flinch as it bounced off his snout.

"Looks like we have accomplices," he sneered. "Any more of you?"

"Just one more," announced Jynx from by the door.

We all turned to see the little feathered dinosaur wielding two sticks of dynamite, the fuses fizzing on each.

"Wait, Jynx—" I pleaded.

Ignoring my protest, she tossed them.

"Move!" I yelled.

The three of us dove back into the piles of treasure as, with a remarkable level of accuracy, a stick landed between the legs of each raptor. Their eyes widened as they looked down and then towards each other.

The explosions were devastating. Coins and jewels were launched around the vault like hail in every direction. We all cowered with our hands over our heads as we were pelted with treasure. My ears rang from the shockwave. I looked back to see that one such unidentified missile had punched a hole through my sail.

"Ah, that's going to sting," I groaned.

"Is everybody okay?" called Carol.

"I'm fine," replied Robyn.

"I'll live," I added.

Where the raptors had stood was now a blackened crater with no sign of the guards.

"Are… are they dead?" asked Carol.

Jynx looked at the blacked craters, where only a few feathers remained of the two guards.

"What am I, a doctor?" she replied with a shrug.

"What is going on here?" hissed Boggs from the doorway, gazing at the destruction we had caused.

"Speak of the devil," replied Jynx. "We had a few complications. I sorted them out."

"With explosives, I see. You were supposed to wait for me."

"Oh, yeah. Why was that again?"

"Because I have the *key*!"

Boggs dangled a large bronze key in front of Jynx. This, presumably, opened the security door and negated the need for blowing the living coprolite out of the vault.

"That *would* have made things easier," concurred Carol.

"Yes, and now half the fortress will have heard you. What are *you* three even doing here?"

"We decided to come and save Benjamin," I replied.

Boggs dragged his massive claws down his cheeks and groaned loudly.

"Why did we even bother to make a plan? Get out of here before someone else comes to check out all the commotion."

Surely enough, we heard more voices from along the corridor.

"Go, *now*," Boggs hissed. "I'll buy you some time."

Robyn nodded anxiously before we fled into the elevator. Jynx pulled the lever and the platform shuddered further downwards. As we reached the lower level, we were immediately hit with a pungent odour. It stank of sweat and animal waste. It was dark, but once my eyes had adjusted to the gloom, I could see an almost endless row of barred prison cells along a cramped and narrow passageway. We crept silently out of the elevator, Jynx glancing around.

"No guards?" she whispered. "What a bunch of knuckleheads."

I didn't entirely share Jynx's optimism—it seemed too good to be true that there wasn't a single guard in sight.

We walked along between the cells and gazed at the myriad of prisoners. An enormous elephant with long, straight tusks and a pronounced forehead lay on its side. With visible ribs and spine and laboured breathing, it was clearly starving. It was a *Palaeoloxodon namadicus*—possibly the largest land mammal of all time. Yet the majestic giant had been reduced to little more than skin and bone.

In a similar condition in the next cell lay a large, muscular cat with long, sword-like teeth. The famous sabre-toothed cat *Smilodon*. It admittedly looked a little healthier than its proboscid neighbour—perhaps it hadn't been incarcerated for as long as the elephant. Its copper-coloured coat was glossy and dappled with dark spots.

Many more creatures had been locked away and seemingly forgotten—a large, stocky kangaroo, a huge orangutan, a beaver as large as a panda. As I walked past cell after cell, I realised what these poor creatures all had in common—they were mammals. This was where the king had sent them all to rot.

"I recognise these mammals," Jynx whispered.

"You do?" I asked.

"They're Stromer's old crew."

"We should spring them too," said Robyn.

"One thing at a time."

Eventually, we came across the slight, dog-like marsupial we sought.

"Benjamin!" Robyn cried.

Benjamin raised his head and gazed blearily at his visitors. His eyes widened upon recognising us.

"Aw, all right, mates?" he said cheerfully, leaping to his feet. "What's the John Dory?"

I hushed them both.

"Quiet," I hissed. "The guards won't be far away."

"Oh, Benjamin," Robyn whispered. "I'm so sorry you ended up here, and that it took us so long to come. We're getting you out."

"*Awesome*. And don't worry about it. I've met new friends here—and I've really learned to appreciate the simple pleasure of bread and water. Even the smell isn't too bad once you get used to it."

"Always looking on the bright side," I said with a smile.

"Let's get you out of here," Robyn said, beaming.

"Uh, how?" I asked, looking at the thick, iron bars and padlocked door. "That door looks pretty strong."

"Can you break the lock?" she asked me.

I clamped my jaws around the padlock and tugged at it with all my strength before shaking my head in disappointment. The lock didn't budge.

"It's too strong," I admitted.

"Yeah, I doubt you could break it," Benjamin confirmed. "There's a woolly rhino sheila over there who tried for days to break her door down. If she couldn't do it, I don't reckon anyone could."

"Maybe we could blow the door off?" Robyn suggested, gesturing towards Jynx.

"I don't just carry around extra sticks of dynamite, you know," Jynx said. "Well, actually, I usually do, but I used up the last of it on those spicy chickens upstairs. I'll bet you a shilling I could pick that lock, though."

Jynx set about inserting her long, thin claw into the keyhole of the large, iron padlock which hung from the door. Her tongue emerged from the side of her mouth and her eyes narrowed in concentration. It only took a few minutes, but time was precious, and it seemed like an age.

"Ah *ha*," Jynx whispered as the padlock finally pinged open.

However, as it opened, the padlock popped out of its latch and fell to the floor. The clang of metal on the stone floor resonated throughout the silent dungeon. We all gasped and stood perfectly still, listening for any indication that the sound had alerted the guards.

The sound we had been dreading soon followed—the thudding of footsteps. The torches which lit the dungeon all extinguished themselves simultaneously, plunging us into darkness.

"Oh, boy," Jynx whispered. "I think I've gone done and picked a whole bouquet of whoopsie daisies."

Etheldred the Bloodthirsty

Many years before the Architect's arrival, in the Gondwanan forest, a pair of shadows loomed over a vulnerable clutch of pastel-blue eggs nestled within a bed of damp fern leaves. Casting the shadows were large, carnivorous, theropod dinosaurs who stood balanced on their hind legs. From snout to tail, they were covered in simple, brown, hair-like feathers, and they sported tall, V-shaped crests on their heads. One had dull, grey crests while the other's were a striking shade of blue. Their long arms hung below them, tipped with sharp claws—a sharpness only matched by the teeth in their jaws. Yet despite their fearsome appearance, this was little more than a young couple about to start a family.

"Honey, it's time," announced the father with the blue crests.

Surely enough, two of the five eggs had begun to wobble from side to side, and the rest soon followed suit. The soft, leathery shell of one soon bulged outwards, causing the harder outer casing to crack. After several pushes, a tiny snout popped through into the world.

The father reached down and gently helped peel away a section of shell to reveal his first-born daughter. "Hello there, little one," he announced.

The baby dinosaur chirped as she took her first breath of fresh air. She stared intently at her mother—imprinting on her and building an instant, powerful bond.

"Momma?" she cried, bouncing excitedly.

"Yes, precious, I *am* your momma."

The chick shook herself to fluff out her matted brown feathers and turned to her father.

"Papa?"

"Yes, precious," he replied with a smile. "I'm your papa."

"Oh, darling, she's *perfect*," the mother exclaimed.

Over the next hour, three more eggs hatched, and three more perfect babies were born—two females and two males in total. However, there was some concern over the last egg which, even three hours after the rest had completely emerged, hadn't even cracked its shell.

"Do you think something's wrong?" the mother suggested.

"I'm sure it's nothing to worry about," the father replied. "Sometimes one just takes a little longer.

Many hours later, the shell of the fifth egg finally began to show signs of movement. It bulged slowly and cracked the outer shell, as the others had. The father peeled away the loose shell to reveal another tiny snout. This one, however, was rather different—it was strikingly pale. As the chick emerged, it became clear that she was entirely white with disconcerting red eyes which almost seemed to glow.

"Oh, my," gasped the mother. "What's wrong with her?"

"I... I don't know. A different colour morph, I guess."

"A colour morph? Look at her eyes. She looks like a ... like a *demon*."

"She's not a demon."

"Perhaps not, but she's not *normal* either."

"What should we do?"

The tiny, pale *Dilophosaurus* chick gazed up at her mother, attempting to imprint with the powerful emotional connection as the others.

"Momma?" the baby chirped.

The mother glared at the latecomer with narrowed eyes for several long seconds.

"No," she stated coldly. "No, I am *not*."

The new chick's tail drooped, and her arms curled into her chest.

"Papa?" she asked.

The father glanced at his partner, looking for guidance. She responded with a shake of her head. He sighed and hung his head low.

"No," he replied. "No, I'm not your papa. I'm sorry, little one."

The new parents scooped their eldest four children from their nest. The mother marched away swiftly, but the father looked back. His eyes were full of doubt, but acceptance, before he, too, disappeared into the forest.

***

Over the following weeks, the white chick roamed the forest in search of parents. She asked every animal she passed, "*Momma?*" Some answered that they weren't, before hurrying away from the unsightly child. Others growled at her, scolded her, and some even tried to eat her. It took many months, but the youngster soon came to accept that she had no parents.

Her frustration grew as she wandered through the primordial forest. She was hungry, but no one had ever shown her what to eat, or how to find it. She chewed on tree bark, leaves, and even soil, all in the hope of stifling her gnawing hunger, but nothing stayed down.

"Hey, kid," came a call through the trees.

The chick turned to see a tall, fat bird with a naked, grey head and ridiculously tiny wings waddling through the undergrowth.

"Hey, you," the bird continued. "Are you lost?"

"I don't know."

"What do mean, you don't know? Do you know where you are or not?"

"I don't."

"Well, you're lost then, aren't you? What are you anyway? I'm a dodo."

"I don't know."

"You don't know much, do you? Well, I'm Etheldred. I've just turned three months old, which means I can leave the nest now. Pretty neat, huh? What's your name?"

"I..." The chick paused, not wanting to admit that she didn't know this either. "My name is Etheldred too."

"You sure? It's a pretty uncommon name."

"Yes. And... and *I'm* a dodo too."

Etheldred the dodo laughed.

"No, you're not. I don't know *what* you are. You're freaky looking, anyway, but definitely not a dodo."

The chick looked at her own hands and flexed her fingers.

"I am?"

"Oh, yeah. That white fluff, and those eyes. *Creepy.*"

"I'm creepy?"

"You bet. What's wrong with you anyway? Are you some kind of freak?"

"I'm not a freak," the chick protested, raising her voice.

"You sort of are."

"I'm not a *freak*," she shrieked, puffing her feathers out to appear larger.

"Whoa there, don't get in such a fuss, freak."

The chick, no more than half as tall as the dodo, stepped forwards and swiped her foot with a sharp claw.

"Don't call me that!"

"What the..." The dodo thumped the small chick with her black-clawed foot, causing her to soar across the forest floor and slam into a tree trunk. She approached and loomed over the little *Dilophosaurus*. "You're more than a freak, you're an *abomination*."

The chick lay winded on the ground, gasping for air. Unable to move and watching her attacker pace into the forest without justice, she felt a swelling of rage. It began to burn, as though her skin were ablaze. On that forest floor, she cried out for help which never came.

Once able to climb to her feet, she grumbled to herself.

"Never again."

***

Smoke filled the forest as the heat intensified. Flames climbed the scale trees and screams echoed through the undergrowth. Two *Dilophosauruses* fled through the burning jungle.

"What's going on?" someone called through the smoke.

The theropods turned to face the source but were unable to see.

"It's an uprising," the blue-crested male replied. "Richard has overthrown King Gideon."

"We're heading to the clearing, away from the fire," the female added. "We can protect our family there. You should come too."

"How kind," the stranger replied.

The owner of the mystery voice began to break through the smoke as she approached—a theropod with large crests upon her head, brilliant white plumage, and fiery red eyes which glinted in the flickering inferno.

"But I'm afraid I have no family to protect."

"No," the mother gasped. "It *can't* be."

"Tell me, have you heard the story of the ugly duckling?" Etheldred hissed.

The parents nodded while nervously backing away from the now grown child they had once abandoned.

"The ugly duckling was shunned for its appearance and lived a life of persecution and solitude. Do you know what happened next?"

"It… it," the father stuttered. "It turned into a…"

"A swan? *No.* It grew into a hawk and *eviscerated* them."

With a snarl, Etheldred lunged at her parents, claws extended and teeth bared. The screams could be heard even over the ensuing mayhem, as Pangaea's newly appointed general exacted her revenge. The furnace of rage within her began to dim, but for only a moment. She had imagined it would subside, that her skin would finally no longer feel ablaze with hatred, but it didn't.

Still she seethed. Still she hated. Still she thirsted for blood.

Horror in the Dungeon

"Into the cell," Jynx hissed.

Obediently, we all clambered inside Benjamin's cell, hoping to be hidden by the darkness. A sickening cackle began to ring out, echoing off the walls, followed by a coarse voice which I recognised to be the ruthless albino *Dilophosaurus* from the forest—General Etheldred.

"The *Architect*," she rasped. "I've been waiting for you. You were foolish to come here."

"What do we do?" Robyn whispered.

I could feel her hands trembling as she clutched at my ankle. I didn't have an answer for her—I had no idea how to get out of this one.

"You think you can hide, but I can *smell* you," Etheldred continued. "The stench of the others is thick, but I can still pick you out."

She took a deep breath in as she sampled the air. Her heavy footsteps beat down on the stone floor, growing closer. I could hear a repetitive metallic clinking which I assumed to be her claws being dragged along the bars.

"The smell of the Architect is truly an unnatural one."

We cowered together, barely daring to breathe for fear of alerting her to our location. I prayed she was bluffing; that couldn't truly track us through the darkness by scent alone.

"There are some," Etheldred hissed, her echoing voice impossible to locate, "who believe this world is tied to the Architect, that her death will bring about the end of days. If she dies, we all die. I don't know if it's true—but I am eager to find out."

She took one more long, wheezing breath. We cowered in the darkness, hoping she wouldn't be able to find us in the shadows, praying for an opportunity to escape. Her rasping voice seemed to be everywhere at once.

"I hear what they say about me. Their whispers reach my ears just as clearly as their screams. They think I loathe the mammals. They think I exterminate them out of hatred, but I don't hate them."

There was a pause before the torches burst back into life, instantly illuminating the pale, scarred, and wretched *Dilophosaurus*. She was *inside* the cell, standing directly over us, the glare of her red eyes burning in the torchlight.

"I do it for the *blood*," she snarled.

All four of us screamed as the bedraggled dinosaur lunged for the kill. She latched onto Robyn's leg and shook her viciously. With a swift kick to the head, Robyn broke free, but not without sustaining a nasty ankle injury. She scrambled back against the wall, eyes pinned to the general. Etheldred lunged once more.

I had to do something.

I leapt between the two and immediately felt the general's jaws clamp around my neck. She bit hard and her teeth sank through my skin. I whelped in pain as she tossed me to the side, but I returned the favour with a swift tail-whip to her face. Etheldred seemed to be momentarily stunned. Not physically, but psychologically—surprised that someone had stood up to her. The wry smile spreading across her face revealed a disturbing relish for the fight.

"I do *love* it when they struggle."

Robyn limped for the cell door and shoved it open, through which we all fled. We turned and made a break for the elevator, only to find the way shut. A gate of solid iron bars had been closed across the passageway. I turned back to see Etheldred emerging from Benjamin's cell, a sickening grin across her face and thick slops of saliva dripping from her jaws.

"What *now*?" asked Robyn, her voice shaking.

I snarled in response, indicating that I was ready for a fight. Sure, Etheldred was huge and mean, but I was no teddy bear myself—I could take her. I was the apex predator of the Permian Period.

"Don't be a knucklehead," snapped Jynx. "They call her Bloodthirsty for a reason—you wouldn't last a second."

"Do you have any better suggestions?" I retorted.

"As a matter of fact, I do. Robyn, you're the *Architect*. You can make this any way you want it to be. Right now would be a pretty good time for you to figure out how to do that."

Robyn scrunched her face sceptically. Nonetheless, she focused her attention and strained. Anxiously awaiting Robyn's intervention, I watched as Etheldred padded closer with menacing intent. And yet, nothing.

"I don't think it's working," Robyn yelped in panic.

With an unsettling snarl, Etheldred hurled herself along the corridor towards us. Her muscular body, covered in wiry-white proto-feathers, barrelled forwards with frightening speed.

"I think the time for plan B might be up," I said, as I prepared myself for the inevitable battle.

"No," Robyn replied defiantly. "*No!*" With that, she screamed out, tensing every muscle in her body.

Etheldred began to slow as she noticed the padlocks on the cell doors vibrating violently. The sound of rattling iron quickly swelled, like a thousand bells ringing at once.

With a bang, one padlock exploded, showering its innards across the corridor before clunking onto the floor. One by one, all the other locks followed suit, sending bright sparks into the air each time. The corridor was illuminated by the crossfire of sparking padlocks. Metal pinged and clattered, and the newly unlocked cell doors creaked.

There is a saying amongst you humans about opening a can of worms. This is a metaphor for committing an action which then creates some manner of chaos. This is a terrible metaphor since, if you were to actually open a can of worms, they would likely just sit there wriggling as worms tend to do. Therefore, what Robyn did wasn't at all like opening a can of worms, but rather like opening a can of angry, grenade-wielding ferrets.

Dozens of prisoners of all sizes and species burst from their confinement. Once out of their cells, it seemed to take a moment for them to appreciate their newfound freedom, but they quickly turned their ire towards their captor.

I stood tall and stared into Etheldred's eyes. Perhaps Jynx was right—a straight fight may have been foolish, but now I had newfound allies. The sabre-toothed *Smilodon* leapt out of the cell to my right and stood by my side. We gave each other a knowing nod and charged together at the general.

Outnumbered, I expected Etheldred to run, but instead she charged right back. With a great roar, the *Smilodon* pounced at her, his vast, muscular frame straining beneath his dappled fur. He landed a powerful, two-pawed blow onto the general's head. She quickly retaliated, snapped her jaws around his forelimb, and tossed him to the side. I then barrelled into her flank, ramming her with my head and knocking her over. While she briefly lay there, I bit hard on her leg, my sharp teeth piercing her pale skin.

Soon, a sea of fur was surging onto the general—weasels, cats, wombats, monkeys—all biting and clawing at her feathered hide in an intoxicating flurry of rage. The sabre-tooth rose to his feet once more and stood over her. He reared his head back and drove his fearsome canine teeth into her shoulder.

But Etheldred wasn't defeated. With a scream of rage, she kicked me in the face with her free foot, forcing me to release my grip on her leg. With impossible strength, she hauled herself to her feet, shaking the mob of attackers off. With the sabre-tooth's great fangs still embedded in her shoulder, she slammed the cat into the metal bars of the nearest cell. The *Smilodon*'s canines shattered upon impact and he fell, fangless and dazed, onto the stone floor. The *Dilophosaurus* turned to me, injured and bleeding but dangerous, nonetheless. Indeed, not only did her injuries not seem to slow her, she cackled loudly. She really did enjoy the hunt.

"You are almost worthy opponents."

I turned to face her side-on. I whipped my tail towards her—a tactic which had worked well a moment ago—but she had grown wise to it. With a snap of her jaws, she grabbed my tail and bit. I yelped and tried to scramble away, but she only bit tighter. With a vicious shake of her head, I felt a crunch in my tail followed by an agonising tear. I looked back in horror to see the tip of my tail now dangling from General Etheldred's grinning maw.

With a crash, a famished but nonetheless enormous woolly rhinoceros charged out of its cell, trampling one of its fellow prisoners in its haste. It wasn't clear if it had intentionally attacked its own, or if it was simply blinded by rage. It roared before charging towards us. The beast filled the corridor and, to avoid being collateral damage, I dove into another of the open cells. Scanning the corridor, I breathed a sigh of relief to see that Robyn, Carol, and Benjamin had done the same into the opposite cell.

Etheldred turned and fled, seemingly unhampered by her injured leg. As she reached the gate, she bit onto a long rope which hung from the ceiling and tugged at it fiercely. This resulted in a loud bell ringing out from somewhere above—another alarm.

"We've got to get out of here," called Jynx.

"I can't say I have the urge to stay," Carol agreed.

Etheldred frantically attempted to unlock the gate. What had been intended as a trap for us now prevented her own escape. She was too late. The enraged rhino slammed into her and sent both of them crashing through. The general scrambled to her feet and fled. She paused for the slightest of moments at the opening to the elevator before glancing back at the vast, horned beast. Evidently, she didn't have time to operate the machinery before being gored, so she chose to dart along a nearby passageway instead.

Alongside a swarm of escaped mammals, we took our chances and made a break for the elevator, clambering over the bent and twisted remains of the iron gate. Despite the elevator platform being extremely large, we barely all fit. The lever was pulled, I couldn't see who by, and the chains began to haul the platform upwards. It was agonisingly slow—partly because of the weight, partly because we so needed it to hurry.

I curled the remainder of my tail and winced at the sight of its bloody stump. Robyn dropped to her knees and placed her hand above the injury.

"Oh, *Ed*."

"I'm okay," I replied, despite the tell-tale tremor in my voice. "Let's just get out of this place."

The Wrath of the King

When we reached the courtyard, we found it to be surprisingly quiet. Night had fallen, and only a few flaming torches lit the grounds. The bells continued to ring out, but there was no sign of any security. Relieved, we sprinted out and turned towards the main gate at the tail of the vast sauropod.

On the beach below, I could see that the battle between the raptors had moved out of the fortress, but it raged on nevertheless—the pterosaurs now aiding in that particular fight.

We made a break for the gate but had to halt as two great shadows rose from the *Breviparopus*'s tail. The familiar silhouettes of Sir Barnum and Lord Gigas, illuminated on either side by two flaming vats of tar, emerged through the gate. They parted and, through the gap between them, marched the king, hauling himself on all fours and dragging his tail.

"You should have gone home, child," Richard growled at Robyn.

"This can't be good," I said.

"I have ruled these lands for *aeons*," the king continued. "Did you really think I would let you take it all away?"

"I never wanted to take anything," Robyn protested. "I just wanted to help my mum."

"*Liar!*" he roared. "You take me for a *fool*? You sought to overthrow me, but you have failed."

"I don't know how good your maths is, mate," piped up Benjamin. "But I reckon you're fair dinkum outnumbered here."

Cheers erupted from the angry crowd of mammals behind us, each one baying for the king's blood. Their confidence was quickly checked as a sickening cackle leaked from Gigas's mouth.

"They think they're a match for us," he snarled.

Richard coughed hard for several seconds before spitting out a large ball of green phlegm. "Lord Gigas," he burbled. "Show them the error of their ways."

Gigas padded forwards. I noticed he now had only pink scar tissue where his left eye had once been—courtesy of Stromer's claw. Unfortunately, the injury had only made him meaner and, without a hint of hesitation, he snapped his jaws into the crowd. One by one, he crushed the mammals in his monstrous jaws. Several were thrown high into the air and off the ramparts, falling to the beach below.

Gigas was enormous and immensely powerful—none of the escapees had any hope of defending themselves. For the tyrannosaur, this was little more than sport. The crowd began to panic and scatter, creatures great and small attempted to flee but had nowhere to go. Screams filled the courtyard as Gigas continued to pick the prisoners off.

"Jynx, take the Heart," Robyn yelled, thrusting the glass slide into the *Archaeopteryx*'s hands. "Fly it away."

Jynx nodded somewhat reluctantly. She grasped Luca and leapt into the air, spreading her wings and performing several powerful wingbeats. But she wasn't fast enough. A large pterosaur speared through the air and pounded into Jynx, sending her back to the courtyard floor and launching the Heart skywards. A second pterosaur, a white, bird-like creature with fur-like feathering, swooped and grabbed Luca in its beak. I watched in agony as Luca was delivered straight into the outstretched hand of Sir Barnum.

"*Luca!*" I shrieked.

"Robyn, you have to run," Carol commanded.

"No, I have to help them," she argued. "I'm not running away anymore. I *always* run away."

"What are you going to do? Fight a *dinosaur*? They need you safe, Robyn. You need to be away from here to help any of them."

"She's right," Jynx groaned, climbing back to her feet. "We can't win this fight. You need to go."

Robyn let out a long exhale as she accepted that they were right.

"Then we get everyone else out of here too."

I nodded in approval.

"We still have the numbers," I said. "We can rush the gate if we all work together."

"Everyone, make a break for the gates!" Carol called out.

Jynx took to the sky once more, swooping above the panicking crowd. "Charge the gates!" she cried. "Follow the Architect."

The remaining crowd, desperate for an escape from the rampaging tyrannosaur, heeded this instruction and poured towards the gate. Unfortunately, it seemed King Richard had planned for this. He grasped one of the vats of burning tar and, with a hateful snarl, heaved it to the ground. A great sea of fire burst over the courtyard. The wall of flame rose between us and the gate, trapping us.

"What *now*?" I gasped.

"All right, let's not panic, mates," said Benjamin. "We just need some water."

"Do you *see* any water, Benjamin?" I yelled.

"Ah, a fair point. Maybe we could—"

Before he could finish, the great, black jaws of Gigas appeared from above and closed around Benjamin's back. The beast bit with a crunch and the marsupial's limbs fell limp. With a swing of Gigas's head, Benjamin was tossed against the courtyard wall. He impacted with a sickening thud and slumped onto the ground.

"*No!*" Robyn screamed.

I rushed to Benjamin's side, immediately guilty that my last words to him had been so aggravated.

"Oh, Benjamin," I whimpered. "Oh, no, no, *no*."

With the *Tyrannosaurus* still looming over us, I waited for his inevitable strike. But I wasn't going down without a fight. I knew I didn't stand a chance. I knew he would kill me anyway, but I wasn't going to make it easy for him. I stood, planted my feet firmly, and growled at the towering theropod.

"Your amateur coup is over," Gigas hissed with a grin.

But then, with a great roar, an enormous, four-legged colossus plummeted from the clifftop above—a vast reptile with a horn upon the end of its nose. It landed atop Gigas, causing the great lord to crumple into the ground.

"*Gideon!*" screamed Jynx, the elation in her voice unmistakable.

"*You!*" roared Richard from beyond the flames.

"Is that all you have to say to your long-lost brother?" Gideon replied. "Aren't you surprised to see me?"

"Brother?" Robyn whispered into my ear.

"Disappointed," Richard replied, "but not so surprised. I knew you'd crawl out of your cave one day."

"I figured the time was right to return Pangaea to the people."

"Pangaea is *mine*."

The muscular silhouette of King Richard heaved the second vat of tar over, and yet more flames tore across the courtyard. We found ourselves trapped between two raging walls of fire. The heat was searing as flames closed in all around.

Gigas, still on the ground, was engulfed, the blaze climbing onto his side and igniting his scruffy feathers. He roared, standing tall and fleeing from the wall of fire before rolling around on the courtyard floor in an effort to put out the flames.

The burning liquid seeped ever closer to us as the fire closed in on both sides. Overwhelmed by the soaring temperature, I cowered as the blaze inched towards me. I could see Robyn's shorts begin to crisp and blister as they were licked by the flames. Those in the crowd began to sob as their fate seemed increasingly clear. Carol grabbed onto Robyn and hugged her tightly.

"I'm sorry," Robyn sobbed.

"Don't you *dare* be sorry," Carol replied. "I love you, honey."

"I just wanted to save you."

"You still can," called Jynx from above. "Like with the padlocks. Remember, Pangaea is *yours*."

Through the crowd, Gideon approached and pressed his colossal, horned, lizard-like face against Robyn's forehead.

"She's right, dear child. Now is the time, Architect. *Now is your moment. Be* who you *are.*"

"You can do it," I added. "The locks—*you* did that. You can get us out of this."

With tears streaming down her face and evaporating in the heat, she nodded. She looked around, desperately searching for a solution. I could see her panic until her face relaxed and her eyes widened. I knew that face—she had a plan. Robyn clenched her eyes shut.

"Water," she whispered. "Benjamin said we needed water."

There was silence for a moment. The world seemed to pass in slow motion. Flames crackled and licked at our faces while orange embers drifted through the smoke-filled air—and then came the rain. Only a few drops at first but, within a seconds, it became a torrential downpour with raindrops the size of golf balls. The tar hissed as the falling droplets burst into jets of steam on impact. The flames quickly sizzled and died.

Richard's eyes widened with rage, the remaining flickers of flame reflecting brightly in his gaze. Behind me, Gigas had extinguished himself and stood over us once more. Half of his body was now featherless and blistered, oozing blood.

"Barnum, Gigas, *finish* them," Richard roared impatiently.

It hadn't been clear to me why Sir Barnum hadn't joined Gigas in the first instance. I thought the king simply deemed two tyrannosaurs unnecessary, but the true reason became apparent as I looked into Barnum's eyes. Despite clearly being fiercely loyal, he hesitated, staring at the cowering crowd. Barnum was a warrior, a knight, and while he had committed some wicked acts at the behest of his master, I could tell he lived by honour. I saw it in his face—what Richard requested of him conflicted with his personal code.

"Sire, perhaps returning them to their cells would be more appropriate," he suggested. "We have them quelled."

"You dare to *question* me?"

Barnum paused and flared his nostrils in frustration.

"Of course not, Your Majesty," he conceded without conviction.

He strode forwards, standing tall above Robyn and staring deep into her eyes. With a frustrated growl, he stepped over us and lunged at Lord Gigas. Gigas's demeanour changed in an instant. He had been comfortable picking off his weak prey one by one. Even having been injured, he looked like he relished the opportunity to continue the massacre.

But Barnum? Barnum wasn't prey. He was an opponent—a powerful opponent. Gigas panicked and bit onto Barnum's helmet, but the knight quickly slipped from his grip and clamped his jaws around the back of Gigas's neck. He dragged the lord towards the far wall of the courtyard and heaved him over the top. There was silence for several seconds before I heard the deep *thump* of Gigas landing on the beach below. The fall was long, and the tyrannosaur was heavy; he was surely dead. It was remarkable how quickly the fight was over—Barnum had taken only seconds to overpower his former partner.

The king's rage turned to fear. His eyes widened and he glanced around nervously. Not only had the Architect mastered her abilities, but his strongest gladiator had betrayed him. He glanced behind him, down at the beach, to find his legions of raptors gone, left behind by the forging sauropod.

"Surrender, Richard!" Gideon bellowed. "You're all out of allies."

"I'd sooner *die*," the king snarled.

Gideon emitted a deep growl from within his belly. "So be it."

The two beasts were vast—even compared to the tyrannosaurs. They charged at one another, colliding with a colossal thud which sent shockwaves through their flesh. Both rose onto their hind legs and flailed at each other with giant, clawed paws. Gideon returned to all fours first, allowing Richard to clamp his long jaws around the back of his neck. The *Iguanodon* retaliated by thrusting his nose-horn upwards into the king's chest and tossing him high.

The ruler of Pangaea crashed onto the courtyard floor and rolled over twice.

"You took *everything* from me!" Gideon roared.

Richard lay there for several long moments, gasping for air. While he was undoubtedly strong, he was showing his age. However, as Gideon approached, panting and slow, it was clear the old hermit was feeling his age just as acutely.

"I only took what you lost on your own," Richard snarled. "Pangaea had already turned on you. I gave them what they wanted."

"And what did they want? To starve? To labour in mine shafts? To be exiled from their homeland?"

The *Megalosaurus* hauled himself to his feet with a groan.

"They wanted progress—to be more than hunters or farmers. They wanted to aspire."

"At what cost?"

"At *any* cost."

"And that's why you were never fit to be king," Gideon growled at his old foe.

They charged once more, but with significantly less enthusiasm. They remained on all fours this time, pushing and pawing at each other.

I gazed up at the dominating mass of Barnum beside us. It wasn't clear to me whose side he was on, and it seemed it wasn't clear to him either.

"Help Gideon," I pleaded. "You know Richard won't forgive what you did—you've chosen a side."

He looked uncomfortable at the prospect. "I protected the citizens, that's all. This isn't my fight."

"But it's the *right* thing to do," Robyn protested.

"*Is* it?" he snapped. "You don't know that, kid. This is between them."

While the behemoths were still lethargic in their attacks, the intensity had increased. The king seemed to be gaining the upper hand, gripping Gideon's face in his jaws and pinning him to the ground. The vast mass of battling reptiles stumbled towards us, causing the crowd to scatter.

"He needs help," Carol cried. "*Someone!*"

As I looked around, it was clear why no one answered the call. The few mammals who hadn't been dispatched by Gigas were nursing injuries, and most were far too small in stature to possibly affect a clash between such leviathans.

"They're not strong enough," I replied. "They'd be trampled before they even got close."

I glanced towards Robyn. She had a look in her eye, an oddly vacant stare which I recognised well. She was deep in thought.

"Robyn?"

"We need someone... *bigger*," she muttered.

I didn't understand until she turned and stared up the long neck of the *Breviparopus*. I replied with nothing more than a gentle nod.

"Jynx," she called.

The black-and-white *Archaeopteryx* swooped almost immediately.

"I need your lockpicking skills again," Robyn said.

"For what?"

Robyn gestured towards the head of the colossal sauropod. Jynx followed her gaze and then looked vacantly back at Robyn for a moment. Her eyebrows rose as she realised what the girl planned.

"Kid, you're insane," Jynx replied with a wry smile. "I like it."

With a powerful thrust of her wings, she launched off the ground and hurtled upwards towards the head of the long-necked giant. A lone *Pterodactylus* swooped for her again, but she was prepared this time and pirouetted out of the attacker's path. She soon disappeared—too far for me to tell her position in the darkness. However, it didn't take long for her handiwork to become apparent.

A huge, metallic *clunk* echoed off the cliff face. The chains which held the vast sauropod in captivity fell from its neck and landed on the beach with an immense clamour. The sauropod stopped for a moment, staring down at its broken chains. It was free but, for a few moments, it didn't seem to know what to do with that freedom. Finally, it bellowed a great, relieved roar and shook itself violently.

All around, stone by stone, the fortress began to crumble. The tower came down first, falling over the side, but with enough huge stones landing on the courtyard to cause real concern.

"This isn't what you had in mind, right?" I asked.

"Not quite," Robyn conceded.

"Everyone *run*," Carol yelled.

Richard was the first to heed this warning. He released Gideon from his jaws and fled through the gate and down the sauropod's great tail. Along with Gideon and the surviving mammals, we hurtled down the *Breviparopus*'s bumpy, armoured tail after the fleeing king. With crumbling bricks falling all around, we mercifully reached the wet sands of the beach below.

Richard turned and watched as his mighty fortress disintegrated.

"*You*," he snarled, his burning eyes fixed on Robyn.

He pounced towards her, only for Gideon to intercept him with a pounding shoulder charge. Richard rolled over before landing back on his feet. Once more, it was Gideon and Richard who faced off. They charged again for what was to be the final time.

Chicxulub

Unlike me, you are a mammal. Or, at least, I assume you are. And mammals have come to dominate the role of megafauna in the modern world, but have you ever considered how?

Mammals aren't new. They first appeared in all their furry, milky glory as far back as the Jurassic Period. They were mostly small burrowers and scavengers which eked out a meagre living under the shadow of their monstrous, reptilian overlords for tens of millions of years.

So, how did they emerge from this subservience? With a little help from the Chicxulub impactor—a space rock the size of Manhattan. Sixty-six million years ago, this asteroid struck the east coast of Mexico twenty times faster than a bullet. The atmosphere was set ablaze, the ground liquified, and sulphur was ejected into the skies. The giant dinosaurs, for all their grandeur, couldn't survive.

It was in this power vacuum that the mammals seized their opportunity. With their oppressors gone, they could rise to heights never before possible.

Because often, to build a new world, the old one must be destroyed.

Vengeance of the Oppressed

Richard gasped and limped away from another round of battle, spitting a mouthful of bloodied sand onto the ground. I wasn't sure if either of these giants would survive another clash. Nonetheless, Richard gritted his teeth and dug his feet into the sand, preparing to charge. However, he instead relaxed his stance and gazed upwards, his eyes wide and jaw hanging slack.

The ground quaked as the *Breviparopus* turned to face us. From such a height, it wasn't clear on whom its tiny eyes were focused, but I was willing to bet it recognised its captor. A deafening rumble began to emanate from the giant's stomach, which then seemed to rise up the creature's incredibly long neck.

"No," Richard gasped.

"Is it...?" began Carol.

"No *way*," I added.

"Uh, we should move," concluded Robyn.

We scrambled to be as far as possible from Richard, who was himself frozen to the spot. He seemed to make no effort to avoid his fate and, after a twitch of his head, his neck twisted upwards in an unnatural fashion, as though he were powerless to stop himself. He groaned as his head seemed to lock into place.

"He's stargazing," explained Barnum.

"He's what?" I replied.

"A seizure of sorts. A symptom of his illness."

The vast sauropod opened its mouth and retched. An elephant-sized glob of yellowish, lumpy vomit was released from the height of a tall building. The paralysed Richard could only watch as it hurtled down on him. It pounded into the sand, driving the king deep into the beach and exploding into a huge crater of vomit and sand. I could no longer see Richard, but he was most certainly gone, pummelled deep into the earth.

We stood in quiet shock for several moments as the *Breviparopus* turned and strode away, shaking the earth with each beating footstep.

"Is… is he gone?" asked Jynx.

"He's gone," replied Gideon.

"The Heart had cured him," added Barnum. "Until he worked it too hard."

"His greed finally got the better of him," Jynx said. "I never thought I'd see the day. I almost thought he was invincible."

"Who knew a half-tonne of vomit was his weakness?" I said.

"You weren't joking about the sick thing, huh?" asked a bemused Carol.

"Nope," Robyn replied quietly, still taking in that fact herself.

Then came a mumble from the rubble. Robyn gasped as she spied the slight body of Benjamin lying amidst the devastation.

"Oh, no," I whispered to myself before darting to be by his side. "Oh, Benjamin."

"Ed," he croaked. "Tell my kids I love them."

A tear formed in my eye as I nodded.

"I will, I promise."

With one final gasp for air, Benjamin fell limp.

"No!" Robyn cried.

Benjamin's abdomen began to convulse. At first, I thought this to be some kind of post-mortem seizure. However, after a moment, a recognised it for what it truly was: laughter.

"You idiot!" I yelled as Benjamin begin to giggle more loudly. "I should kill you myself!"

"Benjamin!" Robyn squealed.

She scooped him into a tight hug.

"Easy, tiger," he protested, clearly still in some actual pain. "I'm not dead, but that did hurt quite a bit."

She eased him onto the ground and began to ruffle his head like a dog instead.

"We thought you were dead," I moaned.

"Yeah, nah, only a little bit, mate," he replied with a smile. "The big drongo will have to do better than that."

"How are you not?" I asked, baffled at Benjamin's death defiance.

Before he could respond, the crowd of freed mammals began to gather around us.

"Where's our captain?" shouted someone from the crew.

"They don't know," I whispered.

"Everyone, he… he was with Mary when she—" Robyn began.

"I'm sorry," Jynx interjected. "They were taken by the sea."

She allowed a single tear to form in her eye before slumping to the ground. It seemed now that the job was over, she would finally allow herself to grieve.

"But without them, you wouldn't be free," announced Gideon, striding through the crowd and placing a vast claw onto Jynx's shoulder as a show of sympathy. "Not just from your cells, but from Richard himself. They made a great sacrifice."

The remaining crew members looked to the ground in silence.

"Be proud. They are the saviours of Pangaea," he continued. "Long live the queen."

Gideon bowed his head towards Robyn.

"*Oh*. Oh, no, no, no," Robyn replied frantically. "Get up."

"What do you mean, no?" I asked. "That's what the scripture said, right? Take the throne."

"I can't be queen," she hissed.

"Why not? Why not be queen?"

"I'd mess it up, Ed. I don't even have the guts to stand up to Hannah Owen. How could I ever be a queen? A queen should be brave."

"Robyn, you busted a pirate crew out of prison. You don't think that was brave?"

"Well then, maybe it was too brave. Look what happened to Stromer. Look what happened to Mary. Even the big, creepy sloth; he didn't deserve to die, did he?"

"But Robyn, Stromer and his crew made their choice. They did it to see you on the throne."

"I just don't want it, *okay*?" Robyn reiterated.

"Then what? Leave them to some another tyrant?"

"Gideon," she replied with a nod. "Gideon will be king."

"Gideon?" I asked, bewildered. "Robyn, it should be you. You *know* it should be you."

"I don't *want* to rule a kingdom, Ed—I'm twelve years old. Gideon can rule, he has before. He'll bring in the change Pangaea needs."

"My lady, if it is your wish—" began Gideon, striding towards us.

"The mammals will be treated as well as everyone else. Right?"

"Of course. Everyone shall be equal in my Pangaea."

"And you'll close the mines, stop the overfishing. You'll let Pangaea heal?"

"You have my word," he replied with a bow.

"My lady," announced the deep, bass-heavy voice of Sir Barnum from behind us. "Please accept my apologies for my past actions. I've always tried to live honourably, but the path isn't always so clearly laid out before me."

He reached out his hand, which was curled into a two-fingered fist, opened his palm, and tilted his hand to the side until Luca dropped. Robyn caught the glass carefully and, after a quick inspection to make sure the slide wasn't damaged, smiled at Barnum to show her appreciation. With that, the great tyrannosaur turned and walked away along the beach, quickly fading into the darkness.

Robyn then let out a sharp gasp and put her injured foot forwards.

"What's up?" I asked.

"My foot," she replied. "It tingled and then… it doesn't hurt anymore."

"Luca," I concluded, gazing at the glass slide in her hand. "He *does* heal."

"What will you do now?" Gideon asked Robyn.

"I'm going to cure my mum," Robyn replied, her eyelids now heavy with exhaustion. "And then I'm going home."

Robyn paced over to her mother with a soft smile. She pressed the glass against Carol's forehead and whispered into it, a single tear rolling down her cheek.

"Luca, please cure her. Give us back our future. *Please.*"

The glass began to glow a soft blue. Carol breathed in deeply, heaving her chest and drawing her shoulders back as if she had plunged into freezing waters. As she exhaled, a blue mist escaped from her mouth.

"How do you feel?" I asked.

"I feel…" Carol began. "Amazing."

Robyn hugged her mother tightly.

"It works," she sobbed. "It really, really *works.*"

With a few quick wing beats, Jynx fluttered onto the top of my sail, looking Robyn in the eye.

"You fulfilled your potential," she said with a smile. "I knew you'd do it, even if *you* didn't."

"You didn't even want us here," I teased.

"That was obviously a test," Jynx replied. "And you passed."

"It was *not* a test," Robyn said with a giggle.

"Okay, fine, it wasn't a test," she conceded with a grin. "I was wrong, but I'm glad I was."

"I guess I should return Luca now."

Jynx looked at Robyn and then Carol before offering a kind smile.

"I'm sure the Heart can wait for a mother and daughter to spend some time with one another. Give it to me. We'll keep it safe in the citadel until you return. Pangaea will survive another few hours without it—besides, I think the little guy needs some recovery time before being put back to work."

Robyn smiled and placed Luca's glass slide carefully into Jynx's small, clawed hand. With equal care, the little dinosaur tucked it away inside her thick chest feathers.

The Black Dress

Right about now, I suspect you'll fall into one of two groups. Those of you in the first group will be thinking that this was a lovely ending. We beat the bad guy, we saved Carol, and Pangaea can heal. Those in the second group will be thinking that despite this apparently satisfying conclusion, there's a concerning number of pages left, which can't be a good sign. To those in the latter group, I say—don't be so cynical! But also, yes. It's not a good sign at all.

You see, life is much like attempting to pet a strange cat. You can't choose to not pet the cat because cats have successfully brainwashed all of you foolish humans. You *have* to try, you *have* to find out if the cat will allow you to pet it. And it might—the experience may be one of great satisfaction. Alternatively, that cat may try to murder you in several different ways including, but not limited to, clawing, biting, knifing, chain-sawing, and running you down with your own car.

The point I'm somewhat laboriously trying to make is that life is unpredictable. The number of outcomes from even mundane activities is infinite and potentially painful. Today's outcome was most certainly like the most vicious of cats.

***

Having now mastered some control of the Pangaean ether, Robyn elegantly formed a neat, wooden door in the Burgess coast cliff face. Opening it, she revealed the lonely beach, the sea shimmering in the summer sun. Once we said our goodbyes, to raucous cheering, all three of us returned triumphantly to Lyme Regis.

"You always did love this beach," remarked Carol.

"There are never any people," Robyn replied.

"It is peaceful, isn't it?"

"We should get back to Michael," I said. "Let's give him the good news."

"We should," agreed Carol. "But first, let's have a little something to celebrate. Wait here."

Carol left and, after ten minutes or so, returned with three ice cream cones. Mint chocolate chip—Robyn's favourite. We sat together on a large boulder and gazed out into the sea. After the mayhem of the past few days, these few moments of calm were just what we needed.

There was a pleasant surprise in store for me, too, as I picked up the ice cream cone.

"Whoa," I whispered.

"What?" asked Carol.

"I've only ever eaten in Pangaea," I replied. "But this is real."

"I guess I'm not the only one who's mastered their abilities," said Robyn with a smile.

Extending my tongue, I lapped up my first taste of ice cream. It was exactly how I imagined it would be—basically if heaven were a food. It was cool and sweet, perfect in the midst of a heatwave.

In the distance, I saw the tell-tale series of blowhole sprays of dolphins.

"Dolphins!" Robyn yelped, pointing at the leaping pod.

"So beautiful," said Carol. "They've always been my favourite. Remember when we went out on the boat tour to see them?"

"That was so cool," I agreed.

"You were there too, huh?" said Carol.

"I got in for free," I replied with a smirk.

"We were so close," added Robyn. "We could have almost touched them."

"You were terrified you might fall out of the boat," I teased.

"I was," Robyn said with a chuckle. "At first."

"Why only at first?" asked Carol.

"Because you were there," Robyn replied. "I knew nothing bad would happen as long as you were there."

Carol reached an arm around her neck and pulled her in close, kissing the top of her head.

"Remember how I was afraid of those birds in London?"

"The parakeets?"

"Yeah, the little green ones. Where was it again?"

"Hyde Park. That was the day we went to the Natural History Museum."

"That's right, and they swarmed us on the way back to the hotel."

I giggled. "One landed on your head."

"But then you made us come back and feed them," Robyn continued. "And they didn't scare me anymore."

"That was fun," Carol agreed.

"Could we go again one time?"

"I'll book the train tickets as soon as we get home. Speaking of which, we really ought to go home now."

Once home, Carol ordered Robyn to change into clean clothes before speaking with her father. We sprinted up the stairs, eager to tell him the good news.

Stepping into the familiar surroundings was both comforting and slightly underwhelming. It felt safe, if far less exciting than Pangaea. An ordinary space, but one I knew every inch of. Indeed, the only thing that wasn't familiar was the elegant black dress which hung from the door. It was a little dark and feminine for Robyn's taste, I knew that much, but its flowing lines and lace sleeves were admittedly pretty. It wasn't clear what the occasion was but, with Carol cured, we certainly had reason for celebration.

We trotted down the stairs, where Carol met us. Wandering into the kitchen, we found Michael wearing a sharp, well-fitting, black suit. I hadn't seen him so well dressed since Robyn's aunt's wedding a couple of years back.

As a side note, that was a night most memorable for Carol becoming somewhat tipsy and belting out a breathtakingly loud—but remarkably in tune—rendition of Fleetwood Mac's "Go Your Own Way" in the taxi home from the wedding. This was in response to the driver taking a wrong turn, which Carol clearly found hilarious. Thankfully, the driver in question had a good sense of humour and even sang along to the parts he knew. Robyn was far too shy for backseat a cappella karaoke, but she did laugh herself to tears.

Now I thought about it, that was probably the last time Carol had let her hair down—being only a few weeks before her diagnosis. I hoped we would have other nights like that soon. I couldn't wait to see her laugh again—to see her *really* laugh. A laugh without the subtle but ever-present sadness which had hidden behind every smile since the cancer darkened our lives. Better yet, I would even be able to join in now that she could see me.

Robyn almost skipped in excitement at the news she had for her father.

"Oh, good, you're home, pumpkin," he said, glancing up from fixing his cuff links. "Could you go get dressed?"

"Oh, sure," she replied with a broad smile. "But first, I have something amazing to tell you."

"You do?"

"It's Mum. She's *better*."

Michael looked up once more, this time with an eyebrow raised and his lips pursed tightly. It was clear he didn't believe her. I thought he would have been rather excited, but his expression was more one of worry—perhaps he feared false hope.

"It's true," she continued. "It's hard to explain, but Pangaea—the place in my drawings—it's *real*. I know it sounds, well… I didn't really believe it either, but Mum saw it too. She came with me and—"

"All right, Robyn. Can you *please* go and get dressed?" he insisted in a sterner tone.

"Just wait, it's important. There was this… he's called Luca, and he cured her, Dad. He cured her cancer. Isn't that—"

"*Enough!*" Michael erupted. "We don't have time for your imaginary *nonsense* today. Go and *get dressed!*"

We stood, stunned. Why was he acting like that? Was it *so* unbelievable? I suppose it was, to be fair. But still, it seemed like an unfair reaction. More irritating still was Carol's lack of a response. Perhaps she was as shocked as us. Robyn furrowed her brow in anger before turning around and marching back up the stairs. I padded after her into her bedroom.

"What was *that* all about?" I asked.

In response, Robyn booted a green stuffed *Triceratops* across her room and watched it bounce harmlessly off the far wall.

"Why wouldn't he *listen* to me?" she remonstrated. "It's such good news—he should be happy. What could be *so* important?"

Carol soon crept into the room too.

"Robyn—"

"Why didn't you *say* anything?" Robyn fumed.

"I'm sorry, I just—"

"You just stood there. He doesn't believe me, but he would've believed you. Why didn't you say something?"

"I couldn't."

"Of *course*, you could, you're an adult. Adults might not believe kids, but they believe other adults—*you* could have said something."

"Robyn, it's not that I didn't think he would believe me. I couldn't say anything."

"Why *not*?"

It hit me like a train loaded with a hundred tonnes of pure, solid heartache—I knew why Carol hadn't said anything. The fact that I knew suggested Robyn now did too, but her continued pressing made it clear she wasn't ready to accept it. My mind wandered back to the night we returned after the Heart was stolen—when Michael warmed Robyn with hot chocolate and blankets and spoke to her softly. I thought she had ignored him, distracted by more pressing issues, but no. She had heard and so had I. We had simply rejected it, wishing so hard for it not to be true it was as if we didn't know at all.

"*Robyn, listen,*" he had said. "*I have something I need to tell you.*"

"You can still tell him, Robyn continued. "Tell him now that it's all true. Tell him you're *better*. Don't you want to see his face when he realises the truth?"

"Robyn..." I interjected.

"*What*, Ed?" she snapped.

"*While you were gone...*" Michael's voice echoed in my head.

"He wouldn't hear her," I said.

"What?"

"Michael wouldn't have heard Carol."

Tears began to stream down Robyn's face as she slowly came to accept what she knew. She shook her head gently.

"*Your mother. She took a turn for the worse.*"

~ 356 ~

"No," she whispered. "No, he'd have heard. Of *course*, he'd have heard. Why wouldn't he hear her? She's *right here*."

"I don't think she is, Robyn."

"Tell him, Mum," she said, sobbing now. "Tell him he's wrong."

Carol shook her head with a solemn smile.

Robyn slumped onto her bed and wiped the tears away with her sleeve.

"I'm so sorry, pumpkin. She's gone."

"You're not really here, are you?" Robyn wept.

"Not really."

"All this time…"

"I'm so sorry, honey."

"But why?"

"It's what you needed. You weren't ready to accept it."

"The dress. That black dress. What's it for? What am I getting dressed for?"

I leapt onto Robyn's bed beside her and placed a comforting paw gently onto her shoulder. I knew what it was for, and so did she.

"Your funeral," she whispered, red eyes fixed on Carol.

The imaginary Carol paced over and crouched in front of Robyn. She placed a hand on her daughter's cheek and kissed her gently on the forehead.

"You weren't ready to say goodbye, and that's okay. But the time has come. You can't avoid it anymore."

"I'm *still* not ready."

"I know. I don't think your father is either. Go and be with him; you two need each other more than ever now."

"It's not fair."

"I know, sweetie, but now it's time to be brave—just like in Pangaea. Put on that dress, and be *brave*."

Robyn nodded slowly.

"I'll try, Mum," she replied, her face scrunched and glistening with tears, her words almost unintelligible through her sobs. "I'll try."

I noticed now that Carol had begun to fade. I could see the wall behind her growing clearer and clearer.

"No. No, no, *no*. Not yet, Mum, not *yet*."

"It's okay, sweetheart, everything will be okay. Go and *live*, be everything you can be. I know you'll make me proud."

"I *need* you, Mum."

"I love you, Robyn," Carol whispered before she faded entirely.

Robyn fell from the bed onto her knees and cried out, tears flooding from her eyes and pooling onto her lap.

I wrapped my body around her and hugged her tightly.

"I need you," she wept.

It didn't take long for Michael to come running in, having heard her wailing, and he, too, crouched and embraced her, his arms passing straight through me.

I'm not sure how long we all sat on that floor. It felt like hours. For that time, we simply embraced and cried in near silence. It was all we could do. Having one another was the only solace we could find.

The New Regime

The newly crowned King Gideon strode through the Gondwanan forest for the first time in an aeon. Doctor Boggs and Jynx proudly strutted close behind. The citizens of Pangaea, upon hearing of his ascension, had gathered all along the new king's route to cheer and celebrate. They whistled and tossed flowers, and some broke down in tears of relief, hopeful for a new future.

After a considerable journey, Gideon approached the gates of Tanis. He had dreamt of this day for as long as he could remember, the triumphant return to his capital.

It was nothing like what he remembered. For one, the city had grown enormously—indeed, it was barely a village when he was banished. The sheer scale of the urban sprawl caught his breath. The vast golden citadel loomed tall over the skyline—impressive, but an imposing reminder of the previous king.

As he strode through the gates, the people began to gather outside their homes, standing in the cobbled streets chattering nervously. They didn't cheer and celebrate his arrival as those outside the city walls had. Instead, they whispered and glanced at their new monarch with suspicious eyes.

"They don't seem best pleased at my arrival," Gideon murmured.

"I'm afraid this is Richard's stronghold," explained Boggs. "For all the evil he is responsible for, these people are fiercely loyal to him. He built this city, he gave them education and healthcare, ample food and fuel. They will not accept his deposition quickly."

Soon, the royal party reached the town square, dominated by a magnificent gothic cathedral. A large crowd had gathered there and began to grumble as the king arrived.

"Go home, usurper!" one called.

"Murderer!"

"Go back to the swamp!"

"How *dare* you?" Gideon roared. "I was placed on the throne by the Architect herself!"

"Liar!"

"Charlatan!"

With a frustrated growl, Gideon marched through the square. The crowds began to throw all manner of objects at him, from vegetables to eggs and even rocks. Boggs hurried the new king through the square, trying his utmost to shield his master with his own body.

***

As darkness fell, Gideon stood on the balcony of the golden citadel, overlooking the city. Even from up there, he could hear the dissenting chants of the citizenry.

"Ingrates," Gideon scolded. "They have grown fat and spoiled in their city of gluttony. The realm starves while these people prosper and now, they think themselves entitled."

"Sire," replied Boggs. "I am sure the citizens will come around in time. We simply—"

"No. They must have their vices removed. This vile city is the cause of their greed, a symbol of Richard's cruel robbery of the people. It disgusts me. Burn it down."

"My king?"

"Burn it all down!"

"Sire, the city has homes, schools, hospitals—"

"Do the people outside these walls have such luxuries?" he boomed. "Jynx, do what you do best, burn it *all* to the ground. We will live as equals in my Pangaea. I will save this realm from itself."

Jynx nodded obediently and flew at speed off the balcony. One by one, small, incendiary explosions dotted the skyline. The orange flickers of the ensuing blazes began to stretch out across Tanis.

"Gideon—" began Boggs.

"You will address me properly, Doctor."

"Your *Majesty*, this is wrong. You can't expect to win over the people by setting their city ablaze."

"Win them over?" Gideon snarled. "I am their *king*. A king whom they have betrayed for an age. I don't have to earn their loyalty; they have to earn *my* forgiveness. And tonight, they will *beg* for it."

Boggs gazed down at the city square as the flames began to lick out of the cathedral windows and the crowd of protestors fled.

"No," he stated. "This isn't right, Gideon. This wasn't the plan. I won't stand for it."

"This is beginning to sound a lot like treason," Gideon snarled. "I knew you were by Richard's side for too long—your allegiance is still with the tyrant, is it not?"

Boggs shook his head sadly. "I'm beginning to fear we've simply replaced one tyrant with another."

A Final Farewell

When our eyes dried, when we finally had no tears left to cry, an eerie silence fell over Robyn's bedroom. The doorbell rang from downstairs, which Michael reluctantly told Robyn he had to answer. He said so almost in a whisper. We listened as he stepped downstairs and opened the door to the sound of a friendly postman unaware of the anguish within those walls. Without speaking a word, Robyn stood and changed into her black dress before skulking downstairs.

Michael apologised for yelling, knelt, and gave Robyn another long hug. He stroked her auburn hair gently as he embraced her, and still Robyn remained silent.

Soon, a black hearse pulled up outside our house followed by a Jaguar limousine. Through the window of the hearse, I could see a wooden coffin and flowers arranged to spell "Carol." Robyn didn't even look at it. We stepped silently towards the limousine, where a tall man wearing a black suit and a top hat held the door open for us. The drive to the funeral was long, but somehow not long enough. I never wanted that journey to end as I knew our destination meant saying a final farewell to Carol.

The ceremony itself was somewhat of a blur. We sat inside the chapel amongst family, friends, and others I didn't recognise. Carol had never been an especially devout Catholic, but she considered it part of her identity, so, a Catholic funeral it was.

It had been a long time since I had witnessed a Catholic ceremony, and it felt odd. The priest—a short, balding, middle-aged man draped in a purple robe—lapped the chapel, chanting in Latin. Some of the congregation chanted back, their robotic voices echoing off the domed ceiling. I was aware of the coffin in front of the pulpit, but I couldn't bring myself to look at or truly process who lay within.

The congregation continually stood, sat, and knelt according to a seemingly arbitrary schedule. The priest spoke about God and Jesus, read from the Bible, and introduced hymns to which neither I, Robyn, nor Michael knew the words. The priest's speeches sounded to me as though they were underwater—distorted and distant. I listened, but my mind was far away—I didn't take much of it in. That being said, I did notice he barely mentioned Carol at all, bar occasionally shoe-horning her name into his preachings—almost as if he intermittently remembered this was a funeral and not simply another Sunday mass. The whole ceremony seemed incredibly impersonal. I couldn't help but feel like Carol deserved a better service.

When it was over, Carol's coffin was carried out by four pallbearers dressed in black suits. Michael stood at the front, his wife's wooden casket resting upon his shoulder. His expression remained strong, his jaw clenched tightly. He held it together until the moment came to place Carol back into the hearse. Perhaps this felt like the last goodbye, and his stoic performance failed. His face crumpled and tears poured from his eyes. Those around dutifully wrapped their arms around his shoulders and offered tissues, but Robyn simply looked on silently. She gazed blankly into the hearse.

Soon, we were on the road once more. On any other day, we would both have been rather excited by the prospect of riding in a limousine, but today it barely even registered. The hearse drove in front, the casket containing Carol visible through the rear window.

We then found ourselves in the graveyard. I barely remembered how we got there. It was hot and sunny, the heatwave still in full swing, which felt contradictory to the sombre mood of the moment. Yet more speeches were made by the graveside, and the priest recited some biblical texts as the coffin was lowered into the ground. Michael's tears seemed to have been replaced by a quiet shock as he fed down one of the supporting ropes. One by one, the attendants took a handful of dirt from a wooden box held in the outstretched hands of the priest and tossed it into the grave. When it was Robyn's turn, I peered into the hole. It was deep—much deeper than I had expected. I didn't know how to feel. It seemed like a bad dream. Like it wasn't real. While I knew it to be true, I couldn't grasp the finality of it all.

Robyn's handful of dirt fell for an age into the chasm which was Carol's final resting place.

"Goodbye, Carol," I whispered.

***

The next thing I knew, we were home in the bathroom. The tap was running—filling the sink to the extent that water was dribbling through the overflow drain. Robyn stared vacantly into the mirror as if she had forgotten about the running water.

"Robyn, are you all right?" I asked. "You haven't said a thing all day."

"Wallowing in her failure, perhaps," hissed a voice from below.

I flinched in fright at the unexpected guest in our bathroom. A black, glossy, scorpion-like creature crawled out of the sink water. I recognised him as the sea scorpion from the Mausoleum, the one who guarded Luca. Jækel, he was called.

"What are *you* doing here?" I asked.

"We had a deal," he replied. "You were to return Luca with haste."

"We've had other things going on."

"Oh, well, don't mind me then. I'm only concerned with the fate of my world."

"Keep your exoskeleton on. Gideon will return it."

"You entrusted Luca to the *usurper*?"

"Gideon helped us. Why wouldn't we trust him?"

"Fools. I offered but one piece of advice: beware the *Bishop*."

"What are you... Robyn?"

I looked up to see Robyn still gazing blankly into the mirror. She barely seemed to have acknowledged Jækel's presence.

"Gideon is…" I continued.

"You gifted the Bishop with the power of life and death. You *fools*."

"He can't be—"

"There is something you should see," Jækel croaked.

He scuttled up the tiled bathroom wall and placed a claw into the rippling water. As he did, the water darkened. I reared onto my hind legs for a better look and saw an image beginning to form. In the sink, I could see Gideon in his old shack in the swamp. He was speaking with the *Therizinosaurus*, Doctor Boggs.

"Is it true?" Gideon demanded.

"It's true," Boggs replied. "The Architect dines with Richard in the citadel as we speak."

"He's *feeding* her?"

"She doesn't seem to be aware of the scripture. Richard is biding his time—I have advised him it would be unwise to kill her until we have learned more about her intentions."

"Never mind that. We would all cease to be if she were to be killed."

"Perhaps, but Richard has never been a man of faith; he doesn't believe her to be omnipotent."

"You'd think the Knight would have more conviction. He was the first to be created, after all. Why has she come now?"

"A personal matter, it would seem. She seeks medicinal aid for her mother. The king has suggested the Heart could be her solution."

"He offered her the *Heart*? Why would he help her?"

"He wants her quest in Pangaea to be a brief one."

"The Architect can't leave—and certainly not with the Heart. We *have* to make sure she stays. She has to see him for the monster he is. Then she will fulfil the scripture and bring about his fall."

"How do you propose we stop her from leaving?"

Gideon paused for a moment in thought.

"The Heart," he stated. "You have Richard's ear—convince him *he* needs the Heart. He's ill himself, is he not?"

"Indeed."

"If it can cure the mother, why not him? I'm surprised he hasn't considered this already."

"Such is his fear of the Architect, having her gone is his only priority."

"So, *change* his priorities; that's why you're there. Make him want the Heart *more* than he wants the Architect gone. If he wants it, he'll take it. That's what he does—and then the Architect will see who the king truly is."

"Does this not seem a little... unethical?" questioned Boggs. "What if the mother doesn't receive the Heart in time? As I understand it, she is dying."

"It's all for the greater good, my old friend."

The water rippled, the image of Gideon replaced by what appeared to be a prison. Behind the bars were countless creatures, but I recognised a few: Sir Barnum the tyrannosaur, Doctor Boggs, the *Velociraptor* from the inn, several *Utahraptors*—it seemed anyone with any past allegiance to the king had been imprisoned.

Another surface oscillation, and we now saw the city of Tanis ablaze—crackling flames lapping out of rooftops, residents fleeing, windows shattering.

The image rippled for the last time, returning the water to its transparent state, the horrors of Gideon's reign reduced to no more than a drain plug.

"What was that?" I asked.

"I have eyes everywhere," Jækel replied. "That was a memory from one such pair of eyes, and a glimpse at the world ruled by the Bishop."

"The greater good?" Robyn murmured—the first words she had uttered all day.

"Robyn?" I replied.

"He said it was all for the greater good. Letting my mum die was for the *greater good*? I could have *saved* her!"

"Robyn—we did everything we could."

"We did," she hissed, with a new ferocity in her voice. "But we were *sabotaged*."

She slammed her fist into the sink, splashing water onto the mirror.

"We had Luca," she ranted. "I had him in my *hand*. We still had time then, but—"

"Robyn—"

"I still had time… but he took my last chance from me."

"We don't even know if it would have—"

"My mum is dead because of *Gideon*," she snarled. "He used me… and I'm going to make him pay."

"I'm not sure what that means, but it doesn't sound like a good idea. We need to talk this through."

"No, Ed, we don't. I'm *done* talking."

The Fall of Tanis

Robyn raised a hand and dragged it diagonally down the bathroom wall, ripping open a jagged wound directly into the burning city of Tanis. We stepped into the cobbled streets which were still damp from recent rainfall. Steam rose from the ground as the rainwater evaporated under the heat of the nearby inferno. Though it was night, the sky glowed orange and the golden citadel glinted in the shimmering flames.

Robyn marched through the city streets towards the citadel. With every step, the cobbles beneath her feet cracked and crumbled.

"*Gideon!*" she screamed, as we reached the citadel. "*Show yourself!*"

With a flick of her hand, the huge, wooden doors ripped off their hinges and blew inwards. Robyn stormed inside the throne room with me scuttling after her.

"*Gideon!*" she roared once more.

"Miss Robyn?" came a tuneful voice from behind.

"Jynx," she snarled.

Robyn raised her hands from her waist, causing iron bars to burst from the ground and encircle our old ally. From the staircase, King Gideon's familiar, hulking frame came into view.

"Robyn? What's the meaning of this?" he demanded.

"*You*!" Robyn shrieked. "I know what you did!"

"I don't understand."

"You killed her!"

"Who?"

"My mum," she replied, a crack in her voice betraying the sorrow hiding beneath the rage.

"My lady, I assure you, I did no such thing."

"I reckon she knows the mum wasn't real," clarified Jynx.

Robyn swung round and glared at the tiny, feathered theropod.

"You *knew*?"

"I'm afraid I did, darling. It didn't seem like it would've helped you all that much to know."

Robyn clenched her hand into a fist, causing Jynx's cage to twist and wrap around her tightly, almost crushing her.

"*Robyn*!" I scolded.

"Stay out of this, Ed."

Robyn marched towards the king and raised a hand as if to grip an invisible cup. Gideon grasped at his throat and began to levitate. As she squeezed her hand tighter, the king wheezed and struggled to breathe.

"Robyn, *stop*," I cried.

"Go away, Ed." Robyn ranted. "He used me, he used you. He used everyone. He *deserves* what's coming to him."

She waved her free hand, and I flew backwards through the air, all the way outside. After thumping onto the cobbled street, I climbed to my feet. Robyn was grieving, I knew that, but I couldn't let her become a monster. I had to save her from herself—though I feared I was already too late.

I looked to the sky to see a thick cloud cover which seemed to glow ever brighter. The few residents to have not already fled the burning city began to gather around me, gazing at the ominous sky and chattering loudly in panic. It was no longer just the flames colouring the sky; there was a new light source of some kind.

The glow intensified before a large hole was punched through the clouds. A burning rock around the size of a car streaked through the atmosphere, a trail of fire and smoke in its wake. It travelled with immense speed and, no sooner than it had become visible, it slammed into the side of the citadel and exploded on impact. I ducked for cover, as did the crowd around me. Fragments of gold and marble were flung far and wide, crashing into buildings and smashing windows.

This was only the first of many. The entire island upon which the citadel sat was bombarded with a hail of fiery rocks. One of the two towers flanking the main structure was the first to fall. After being struck near its base, it toppled and crashed into the lake, raising huge swells of water which burst into the city streets.

After a deafening creak, the main structure of the citadel began to collapse. The pointed roof of the golden structure bowed onto its side before dropping onto the level below. The impact caused a chain reaction of collapsing floors which accelerated with ferocious speed. It took no more than a few seconds for the rest of the citadel to crumple into a dense cloud of dust and rubble. There were gasps and screams from the street as Pangaea's symbol of power disintegrated.

I watched, eyes wide with terror, as the dust cloud poured onto the streets, forcing me to cower and shield my face. Stone and ash pelted my back as the suffocating debris consumed me, but I feared it wasn't yet over. The glow above my head grew ever whiter and blindingly bright, even through the dense dust. I could feel Robyn's fury growing stronger. Worse was to come.

For a moment, the city was eerily quiet. The few remaining citizens had now wisely fled. I wandered into an alleyway and found a ladder which I assumed was some kind of fire escape. Climbing to the roof of a tall bell tower, I attempted to rise above the stifling cloud of debris.

From there I could see it. The clouds in the sky had cleared—dissipated by the meteorite shower—so what now approached was horrifyingly visible: an asteroid of unspeakable proportions.

"Oh, Robyn, *no*," I whispered, sick at heart.

On the streets below, Pangaeans streamed towards the city limits in their thousands—fleeing for their lives. Above, the complex network of cable cars whizzed outwards, carrying evacuees from the citadel towards the safety of the forest. I prayed they would all be out of harm's way in time. Thinking back to the mausoleum, I remembered the comet above the citadel engraved into the entrance. It seemed as though Robyn was to save Pangaea from its end. I had never imagined her destiny was to bring it about.

As the asteroid reached the atmosphere, the air around me seemed to ignite and the sky burst into flame. The vast space rock slammed into the citadel, launching the surrounding earth high into the air. A huge wave pulsed through the ground, as though the surface of Pangaea had been liquified. Glowing magma and sulphurous, yellow smoke spewed from the resultant cracks in the earth, while buildings crumpled and toppled as their foundations were shattered.

A wall of red-hot, liquid earth raced towards the bell tower upon which I stood. I was motionless, like a stunned animal waiting to become roadkill. There was nowhere to run. The building beneath my feet shook violently, preparing to swallow me.

I closed my eyes and grimaced.

***

When I awoke, I found only darkness. I couldn't even see my paws waving before my eyes. I assumed this to be death—it was peaceful, if a little uninteresting. But death hadn't come for me. Rather, I had been encased in what seemed to be a hollow ball of solid rock—like a chick in an egg.

I waited in what I came to consider my tomb for what seemed like forever, wondering what had gone so wrong. I thought about Robyn, about the atrocity she had committed, about what pain she must be feeling. I considered Gideon's plot—perhaps, as he said, it was for the greater good. Could he have been right? Was releasing Pangaea from Richard's tyranny worth a single life? Were I more detached from the situation, I would have probably agreed, but then the memory of Carol invaded my mind and quelled any such notion. Carol was special. Her life was worth more than any cause.

Finally, a loud *snap* rang out above me. A splinter of orange light glinted through a tiny hole, which quickly cracked and spread like a lightning bolt. The stone split down the middle, all the way around, until it was in two halves. Each half fell away to the side and, before me, stood Robyn—covered in soot and her clothes singed and torn.

Glowing embers floated through the air. We were now in the forest outside the city walls and, in the distance, there was only a smouldering crater where the citadel had once been. Now, not only was the city on fire, even the surrounding forest was ablaze. It soon began to rain, but it wasn't water that fell from the sky. Molten glass showered the ground, glowing yellow and splashing into broiling puddles on impact before solidifying into smooth, rippled plates.

"What have you *done*?" I gasped.

"What I should have done the first time I came here. It's over now."

"But... this? Robyn, look around you. Look at the destruction. Think of the people—"

"*There are no people, Ed!*" she screamed. "They're not *real*, *you're* not real. I made them all up in my head! You're all *pretend*."

"I *am* real!" I yelled. "Whether you imagined me or not, I'm *here*. I think and I feel, and that makes me *real*. That makes all these people real."

"I'm going home, Ed."

"Robyn, you have a responsibility to this world. We can't just go home and leave it like... like *this*."

"I didn't say '*we*,'" she replied coldly.

"What?"

Robyn raised her arms and a blackened, burnt tree rose from the ground, exposing its roots. Between those roots was a shimmering portal into her bedroom.

"So that's it? You're running away again? When are you going to stop running from who you need to be? You have a duty to this place, Robyn. Stop being such a *coward*!"

"Goodbye, Ed," she growled without looking back at me.

With that, she strode under the tree root and back into the real world. I chased after her but, before I could reach her, the tree slammed back into the ground. Its brittle trunk snapped and collapsed. She was gone.

"No," I whispered. "No, Robyn. You can't..."

I took a few seconds to process my lifelong friend's abandonment. It cut deep—a betrayal the likes of which I had never imagined. My body tensed with fury.

"Fine," I snarled, before screaming out. "*Fine*! I don't need you anyway."

But I did need her, and I knew that. My trusted companion—the other half of my very being—was gone. I felt naked and exposed. After a few seconds of pacing, I slumped to the ground and thumped my head onto the ash-covered ground.

"Where I go, you go," I murmured. "Always. That's what you said, Robyn. That's what you *said*."

Jækel's Torment

Robyn returned home tired and broken. She looked into the mirror and gazed upon her tattered, scorched clothes and blackened face. She didn't feel regret, but neither did she feel relief or satisfaction as she had hoped. Revenge had only left her hollow. She washed up and changed into new clothes, throwing her burnt outfit into the bin.

She sat on her bed and stared at the wall. Stared at the drawings of Pangaea, of Ed, of all the wonderful creatures she had dreamt. The drawings had become more than colourful sketches. She recognised them, she *knew* them— they had taken on identities. Mother Mary, Captain Stromer, Benjamin... *Gideon*. They were now merely reminders of her failure. She stood, gripped the drawing of Gideon, and tore it off the wall. Then, one by one, she ripped them all down. She growled in frustration as the final drawing, the drawing of Ed, fluttered to the floor.

After scrunching them into a messy ball, she took them outside and stuffed them into the bin atop her charred outfit. She didn't cry. She felt no attachment to them anymore. *Good riddance*, she thought.

"The great Architect," hissed a voice from behind her. "Now the great Destroyer."

She turned to see Jækel, guardian of the mausoleum, slink out of the bushes. The sea scorpion had grown massively and was now the size of a large dog.

"What do *you* want?"

"I promised you there would be consequences for failure."

"Get lost, bug."

Robyn returned inside, only for Jækel to scuttle after her.

"You were the fated one, you know—you were supposed to save us all. Now, look at you. I knew you were no good the first time I saw you. You were never ready for the throne."

"Yeah, well, at least you get to say, 'I told you so.'"

"An empty prize."

"Why are you here, Jækel? Go home."

"Which home would that be? The mausoleum? I warned you it would wane without Luca. The mausoleum is but a ruin now. Or perhaps you mean Pangaea as a whole? The place you dropped an asteroid on and left with neither Heart nor ruler."

"I don't mean either of those places. I mean to nowhere, to nothing," Robyn hissed as she marched up the stairs. "You're not real, Jækel. *Disappear.*"

As Robyn reached her bedroom, Jækel climbed atop her bed and reared up to look her in the eyes—his own eyes little more than inky, black spots on his armoured head.

"According to whom?" he hissed.

"According to me. I made you in my mind, and I can get rid of you just as easily."

"Oh, child," he replied with a dry chuckle. "I think you'll find the monsters inside your own head are the most difficult to banish. The most vicious demons are always those of our own making."

Robyn snorted. "Whatever."

She stopped and gazed at the bare wall. She had missed a drawing which hung crooked by a corner. On closer inspection, this one wasn't one of her prehistoric creations. This one, an old drawing, was more personal.

Were she in a different mindset, she would have likely scolded the artistic skills of her six- or seven-year-old self. In the centre was a crudely drawn figure with auburn hair—a smiling, happy self-portrait. Holding one hand was her father, with a suitably floppy black mop on his head, and holding the other was Carol. It had been so long since her mother had hair, Robyn had almost forgotten that her auburn locks were a maternal trait.

Robyn reached out her hand to pull it off the wall but stopped as her finger grazed the paper. She couldn't bring herself to do it. She couldn't let this one go, yet she so wished she could.

"She is but one of many you've let down," Jækel sneered.

"I don't need this," Robyn huffed. "I'm going out."

"To purchase some house plants, perhaps? It would seem prudent to replace some of the oxygen you currently waste."

Robyn grabbed her jacket and stormed outside. She walked quickly, but Jækel kept up with ease, his jagged legs clicking relentlessly on the pavement.

"You can't walk away from what you are," he seethed.

"Oh, shut up, shut up, shut *up!*" she screamed. "Leave me *alone.*"

***

But Jækel didn't leave her alone. For weeks, he followed her everywhere. When she ate dinner, he was there, drooling on her plate. When she watched television, he crawled across the screen to block her view. When she went for a walk, he would clamp her ankle with a claw, forcing her to drag him around. At night, he lay on her pillow, breathing on her face. Robyn knew arthropods didn't even take breaths—they don't have lungs—he did it purely to torment her.

More unnerving still was that, with each passing day, Jækel grew. Soon, he was as long as a car and dominated her every waking moment. No matter what she did or where she went, Jækel loomed.

She barely spoke to her father. He tried to talk to her on several occasions, but she never heard what he said. Whenever he began, Jækel hissed in her ear. He would remind her of her failure, of how she couldn't save her mother, of how she had destroyed the only place where she belonged and abandoned her only friends.

One day, Michael suggested they go for a drive somewhere. Thanks to Jækel's incessant vitriol, Robyn couldn't make out where he planned to go—for lunch, perhaps. She opened the back door of the car and climbed inside. Of course, she was old enough to sit in the front, but that was her mother's seat. Robyn didn't feel she had earned it.

As she sat, Jækel pressed up beside her. With his newly enormous size, he was crammed tightly into the little Volkswagen. His armoured back strained against the door and his face pressed into Robyn. She winced as his many mouthparts, each like tiny sets of crab claws, writhed around against her cheek, dribbling saliva down her face. For several seconds she sat, before shuddering and throwing the car door back open.

"I-I can't, I can't be *in* here," she stammered as she fled the car and stormed back into the house.

Michael stared from the car, his eyes wide with concern.

"Robyn, what's the matter?" he called as he climbed out of the driver's seat.

"Leave me alone!" she yelled.

In truth, she intended this for Jækel, but her father reluctantly heeded, nonetheless.

Robyn stormed to her room and slammed the door shut behind her, locking Jækel outside. But as he always did, the sea scorpion simply reappeared in front of her.

"Is this my life now?" she asked. "Just this torment?"

"You know why it is this way," Jækel replied coldly.

Robyn paused for a moment and began to sob before replying.

"Because I deserve it."

"Because you *deserve* it," he hissed.

"Will I ever be rid of you?"

"That depends on whether you earn it."

A New Dawn

Sometimes, I wish we could skip back to a few chapters ago, to before everything was turned upside down. You, as the reader, certainly could if you wish. But the trouble with simply re-reading an old chapter is it doesn't truly erase the knowledge of what followed—it's forever tainted.

You see, life is no different. You can choose to dwell on the past but to truly move past hard times; you have to keep turning the pages.

***

It was a morning like any other that week; somehow bright, but bleak all the same. Thick cloud cover allowed through only a flat, grey light which seemed to bleach the landscape. The bitter smell of carbon hung thick in the air and fine ash coated the Gondwanan forest floor. Scattered over the ash were tiny, almost perfectly spherical stones which had rained down in the hours after the asteroid impact. Thankfully, they were little more than gravel at this point, but they had been red hot when they fell, continually lighting new fires. Bare and blackened, the trees had all perished in the ensuing blazes.

While I had spent most of my existence bemoaning how I couldn't taste food, I now realised the real world had one considerable advantage. There I couldn't eat, but nor did I feel hunger. For the first time, I was starving. My stomach ached and felt as though it might collapse in on itself.

I made my way to the fishing port of Hangenberg in the hope that they might have some food reserves. As I passed the treeline and crossed the dunes, I could see I wasn't the only one with this idea. A sea of white tents stretched along the coastline for as far as I could see, while a large variety of animals slept on the streets and squabbled over small scraps.

The scent of fish had gone, as had the cacophony of sea birds. Even the Tethys itself seemed quiet, with only the odd wave heard in the distance. The bustle was gone, replaced with solemn silence.

After making my way through town, I stood at the end of Mary's pier, staring at the grey sea through the open floor. To my surprise, one of her baskets began to wobble on the shelf before a small, badger-like creature crawled out.

"Are you looking for Mary?" she asked.

"Uh, no," I stammered. "I'm not looking for Mary."

"I don't know when she'll be back."

"I... I'm sorry, little guy. I don't think she will."

Another basket tipped over and two more little mammals clambered out.

"Is Mary gone?" one asked.

"Tell me she's not really gone, mister," added another.

"I'm sorry. She… she…" I stammered.

"She fought admirably," interjected a deep voice from behind. "She sacrificed herself for the good of all Pangaea. You should be proud."

I turned to see the vast tyrannosaur Sir Barnum looming over me. Goodness knows how such a giant had managed to sneak up on me.

"I'm starting to wonder if it was worth it," I replied in a hushed tone so the young mammals wouldn't hear.

"She and her crew were brave. That's all that matters."

I turned back towards the mammals who had huddled around each other in grief.

"I'm so sorry for your loss," I croaked. "I know what it's like to lose someone so close. You have to stick together though, yeah? You'll need each other more than ever."

They raised their heads and nodded gently before huddling together once more.

Barnum and I strolled back across the pier and gazed out at the forest of tents.

"Why are there so many people here?" I asked.

"Probably for the same reason as you," Barnum replied. "Hangenberg is the only place with food reserves left."

"The only place in all of Gondwana?"

"The only place in all of Pangaea."

"How did the impact affect all of Pangaea?"

"The impact? The asteroid didn't do this. It didn't really affect anyone outside Tanis."

"So why no food?"

"It would seem the Heart hasn't been returned. The flora is fading, and we will follow soon."

"Oh, no."

"When did you last see it?"

"Jynx took it. She must have taken it to—"

"To the citadel."

"Which was obliterated," I concluded, hanging my head in disappointment. "How long will the food hold out?"

"For this many people? A couple days, perhaps. The large herbivores will go first, which will in turn feed the carnivores for a little longer."

"Jeez, is that what it's come to?"

"Not yet."

I wasn't sure how long Barnum could hold out before resorting to such measures. I knew I was hungry, but he was visibly deteriorating. Such a huge creature needed vast amounts of food to stay healthy. I could clearly see his ribs and even the depressions in his skull.

Through the cobbled streets bounded a familiar little mammal with tan fur and dark stripes.

"Aw, g'day, Ed," Benjamin chirped. He then craned his neck upwards to look at Barnum. "You all right?"

Barnum nodded.

"You're not going to tail whip me halfway across Pangaea again?"

"I won't," Barnum replied with a slight chuckle.

"Good to hear, because, let me tell you, that *sucked*."

"Out of curiosity, where did you land?"

"Hell Creek."

"All the way to Hell Creek?" Barnum said with a sly smirk. "No wonder it took Gigas so long to find you."

"All right, don't be too proud of yourself. Anyway, someone by the dunes said I'd find you here, Ed. You've got a visitor."

"A visitor?"

"Ed?" came a sheepish voice from around the corner.

"Robyn?"

With her hands clasped over her stomach, she skulked out into the street. Her eyes glistened with tears as they darted from side to side at the starving masses. My initial urge was to run and embrace her, but I hesitated. The pain from her abandonment was still raw.

"Could we have a minute, guys?" I asked.

"Oh, uh, sure thing," Benjamin replied.

Benjamin and Barnum retreated out of hearing distance, but they still gazed over curiously.

"Ed, what have I done?" Robyn asked in a pained voice.

"You destroyed Pangaea," barked Jækel, scuttling out from the alleyway. "That's what you have done."

"Jækel? What's he doing here?"

"He's my tormentor," replied Robyn bitterly.

"He's gotten… big."

I took a deep breath and stepped forwards. The image of Robyn's fury haunted me still. I knew now what she was capable of, but I also knew she was better than that. I believed she could make things right.

"Robyn, you can fix this."

"How?"

"Your power that day… it was terrifying. But it was also incredible—you can use that same power to rebuild. Set everything straight."

"She can't," hissed Jækel. "One emotional outburst does not count as mastering your abilities. She hasn't even attempted to understand them."

"What?" I gawped. "Oh, shut up, Jækel."

"He's right, Ed," Robyn said, her head hung low. "I let everyone down before. I'd just do the same again. I don't know how to control it."

I couldn't believe what I was hearing. I glanced at Jækel and then back to Robyn.

"Is that what this overgrown lobster has been telling you? Jækel, go and fossilise."

I strode up to Robyn, rose onto my hind legs, and placed my front paws on her shoulders.

"You are incredible, Robyn. I've always known it and I won't hear anything otherwise. This guy is full of frass—you are the *Architect*. You can't keep running away and you can't keep hiding. It's time to start acting like the queen I know you're destined to be."

Robyn stared blankly for a moment, processing my rant.

"Give up, *Dimetrodon*," said Jækel. "She's not the saviour you think she is."

Robyn narrowed her eyes in defiance. "Maybe I can't fix this," she mumbled. "But I have to try."

"You will fail," he grumbled.

"Oh, shut *up*, Jækel," Robyn cried. "I can't take it anymore. Just shut up, shut up, shut *up*."

I grinned broadly.

"Yeah, shut up, Jækel," I concurred gleefully before flicking a rock at him with my tail. I flinched from the self-inflicted pain. My tail was still tender after Etheldred had bitten off the tip, but the satisfying *clunk* of the rock bouncing off Jækel's head made it entirely worthwhile.

***

After a long hike through the charred remains of the Gondwanan forest with Jækel still awkwardly following us, Robyn and I arrived in the ruined city of Tanis. Benjamin and Barnum had stayed behind to distribute food to the refugees, but they promised to meet us in the city when they were done.

We pressed on through the rubble-filled streets, occasionally choking on the thick, lingering smoke. After balancing over the narrow remains of the stone bridge, we stood amongst the scorched remains of the golden citadel. The crumpled foundations protruded from the ground like jagged shards of glass as dark plumes of soot bellowed into the air and the embers continued to smoulder. The bitter stench of burning was so strong I could taste it.

I could see Robyn's eyes begin to shimmer as she fought back tears. However, a gentle rumbling in the dirt soon had us distracted. Something sharp poked through the ground, pricking my feet. I yelped and skipped backwards. The mound of earth bubbled upwards and, as it fell away, revealed a familiar, oversized red-and-yellow sombrero.

"*Felipe!*" Robyn cried.

"*Hola, señorita,*" he chimed.

Robyn ran forwards to hug him, before thinking better of it while gazing at his pin-like spines.

"The chieftain, he said you were... the spirit of the Pangaea?"

"*Si*, that is me."

"Why didn't you say so?" she replied with a slight giggle.

"I prefer Felipe. It's fun to say. Felipe. Fe-*li*-pe. Feliiipe." He paused for a moment and gazed into space. "Now I have said it too many times and it does not even sound like a real name anymore."

"It suits you," I reassured him.

"You guided us well. We found Gideon, we found the fortress, and we found the Heart." Robyn's face then fell. "It didn't matter in the end though—I couldn't save Mum. She was already gone."

"I know, but that does not mean it didn't matter. You saved the mammals from the dungeon, you set Simon free, did you not?"

"Simon?"

"*Si*, he who carried the fortress."

"The giant sauropod is called... *Simon*?" I said with an eyebrow raised.

"*Si.*"

"Fair enough." I shrugged. "I guess I just expected something a little… grander."

"I might have saved those people," Robyn continued. "But look around, I've done more harm than good. I was just so… so *angry*."

"Sometimes it's okay to be angry," Felipe explained. "Sometimes it's even good to be angry. When bad things are happening, maybe *more* people should be angry."

"But I destroyed a whole city."

"Did you destroy? Or did you reset? This looks like a clean slate to me."

"But the people—"

"Nobody was hurt. Everyone is safe."

"But they're starving," I added.

"So, we should feed them."

"How?" Robyn asked.

"It's all part of the plan."

"Whose plan?" she said.

"I suppose… *your* plan."

"Bit of a convoluted plan," I remarked. "But the cactus is right—you can still fix things. He said no one was hurt, so Luca is here somewhere. We have to take him back to the mausoleum so Pangaea can heal."

"Look at this place," jibed Jækel. "Luca is dead, along with everyone else here. I don't care what the *cactus* says, it's over."

"No," Robyn replied. "No, Luca is here somewhere. He has to be."

"Then let's find him," I said with a nod.

For hours, we dug through the ash, choking on the smoke all the while. Occasionally, a piece of the remaining structure would collapse and we would flinch in fright as the fragments crunched into the ground nearby. But finally, I found what we were looking for. I scooped up a pawful of ash and let the dust sift through my toes. Left behind was a small glass slide with a tiny blue smudge in the middle.

"He's here!" I called.

"*Yes*," Robyn cried.

She scrambled over and grabbed Luca, raising him high and letting the light shine through the glass, illuminating the slide a familiar shade of greenish-blue. However, his glow was almost imperceptibly dim.

"Perhaps there's hope after all," muttered Jækel. "He must be returned to the mausoleum *immediately*."

"I guess we head for the pier," I suggested. "There must be a boat."

"I... I think I have a quicker way," Robyn replied hesitantly.

With a wave of her hand, a window opened in the air. A slowly rotating vortex through which the mountains of Laurasia was clearly visible.

"Whoa, that would have been useful a while ago."

"Well, I reckon I'm finally getting the hang of this 'Architect' business."

"We must *hurry*," urged Jækel.

"Good luck, *señorita*," called Felipe. "Greatness has been chasing you; you only had to stop running so fast."

"Thank you, Felipe," Robyn replied with a faint smile. "For everything. And I really do love your hat."

Felipe reached a stalk over his head and pricked the hat with his spines, lifting it off. He then reached over and placed the huge sombrero on the top of Robyn's head. It was far too large and covered her entire head.

"You should have it," he said with a smile. "It can be your crown."

"I love it." Robyn said, beaming. She pushed the sombrero up so she could see. "And I promise to learn some more Spanish for you," she added with a chuckle.

"*Grazie*," he replied with an appreciative nod.

Unsettled Business

Robyn, Jækel, and I marched through the portal to the snowy entrance of the Mausoleum of the Archean. Stepping directly into the bitter wind was a shock, and I shuddered in the snowfall.

While the mountain had always been cold, it was now frigid and desolate. The evergreen trees were green no more. Their withered, orange needles carpeted the forest floor. There wasn't so much as a birdcall to be heard.

Robyn glanced down at Luca in her hand.

"Time to get you home, buddy," she whispered. "Sorry it took so long."

"Wait," called a familiar voice from behind.

I turned to see the giant ground sloth Cuvier on the other side of the portal, in the ruins of the citadel.

"Cuvier?" said Robyn. "You're alive. And Stromer?"

Cuvier shook his head.

"Mary?" I asked.

"Only me," he replied, his eyes heavy with sadness.

"I'm sorry," Robyn said.

"They believed they were doing the right thing," he growled as he stepped through the portal into the snow. "They believed because of you, and now they are dead."

He towered over us with his vast, scarred frame, his metal prosthetic claws glinting in the light.

"Back up, big guy—" I pleaded.

"They were right," he said. "It was the right thing. I will help you to return the Heart."

"Oh," Robyn replied with a relieved sigh. "Thank you."

"Although we just have to drop it off inside," I added. "It won't be difficult."

"I wouldn't be so sure of that," hissed a troubling and familiar voice from above.

We looked up to see the pale, crested reptile standing upon a ledge in the stone walls, almost invisible against her snow-covered background.

General Etheldred leapt down, landing before us with a dull thump. "Nice hat," she sneered.

Robyn gripped her comically large sombrero in defiance.

"What do you want?" I barked. "It's over, the king is gone."

"Indeed, he is. The king is dead… long live the *queen*."

"Exactly," I replied, glancing at Robyn.

Etheldred cackled loudly as she began to circle us.

"The Architect? The king named me as his successor."

"You?" Robyn asked.

"I obeyed every whim of that old man for an aeon," she continued. "I *earned* the crown, and you won't get in my way."

"We don't have time for this," urged Jækel.

"Cuvier," I said. "We might need your help after all."

"Cuvier?" remarked Etheldred. "I know that name."

With a flick of his wrist, Cuvier's steel claws rang, and he stepped forwards.

"Ah, yes," hissed Etheldred with a wicked grin. "Now I remember. I like what you've done with the hand—I still have the original in a jar somewhere."

Etheldred and Cuvier took a moment to size one another up. The giant sloth had a huge weight advantage, but the general didn't seem at all fazed. She wasn't just ruthless—over the years she had become a skilled warrior.

Cuvier hurtled through the portal and leapt at her, the pair tumbling through the snow. He stood and swiped at her several times with his prosthetic, steel claws, but she was agile enough to evade each one. She slid between his legs and leapt onto his back, gripping with her razor-like claws.

The general bit hard on the back of his neck, only to find the skin to be loose and filled with a chain mail of bone. Her jaws still clamped, she thrashed her head but caused little injury. In her search for a weak spot, she scrambled upwards until she was atop his head. Cuvier retaliated by pointing his head down and pounding it into the snow.

"Get the Heart inside," he barked at us. "I'll take care of this beast."

Robyn nodded and, with another swish of her hand, another portal opened, this time taking us directly inside the mausoleum.

We walked once more atop the surface of the sacred pool, while Jækel slipped beneath and swam ahead. While it had been blindingly bright before, the mausoleum's interior was now in near-total darkness, the only light coming through Robyn's portal.

"Dear child," announced the hauntingly beautiful voice of Luca the instant we entered. *"You have done well."*

"I have?"

"She *has*?" added Jækel.

"To build something new, Architect, you must first destroy the old. Return me to my pedestal and go. Go and build a new Pangaea—a better Pangaea."

Robyn smiled and placed the slide back under the microscope where we had found it more than a week before.

Luca instantly began to glow his signature greenish shade of blue.

"Perhaps I was wrong about you, child," said Jækel, almost in a whisper. "I should have known Luca would judge you well. Go. Fulfil your destiny."

Curiously, the giant sea scorpion began to shrink, eventually returning to the diminutive size he had been when we first encountered him.

"But don't come back," he added.

"Goodbye, Luca," Robyn said with a hopeful smile.

"*Farewell, Architect,*" Luca boomed.

***

Crushed against the ground, the pale *Dilophosaurus* grabbed the sloth's nose ring and twisted, causing him to roar in pain. She wriggled from under him before stabbing a claw into his hind leg.

"I'll say something for you, sloth," Etheldred croaked, rising to her feet before him. "Even when I took your hand, you never screamed. You're the only one who didn't break."

With a furious roar, Cuvier pounded forwards, slashing wildly with both hands. Etheldred dived to his side and sliced along his flank with her razor-sharp claws. Cuvier yelped and dropped to his knees.

"I did not scream," he replied, panting and gripping his wounded leg. "But that does not mean I was not broken. I was broken in my mind. Broken in my soul. Every time I close my eyes you are burning me, you are cutting me, you are taking my hand. You break me every day. But today I finally return the favour. Today I banish you from my nightmares."

"Or perhaps today is simply the day you lose your other hand," she sneered.

"You are a monster, General. An abomination."

Etheldred's smirking expression hardened.

"You know, a long time ago, when I was but a chick, I was called that word—*abomination*. By a dodo, of all things. She was three times my height, much like you are now. Do you know what I did?"

"*Non*. And I do not care."

"I hunted her for months, before tearing out her gizzard with my bare claws. She was my first taste of meat... of *blood*."

"Come and get some more, then," Cuvier snarled.

Etheldred leapt for Cuvier's face, having identified that as his weakest point. As she flew through the air, Cuvier raised his hand and caught her by the throat. For a moment, the general paused in shock before Cuvier rained down a pounding head butt—smashing his thick skull into hers. He released her, allowing her to drop to the ground. She was still conscious, but dazed, her head crests shattered. She stood still with a vacant expression.

"*Adieu, Générale,*" Cuvier growled as he sliced his metal claws through the air towards the general's neck.

The snow muffled the thump of General Etheldred's head landing on the ground, and yet it seemed to echo across the mountain.

***

Robyn and I stepped back outside, the rippling portal snapping shut behind us. Cuvier sat in the snow, breathing deeply. I quickly noticed the headless general lying in the snow behind him.

"Yikes," I said.

"Are you okay?" asked Robyn.

"*Oui,*" Cuvier replied. "I think I will be."

"Thank you for everything. I wish Stromer and Mary could have been here too."

Beneath our feet, glowing blue veins of light ripped across the ground. As they did, moss spawned on the rocks and pine needles burst out from the bare trees. Luca had begun to repair Pangaea. Robyn looked down at me with a proud smile.

"It seems their sacrifice was not for nothing," Cuvier added. "If you could help me, I would like to go home."

"To Haţeg?" she asked.

Cuvier nodded.

"Okay."

Robyn closed her eyes and held her hand out as though expecting a high-five. The air shimmered before revealing a crisp image of the Hațeg beach, the crumbling lighthouse in the distance.

"Farewell, Architect," Cuvier announced.

The great sloth disappeared back through the portal to his island home. The doorway in the air fluttered before snapping shut behind him.

"Do you think he'll be okay?" Robyn asked. "His best friend is gone. In fact, I think Stromer was his only friend."

"He's a tough guy," I replied. "I'm sure he'll be fine."

"I hope so."

We watched as the forest below began to flourish, the smell of pine and the sound of chirping songbirds returning minute by minute.

"We did it, Ed," Robyn whispered. "We did it."

New Tanis

Upon our return to the ruins of Tanis, I could see that Luca's revival had already begun to heal the surrounding forest, but the city itself still lay in ruins. We stood amongst the smouldering remains of the citadel, the sun hanging low in the sky and casting long shadows. Felipe was nowhere to be seen, but I supposed he had done his job.

"Shall we rebuild it?" I asked.

"No," Robyn stated. "A golden citadel? It seems a little... unnecessary. Greedy, really. That was Richard's problem—he was greedy. We should build something new, something that's for everyone, something which represents how the *new* Pangaea should be. Something... something that would make Mum proud."

After a few moments stroking her chin in thought, she closed her eyes and pressed her fingertips into her brow. The ground rumbled and bulged, and the dirt churned as huge wooden shoots burst through the soil. They rose like great wooden tentacles which twisted around one another into a vast spiralling tree above us. Branches grew out of the main shoots, forming an intricate spiral staircase around the trunk. The occasional window and balcony structure stretched outwards from the high branches.

I gazed at the colossal structure which now towered over the ruined city. Rich greenery had erupted from the canopy and draped elegantly from hundreds of outstretched branches.

I gasped. *"Wow."*

Robyn dropped her hands and exhaled before taking several deep breaths. She opened her eyes and gazed at her grand creation. Her eyebrows rose and a smile spread across her face, as though she herself was surprised at how beautiful it was.

"Not bad, huh?" she said with a smirk.

"It'll do, I suppose," I teased. "Though you worried the citadel was a bit much, right? This isn't exactly subtle."

"But this place isn't just for royalty, or lords, or knights. This place will be for those in need—for those less fortunate. So they can be fed, sheltered, and healed. I think *this* is what Pangaea has been missing."

"It's been missing a massive tree?"

"It's been missing *compassion*, Ed. 'Compassion will be the foundation of the new Pangaea.' That's what Luca said."

"You should have taken the job to begin with," I replied with a smile.

"The job?"

"Queen."

"Oh, I still don't want to be queen."

"What? After all this? What about that scripture? You were to take the throne and save Pangaea."

"It didn't say which part of me was to take the throne."

"What's that supposed to mean?"

"*You*, Ed. You're part of me—all the best parts of me. I need to be braver now."

"*Brave*? You leapt from a cliff onto a moving castle, you led a prison break. For God's sake, you overthrew a king—*two* kings, and giant lizard kings no less. How much braver can you get?"

"I'm only brave when you're there to lead the way, Ed. I need to do it on my own."

"I thought you weren't going to run anymore."

"I'm not running." Robyn knelt and placed a hand on my shoulder. "I realise now I wasn't running from being queen, I wasn't hiding from Pangaea at all. I was hiding *in* Pangaea. *This* is my hiding place from the real world, but I know you're right, Ed—I have to stop running. There's someone who needs me to."

"Your dad?"

Robyn nodded.

"I reckon I need him too," she continued. "I've rebuilt this world, and now it's time to rebuild my own. I can't keep shutting it out."

"I think our Architect speaks wisely," came a booming voice from behind.

I turned and laid my eyes on Sir Barnum, who was flanked by the equally tall Doctor Boggs and the scampering Benjamin.

"Long live King Edward," Barnum added.

I gritted my teeth and sucked in a mouthful of air at the sound of my full name.

"Let's stick with 'Ed,'" I insisted.

"King *Ed* it is then." Robyn chuckled.

"Pangaea is divided," continued Barnum. "There is still great tension between the reptiles and the mammals. The people will no doubt wonder on which side your biases lie."

"I'm not a mammal or a reptile," I replied.

"And yet," interjected Boggs, "you are a little of both. That could be just what's needed to restore harmony to the kingdom."

I took a long, deep breath and exhaled gently, slowing my heart rate.

"Okay," I replied. "I'll do it. I'll be the king Pangaea needs, or at least... I'll *try*. But I can't do it alone."

"You won't have to," Robyn replied, glancing at Barnum, Benjamin, and Boggs. "Will he?"

"I will guide you as best I can," Boggs replied with a nod.

"As will I," added Barnum.

"You're not getting rid of me so easy, mate," chirped Benjamin.

"And I made you a coronation present," Robyn announced with her hands behind her back.

"You did?"

She pulled her hand forwards to reveal a large, glass jar filled with yellow fluid and floating, green lumps.

"*Pickles*?" I asked with a wide-eyed grin.

"Pickles," she confirmed. "It only seems fair you get to sample the finest snack in the world."

I trotted over as Robyn twisted off the lid and extracted a single gherkin. I had heard Robyn celebrate the wonderous pickle ever since she had first tried one almost a decade ago. The finest food ever created, from what I could gather. I *had* to try it. I had to experience the very best the culinary world had to offer.

She tossed it through the air, and it seemed to spin towards me in slow motion. I opened my mouth gratefully and snapped it shut around the tiny cucumber. I crunched, and the rich juices burst out into my mouth—sweet, yet bitter, tangy, and… *disgusting*. My throat tightened and my eyes began to water. I couldn't help it, I had to spit it out.

Robyn looked down, her jaw hanging loose, at the half-chewed gherkin on the floor.

"Sorry," I apologised. "They're not for me."

Robyn shrugged before plunging her hand into the jar once more.

"More for me then," she mumbled, her mouth now full of pickle.

"The first item of royal business, Your Majesty," said Barnum. "What do you suppose we do about that?"

He stared down upon the giant, golden statue of Richard in what remained of the town square. While the architecture around it crumbled, the statue seemed to stand prouder than ever.

"Tear it down," I responded without hesitation. "No one wants to remember a tyrant."

"Perhaps that's a little hasty," began Boggs. "Many of these residents remember Richard quite differently. I don't deny he was a wicked king for most, but he also civilised the city. He brought the citizens education, medicine, music. His legacy is… *complex*."

"What do you propose, a memorial? He drove half the kingdom to starvation."

"What if we move the statue?" Barnum suggested. "The old town had a museum. We could rebuild and place it within. It will placate the revolutionaries without alienating the loyalists."

"That's… that's not a bad idea," I conceded.

"Looks like this system is working already," Robyn concluded with a broad smile. "Barnum, did you know Gideon was the Bishop?"

"To my shame, I did not. Nor did I realise Richard was the Knight."

"He was?" I replied. "I guess that makes sense, that's why they hated each other so much."

"Stromer mentioned a third," said Robyn.

"Ah, yes, the Rook," replied Boggs.

"Do you think he's still out there somewhere?"

"Perhaps, but let's hope not."

"Why not?" I asked.

"I know little of the Rook, other than that both Richard and Gideon feared him greatly. A vast beast of great power whom they imprisoned while Pangaea was still young, so the story goes."

"Always bringing the good news, Doctor," I replied with a smirk. "Well let's hope whatever prison he's in is pretty secure."

I gazed down upon the smouldering ruins of Tanis.

"I suppose you should magic up a new city before you go, Robyn."

"Ah, yeah, I should. That might take a while."

"Or perhaps," interrupted Boggs, "the people should rebuild it themselves. Allow them to build their own city, as they wish it to be."

"I guess so. Your Majesty?" Robyn asked.

"That would take even longer. We'd be here until the cows come home."

Robyn flashed me a knowing smile.

"I mean, until the cows freeze over. No, until they turn blue."

"I *knew* you were just winding me up!"

"I agree, though," I replied. "Let them build it as they see fit."

"The residents have been asking for more greenery in the city," suggested Sir Barnum.

"The giant tree isn't enough greenery?" I asked.

"I was thinking smaller in scale," he replied. "Gardens and parks. I think I know the man for the job. A certain dinosaur with a PhD in horticulture. Doctor?"

Boggs smiled at the prospect. "Now, I *am* that kind of doctor."

"Wait," I started. "You're a doctor of… *gardening*?"

With a broad grin, Boggs raised his long, scythe-like claws in demonstration of his aptitude for the task.

"I majored in topiaries."

"Well then, it's settled," Robyn concluded with a slight giggle. "The people will build their own city, under your guidance. *New* Tanis. A new city for a new Pangaea."

A Memory in the Stone

Life has existed on our world for billions of years—complex life for hundreds of millions. In that time, trillions of species of fungi, bacteria, plants, animals, and so much more have lived, died, fed, hunted, reproduced, and succumbed to the cold embrace of extinction. And yet, despite this vast and rich natural history, we would have no knowledge of it were it not for one rare and peculiar phenomenon—fossilisation.

How does an animal come to be preserved for millions of years? How does the evidence of ancient life avoid being eroded by the ever-restless forces of nature?

Well, most of the time it doesn't. Only a tiny, unimaginably minuscule proportion of animals reach the end of their lives in such a fashion as to be fossilised. Firstly, the body of the unfortunate creature must avoid being scavenged by another animal. Given the hardships of life in the wild, it takes extraordinary circumstances for an entire body of flesh to go to waste. So, the animal must meet its end somewhere other animals can't reach. Perhaps buried in a landslide, or fallen into a deep cave, or drowned in a tar pit.

Now we have a fossil, right? Not quite. Even in such a scenario where other animals can't consume the remains, keeping bacteria away is another demand entirely. Even bones will decompose eventually under normal conditions. As such, the final resting place of the animal must also be inhospitable to microbes—perhaps being buried so well it becomes devoid of oxygen.

Should all of these impossibly unlikely criteria be met, something rather magical occurs. Over thousands of years, silt, sand, and other sediments build over the body of the animal, layer by layer. This adds weight, eventually a vast amount of weight. So heavy does the ground above become that the sediment around the creature in question is compressed until the grains fuse into solid rock.

Then, should water begin to seep through the rock and reach the animal, a chemical reaction causes the bones to slowly dissolve and disappear. But while the bones have disappeared, the reaction leaves behind solid crystals of rock where the bone once lay.

What this means is that a fossil is not the animal itself. It's not even the bones of the animal. A fossil is little more than the memory of that animal captured within the rock. Yet while the animal is no longer there, we can still study it. We can still learn from a creature which no longer exists—because the rock remembers. The entire field of palaeontology was built upon the foundations of these memories.

The same is true for people. None of us live forever. However, a select few who live their life in just the right way can continue to shape the world in memory.

The Legacy of a Mother

Robyn trudged down the sandy path to the lonely beach. As she reached the bottom and the rocky shoreline came into view, her heart sank. Sitting on several large rocks were Hannah Owen and her two sidekicks. With a sigh, Robyn turned to leave.

However, after a few steps, she stopped. Was this still who she was? She had toppled kings and battled prehistoric beasts—was she really still afraid of Hannah? She thought for a second and realised she truly wasn't. After taking a deep breath, she marched onto the pebbled beach.

Upon noticing Robyn's approach, Hannah scowled and rose from her rock.

"Hey," she yelled. "Did I say you could come down here?"

"No," Robyn stated with a smile before strolling past towards the sea.

Hannah's jaw dropped and her friends gasped in unison.

"Did you not hear me? Get off my beach."

Hannah stormed over and stood in front of Robyn, blocking her path.

"Are you deaf?"

"Listen, Hannah, I'm happy to share. It's a big enough beach."

"Who do you think you are? *Leave!*"

Robyn smiled despite feeling the presence of her two stooges behind her. She stepped forward, her and Hannah's noses mere inches from one another. Hannah retracted a little, clearly surprised by this turn of events.

"Are you going to make me?" Robyn asked.

The three bullies' jaws hung slack in shock. Hannah especially seemed bewildered at how to react. Her mouth began to form words several times, but she abandoned each one. Finally, she huffed in frustration and marched past Robyn.

"Come on," she commanded her cronies. "This beach stinks."

Robyn smiled—she hadn't expected it to be quite so easy. It seemed Miss Owen only liked prey that didn't stand their ground.

With a deep inhale, Robyn smiled and stared out at the sea. The water was calm, the sky clear, and the air still.

Seagulls squabbled in the distance in an otherwise silent moment. She breathed a deep sigh of relief. Pangaea was safe. She knew she would miss having Ed by her side every day, but she was beginning to feel ready for what lay ahead.

She picked up a flat rock and tossed it into the mirror-like water. Predictably, it plopped anticlimactically. Perhaps she would never learn to skip a stone. But it was a triumphant plop nonetheless. She happily tossed stone after stone for almost an hour.

"You're holding it wrong."

Robyn turned to see her father strolling along the beach.

"I thought I'd find you here," he said, picking up a flat, round stone. "Look, wrap your finger around the edge, imagine you're throwing a wee frisbee. It should fly level, with some spin."

Robyn smiled and took the stone from his hand. As Michael instructed, she held it with her index finger wrapped around the edge of the stone. She threw it—imagining it as a frisbee. It glided, almost parallel to the water, before bouncing off the surface once… twice… and then dipped beneath the sea.

"I *did* it," Robyn exclaimed.

"I guess we can do anything together."

"I guess so," she replied, beaming, before her face dropped once more.

In the distance, just as they had done before, the spray of dolphins appeared on the horizon as a pod bobbed through the waves.

"I miss her," said Robyn.

"Me too, pumpkin. You know, I always thought it was such a cliché when people say someone isn't really gone. That they 'live on in our hearts.' I think I get it now, though."

"You do?"

"Well, she left a mark, didn't she? Had she never been part of our lives, we'd be different people. She gave me you, for a start. And she guided you, raised you, taught you kindness and fairness. All those qualities you have which she taught you; *you* are her legacy. You're her mark on the world."

"I think she probably taught you a thing or two as well."

"She sure did."

"But not how to dance."

Michael laughed.

"Even your mum couldn't work miracles."

Michael wrapped his arm around Robyn's shoulder and pulled her in close.

"I'll always be here for you, you know," he said. "To look after you."

"I reckon Mum would want us to look after each other."

"You know, I think you're probably right," he replied with a smile. "What do you say we make her proud then?"

He held out a fist which Robyn obligingly bumped with her own.

As the sun set, Robyn and Michael stood side by side, skipping stones across the still surface of the sea. They had each other, but more than that, they were armed with the memories and the lessons Carol had left behind. She had shaped them both, and so she lived on in the people they would grow to become.

***

I don't know how, but as I stood on one of the highest of the vast wooden platforms in the great tree above New Tanis, gazing upon the vast Pangaean landscape, I could feel the peace in Robyn's heart. It wasn't that she had forgotten, nor was the pain gone, but she had come to accept her new world and make the most of it. She had found a purpose in the real world.

I shared this notion. Below, the city was being rebuilt, building by building. Where grey, gothic architecture once dominated, low villas laced with vines and topped with luscious gardens now presided. Much like Robyn's, my new world was still broken, and reconstruction was likely to be long and hard. In truth, it was intimidating. It would never be the same as it was, but by my sides were my three advisors, rich in experience of this world. Benjamin smiled at me with the same infectious optimism he always had. Perhaps he was right to be optimistic.

Pangaea was forever changed, and I had no doubt difficult times still lay ahead, but I was going to make the best of it. With people to trust and to lean on, we would make it work.

I owed it to Robyn. I owed it to Carol. I owed it to myself.

Life continues, and I plan to *live* it.

Printed in Great Britain
by Amazon